brothers of paradise

DARK EYED
Devil

olivia hayle

EPIGRAPH

"She kissed me.
She kissed the devil.
Only a beautiful soul like hers
would kiss the damned."

- Daniel Saint

PROLOGUE

You were everything to me, and then you broke my heart.

But I think that part was inevitable. We were destined to love each other. That's fair, isn't it, Hayden? At least that's the way it was for me. I don't think I ever had a choice, really, from the moment I first laid eyes on you, all those years ago.

Sure, I didn't *know* it back then, but that doesn't make my love any less real. The truth is, you've fascinated me since I was ten years old.

I once told you that, remember? And you smiled at me with those amber eyes of yours and asked if I meant fascinating, like how a weird bug is fascinating, and my heart ached at wanting to make you understand just how much I loved you. How much you meant to me.

How much I *still* love you.

Things could have been so different, Hayden, if you would have just let me in when I asked the first time.

If you had given us a chance.

If you hadn't left after the accident.

Maybe, just maybe, you'll let me in this time around. We're older and wiser. Things have happened that even the best of intentions can't erase. But some things haven't changed. Our hearts still understand one another. The distance and the silence hasn't changed that.

Some love stories are simple.

But ours never was.

1

HAYDEN

Hayden, 11

It's hard to forget the day you're saved.

I remember it like it was yesterday; the wind howling in the trees, the sound of heavy rainfall against the tin roof of my uncle's shabby car.

"They've offered me a job," he had told me. "We'll get a place to stay, too."

But the house at the end of the driveway isn't like any house I've ever seen. It's a mansion. A white, sprawling porch wraps around the front, visible even in the darkness.

"We're going to live *there?*"

"No, there's a house down by the beach where we'll live."

"They have their own beach house?"

I can hear the weariness in my uncle's voice. "Yes. Don't make this difficult."

I shrug and turn away from him. I've been nothing but easy. Five moves in the past two years, with five different schools, too. I was the poster child for *easy*.

I haven't seen much of Paradise Shores so far, but one

thing is clear—this is a rich place. People like us don't stay here, not for long.

"They have children," my uncle urges. "Mr. Marchand said he had sons. They should be about your age, I think."

"Uh-huh."

"This will be good. It'll give us some stability."

"Yeah."

Gary blows out a frustrated sigh. "I'm doing the best I can here, kid."

"I know." I bite out the following words, bitter in my mouth. "Thank you."

One day, I won't need to thank anyone. I'll be as rich and as famous as those stars on television, on social media, who could go anywhere and do anything. I'll own a house like this myself.

"Come on. We can't stay out here forever." Gary puts the car in drive and rolls up the wide driveway. His left knee is bouncing.

Gary isn't usually nervous. I lean forward and try to get a good look at the house. It's at least three stories with white, wooden paneling. It has blue double-doors and the porch is flanked by well-maintained flower beds. It looks like a house from a commercial, the ones with golden retrievers and blond children with happy smiles.

"Are you *really* sure this is it?"

Gary scoffs. "Yes, I'm sure, kid."

The front door opens. A tall man stands silhouetted against the light, a child standing to his right. He has a hand on her head.

"Gary?" he calls. "Is that you?"

My uncle swears and pulls his jacket up around his ears. He's buzzing with nervous energy.

"Stay here," he tells me and steps out into the rain. It wets his thin bomber jacket and makes his brown hair stick to his head. It's so different from my ink-black hair, the color from my father's side. It's the only feature I share with him, although he hasn't been around lately for me to double-check.

I watch as he talks with the man, this Mr. Marchand. The girl at his side is peering out into the rain. She can't see me, not through this darkness and the rain. Besides, Gary always tints his car windows.

She disappears back into the house. My stomach growls again, but I ignore it. It's only a nuisance when Gary hears it.

I hate making him feel guilty.

I hate being a burden.

The girl comes running out of the house, a raincoat hastily pulled on and an umbrella in her hand.

She stops by my door and pushes back tresses of long, auburn hair. She's younger than me, but probably not by much. "Hello? Are you in there?"

I take a deep breath and double-check the Band-Aids across my right knuckles. *Don't let them see that you've been fighting,* Gary had said, and shook his head when I'd tried to explain that I was only defending myself.

Then I open the door and set foot in Paradise Shores for the first time.

Lily, 10

"Lily!!" Parker calls from his room, right across from mine. "Have you seen Atlas?"

I scratch the golden retriever behind his ear. "No!"

Rhys snorts from his place in my reading nook and flips another page in his book. "Liar."

"He cut my computer time in half yesterday."

"Ah."

"Lily, are you sure?!"

"Yes!"

"I can vouch for her!" Rhys calls. Somehow, his voice drawls, even when he yells. My brothers couldn't be more different if they tried.

Heavy footsteps echo in the corridor, and then Parker's blond head pops into my room. His eyes zero in on Atlas lying by my feet. "Lily!"

"What?"

"I *asked* you!"

"You did?"

He groans and heads toward the dog. Atlas bounces up,

tail wagging, and Parker pats him on the head. "You know walking him is my chore this week."

"Oh, that's right."

"Screw you, Lily."

"Mom told you not to say that," I counter. I know it's a weak argument, but with three older brothers, I've learned to use whatever excuses I can.

Parker rolls his eyes. "Mom's not listening right now, is she?"

"You cut her computer time in half," Rhys points out, not bothering to look at us.

"*Of course* you're on her side."

Rhys—older than both Parker and me, although not quite as old as Henry—snorts again, like all of this is beneath him. He's getting frighteningly good at that. "I'm on the side of truth."

"When it fits you, asshole."

"Parker!" Only Dad uses that word.

Rhys shuts his book with an audible snap. "What's bothering you today, huh?"

"Nothing."

"Save us both the trouble and just tell me."

Parker plays with Atlas's collar. "I don't think Dad should rent out the beach house."

"It's not like we use it all that much."

"Yes, in the summer we do."

I frown. I have to say, I kind of get Parker's point. The little cottage is right by the shoreline, a stone's throw from our house. Previous summers, Mom would prepare little beds out there for us, and then we'd lie and watch the stars through the window in the ceiling and eat marshmallows. If we were lucky, she would even tell us a story. The best ones were the ones she made up, because you never knew how they ended.

Plus, her stories always involved four very brave siblings.

I look at Rhys. "Why is Dad letting someone else stay there? It's ours, isn't it?"

"It's for the money," Parker answers, his voice gloomy.

"No, it's not, you idiot. Dad found a new groundskeeper. The guy is bringing a kid, too, apparently. So they're going to be living there."

"Is it a girl?" I ask.

"What age is he?" Parker asks.

Rhys rolls his eyes. "I don't know anything else."

"Hey, how come you found out? They haven't told the rest of us yet!"

"Dad told Henry, and Henry told me." Rhys shoots us both a superior glance. "They're coming next week."

"I hate being the last to know things around here." Parker clicks his tongue at Atlas. "Come on, boy. Let's go look at the beach house while we still have a chance."

Rhys waits until they've left my bedroom before he comes over and leans on the back of my chair. He looks over my drawings in silence.

I wait with bated breath for his verdict. Once, he'd called an elf I'd drawn *inspired,* and I'd been on cloud nine all day.

He points at one I'm still working on. "You've gotten a lot better at drawing scales."

The giant dragon isn't done yet, curled around a castle, but I nod nonetheless. "I've been practicing."

"It shows."

Henry and Parker are similar in many ways. Just as good at sports, although Henry is much better at games like Scrabble. Henry had been the one to teach Parker how to ride a bike, when Dad was away at work, even though he was still only a kid himself at the time.

But Rhys? Rhys is mine, and I grin at his pride.

"Thanks."

He musses my hair in response and reaches for his book again.

"Do you really not know if it's a girl or a boy?"

"That's what I said, Lils."

"But you might have just lied to annoy Parker."

The corner of Rhys's mouth curls. "I really don't know."

"Okay." I pick up my pen and get back to work. The long wait for next week has begun, it seems, when we'll find out who the new playmate is. I hope it's a girl, and I hope we'll become best friends.

I'm seriously outnumbered in this household.

3

LILY

Lily, 10

It was a boy, and he became my brothers' best friend.

Hayden spent most of his time with them, playing volley-ball under the summer sun or learning how to sail. In the evenings, they'd lie side by side on the couch in the basement, testing one another's skill at Nintendo.

But I didn't know that when he arrived. No, when he came to Paradise Shores, I was ecstatic. Hayden was the same age as Parker, but I was the only one home when he and his uncle showed up. A friend just for me, I thought. He wasn't a girl—it would have been better if he was a girl—but I'd just have to make do.

I'll never forget the way he'd looked that night, in the rain outside our house. Water dripped down his face, dropped from his thick hair. I could see that his eyes were amber, even in the darkness. I'd never seen that on a person before.

I'd have to try to draw it.

"What are you staring at?"

No one has ever asked me that before. "You."

"Well, look somewhere else."

"That's silly." I offer him my umbrella to share. "It's raining. Come on, let's go inside."

He glances up at his uncle before a defiant spark comes into his eyes. "Okay."

"Are you hungry? I can make you an omelet." Well, I sort of could. Mom tried to teach us the week before and I remember all the steps. I haven't actually done it on my own yet, though. But I feel very grown-up offering him that.

"I don't like omelets."

Well, that's kind of a bummer. I don't know how to make anything else. "Do you like cereal?"

"Yeah."

"Good. Come on, we have loads of different kinds. Parker likes to mix, but I don't." I find his hand in the darkness and pull him toward the house. "I'll even show you where the Cocoa Puffs are."

His hand is careful in mine. I glance back, but he's following me dutifully. We're the same height.

I smile up at Dad as we pass him and the new groundskeeper.

"Lily?"

"I'm going to make him some cereal."

Dad nods. "That's nice of you, sweetheart."

The new groundskeeper shoots the boy a look, like he's telling him something. I don't know what it means.

The boy nods.

"Go on, then," the man says.

I hang the raincoat on Mom's peg and grin at the new boy. "What's your name?"

"Hayden," he says. He doesn't look at me—he's looking at the double-curved staircases that lead up to the second floor. Mom always keeps a vase of lilies on the table between them. It's the flower I'm named after.

"It's nice, right?"

"Sure."

I look him over from top to toe. He seems pretty sullen, this dark-haired boy who doesn't smile, but I'm sure he'll cheer up with a bit of food in him. Henry's the same, when he's hungry.

"Kitchen is this way."

He chooses Cocoa Puffs, and he doesn't mix different kinds of cereal together. It's a good start.

I pour a small bowl for myself as well and hop up on a kitchen stool opposite him. Hayden eats in silence, and if he notices me looking at him, he doesn't mention it.

But my curiosity gets the better of me soon enough.

"Well, my name is Lily," I say.

"Huh." He continues to eat.

"So… You're going to live with your dad in the beach house, right?"

"He's my uncle."

"Oh. That's nice." I've never met someone before who lives with their uncle. I need to tread carefully.

"Are you thirsty? Can I get you a glass of water?"

"Nah."

Mom would know exactly what to say—she's a great hostess. If only she was home! I try to make my voice soft, like hers. "You'll like it here. This is a nice town, actually. And there's a great little cove by the beach. I can show you one day."

He just nods. God, but he's silent! No one in my class at school is this quiet. Maybe something is wrong with him. He shovels another spoonful of cereal into his mouth, and I notice his hands.

"Why do you have so many Band-Aids?"

Hayden's eyes grow guarded. "I cut myself."

"I'm sorry."

"Don't be."

I take my empty bowl to the sink and try to think. He's silent. He's a boy. And he looks pretty… well, disheveled. I know that my mom wouldn't let my brothers wear a shirt that's the wrong size, like his, which hangs awkwardly from his shoulders.

I feel a sudden and very heavy responsibility to be the perfect host. Dad is handling the business side—I'll handle the boy.

"Have you ever played Nintendo?"

His head snaps up. "Once or twice."

"Do you wanna play?"

"Yeah."

"All right," I say, heading for the staircase. "Let's go."

An hour later, when Hayden's uncle comes to fetch him, they find us sound asleep on the couch in the basement, the TV still on.

4

LILY

The present

"Lily! Get in here!"

I roll my eyes at Turner's voice. "I'll take my sweet time, thank you very much."

"No, you won't. Have you forgotten that I'm your boss?"

"Actually, your father is. Technically speaking he's both of our bosses."

Startled laughter sounds from his glass office. "That was a low blow. I'm eating your lunch too as retaliation."

"No, no, I'm coming!" I close my laptop and hurry across the ten feet that separates our offices. Turner is sitting at his conference table, two poke bowls on the table. A sparkling water for me and a diet soda for him.

"You work too hard," he chides. *"Decompress."*

"Well, we have to work hard. The Anderson deadline is in five days."

"It's almost ready, Lily. You've done an outstanding job with the decor, not to mention the landscaping. It passed the house inspection with flying colors."

I nod at his words, poking at my raw salmon. He's right.

But even so, the Anderson development is the first house I've been running lead on since I was hired at Turner's family company. Property development was never my dream, but I took enough architecture classes in college to understand the basics—not to mention the decor part.

It's exhilarating, the mix of responsibility and teamwork that goes into building. It had made Dad happy too. Yet another one of the Marchand kids choosing his profession.

"Thanks." I shoot him a smile. "It's a thrill, isn't it? Building?"

Turner nods. "The biggest. You can spend years on a project, slogging over every detail, but then at the end, when you walk through the finished house…"

"Finally seeing your masterpiece complete," I say, thinking of Michelangelo and the Sistine Chapel that took him four years to paint. Studying art history in college hadn't exactly paid off, according to my dad, but it had been some of the best years of my life.

"I'll let my father know you called his developments around the marina masterpieces," Turner says. "You'll become more popular with the old man than you already are."

I chuckle. "Flatterer. I already know I got this job because of you."

"Okay, so maybe I put in a good word or two. But trust me, the board was in complete agreement."

"Thanks for letting me know."

"Of course." He nods at the ginger in my bowl. "Still avoiding that?"

"Yep. Here." I push my lunch toward him, and Turner carefully picks out the pieces with his chopsticks. If someone would have told teenage me that I'd one day be working closely with Turner Harris, the school's ultimate jock and my brother's dickish friend, I'd have laughed in their face. But things changed, I suppose. Once, I dreamed my future would be spent as Mrs. Hayden Cole and running my own art gallery.

"So," Turner says, focusing on opening his packet of soy sauce. "I'm taking *Catalina* out tomorrow night. She needs to stretch her sails a bit."

"The wind should be good. You and Parker?"

"I haven't asked him yet, actually. I was thinking if you wanted to join…"

"Me?"

"Yeah." He grins. "You haven't sailed in a bit, but I'm sure you remember how to. You guys went sailing all the time growing up."

We did, but I'm still not sure if I know the knots. My leg, too… I healed great after the accident all those years ago, and there's no real pain left, but my leg still won't always co-operate. There's just a faint limp that lingers and sometimes it locks up. If the backstay fails, or if we get caught in downward wind, there's a chance I won't be able to pull my weight.

"We did," I say. "Thanks, but I think I'll stay landlocked tomorrow. I think I need a refresher course before I can play skipper again."

"That's probably a good choice," he teases. "I wouldn't want you to get seasick all over *Catalina*'s shiny new deck."

"Ew, Turner." I shake my head at him. "I'm not a *complete* novice."

"No, you're not." He smiles at me, and it feels laden with more meaning than usual. "Are you going to the Maze Party this weekend?"

"Yes. The whole family is going, actually. I'm sure the Harrises are attending?"

He gives a nod. "My parents will be there, yeah. But I was thinking… how about we go together?"

I'm momentarily confused. The Maze Party is Paradise Shores' biggest event in the summer. A garden party hosted on the lawns down by the beach, filled to the brim with familiar faces and cocktails. There's a small maze, constructed for the children, which gives the party its name. It's practically an institution. Turner and I had been there at the same time on several occasions over the years.

But now he wanted us to…

"Together, together?" I ask stupidly. "Like a date?"

He cocks his head, a faint blush on his cheeks. "If you want to, yes. Or as good friends, as co-workers. I enjoy spending time with you."

My immediate instinct is to turn him down. It's a bad idea for about a hundred different reasons. I've never been attracted to him, for starters. He's also my brother's friend. He was kind of a dick in high school.

And there's a little voice whispering in my head, familiar and exasperating, saying that *he's not Hayden*. Every time I think I'm ready to move on, I hear that voice.

I tell it to shut up.

"I'd love to," I say.

———

You think you won't get over pain, or betrayal, or loss, but you do.

You get up every morning and the sun still shines. The waves still crash against the shore in the distance, and your mom still makes you buttermilk pancakes. The world keeps spinning. And you find that you carry on, too.

After Hayden left, I ended up accepting an offer from Yale, and it was everything I wanted. It had art and design courses. Interesting student organizations, closeness to the city, a lively student council. Close enough to New York, and therefore also Rhys. A semester spent in Paris to study art at the Sorbonne and practice my French.

But it didn't have the seafood I loved.

It didn't have the beach and the ocean.

And it didn't have Hayden.

Not that he would've been there, even if he could. He'd made that perfectly clear. For years, no one had heard anything from him. He didn't show up in Paradise Shores. He wasn't active on social media, not that he ever really was to begin with.

Texting him that first month had been mildly humiliating. I'd sent text after text without getting a reply, not until one day, he texted back eight little words.

I'm going away for a while. Take care, Lily.

Nine words, actually, if you counted my name.

That was all I got. Rhys got even less, and Parker was just confused.

The one picture I got was through Hayden's uncle, inadvertently. He'd showed it to my mom, who'd shown Henry, and somehow it had made its way to me.

It was Hayden in uniform. His thick, dark hair was gone, shaved close to the skull. A hat was tucked under his arm and he stood pin-straight, shoulders back. He was handsome, handsome in a foreign, adult way, in a way I'd only been able to imagine. He stared straight into the camera, eyes solemn and distant, giving nothing away. Was he happy in the military? Had he found his calling?

The man in the photograph gave me no answers, much like his real-life self.

So I put the photograph out of my mind and focused on making something of myself. I spent five years in New York, living across the hall from Rhys and working at one gallery after another. It got boring eventually, and I missed the ocean and my family. So I came back to Paradise Shores and ended up in Harris Property Development, my father's rival. Now I have my own place close to the ocean and I spend nearly every weekend at the family house, making pancakes and eating family brunch.

It's a good life—despite the Hayden-shaped hole in it. So what if I'd never considered Turner before? We were friendly. He was nice, and we laughed together. I'd made the completely right decision in accepting his suggestion for a date.

I would wear my white, lacey dress, my wedge heels, and I'd drink champagne and enjoy myself with Turner. No expectations, no fears.

Tonight, though, I'm snuggling alone on my couch with the TV on. There is no point in stressing about a date that was days away. There's a new documentary about Italian art that I want to watch.

The show has just started when my phone chimes. It's Parker.

Guess who's coming to town this weekend? he sent. **Hayden!**

5

HAYDEN

Hayden, 11

"This is a nice place, isn't it?"

I look around the beach house. We've already unpacked—it didn't take us long. There's a kitchenette and a living room with two large sofas. A gigantic bathroom with the largest shower I've ever seen. Technically there's only one bedroom, but someone converted the large walk-in closet off the living room into a second one with a single bed.

The floors are hardwood, and giant windows open up straight onto the ocean. The sound of waves made it difficult to sleep the first few nights.

"Yes, I suppose."

Gary shakes his head at me. "You'll get used to it, kid. So will I."

I guess I will. Gary and I have lived in worse places. And the years with my father before that, when it was just him and me… this would be nothing like that, compared to empty bottles everywhere and the sudden eruptions of violence.

"Where should we put her?" Gary is holding my mother's picture, framed. "On the counter?"

"No," I say with a frown. She would be staring at us eating.

Gary looks around. "The place isn't that big, kid."

I point to one of the windowsills. "How about there?"

He puts the picture in place and takes a few steps back, hands on his hips. "Perfect. She'll be able to see the ocean, too."

A smiling, blonde woman looks back at us. She died when I was five, and in my mind, she's become a distant memory, a woman who smelled like vanilla and hugs. Gary doesn't look anything like his sister, but he's a good sort. He's made sure her picture was set up in every place we'd stayed in.

"That's good, right?"

"Yeah." I head to the thick brochure on the counter. A giant brick building is on the front, students in uniforms sitting on the grass, laughing happily. "Paradise Shores Preparatory School?"

"That's the one." My uncle lifts the little clip-on tie that came with my uniform and turns it to and fro.

"Who names their town *Paradise* anyway? What kind of stupid name is that?"

Gary chuckles. "I know. This is… Hay, this is batshit crazy. But the school is good."

"Who's paying for this?"

"The Marchands. It's a perk of the job."

I run my hand over the pressed pants. They scream of money, of expensive fabric and high expectations. I have no idea what schools like this cost, but it has to be more than Gary makes. "That's quite a perk."

He reaches over and runs a hand through my hair, mussing it up.

"Stop." I pat it down so it falls over my forehead.

"This'll be good for us."

"Sure."

"All the Marchand kids go to that school. You can carpool in the morning."

Right.

The Marchand kids.

There was Henry, the tallest and most self-important of the group. He'd reached over and shook my hand, as if he was an adult and not a fourteen-year-old with a cracking voice.

Rhys didn't say much of anything, actually, but he'd looked me over from top to toe like he suspected me of carrying some foreign disease.

The blond boy my age, Parker, asked if I wanted to play lacrosse on the back lawn some time. I had said no. Lacrosse sounds awful.

There is an entire world between them and me, and no way to bridge it. I'm not even going to try. We sure as hell won't be staying in Paradise Shores with their wrap-around porches and expensive preparatory schools long enough for me to get to know these kids.

"When?"

"They leave by seven thirty tomorrow. I spoke to Mrs. Marchand, and she'll make sure there's a spot for you." Gary gives me an unusually serious look. "Be good in school."

"Yeah, yeah," I say, looking away. *Be good.* That was always the advice, everywhere we went. But it's hard to act good when you don't feel like you're particularly good. Not that the youngest Marchand seemed to care about that at all.

Lily had looked at me with such curiosity that I felt like asking her if she wanted to take a picture instead. She's kind, though. Better than her stupid brothers, even if she definitely asks too many questions.

She's pretty brave, too. I'd seen her grab a live lobster by the tail and not flinch once as she tied its claws, saying that her father had taught her that. She had shown me her favorite climbing tree just a few days before. It was pretty tall, even if she was too old to climb trees. Lily hadn't liked it when I said that. Her hair had been a fiery halo around her head, her freckled face contorted in a frown. *What do you know?* she'd hissed back at me. *You're probably just afraid of heights!*

I had to climb the tree to show that I wasn't, of course. If Lily noticed that my hands were shaking a bit when I came back down, she hadn't mentioned it. Heights really weren't my favorite thing.

But still. Lily is nice enough, for a Paradise Shores brat.

———

Lily, 13

Hayden reaches out. "Hand me the bucket."

I give it to him, making sure that none of the saltwater tips out. "Did you find one?"

"No, but that is getting heavy by now."

"I can carry it."

"I know you can." Hayden shoots me a pointed look. "But just because you *can* do something doesn't mean you *should*."

I roll my eyes at the clear innuendo in his words. "Not from you, too!"

Hayden shakes his head so that the dark locks fly and reaches down in the shallows. The tide is out, and there's no better time to go mussel picking.

"I won't. But at least tell me what you were actually trying to do."

"I've already had this discussion with Rhys."

"So have it again, with me."

The water is cool against my ankles, soft wave after wave lapping against our legs. I haven't seen Hayden in weeks, not since we left for our summer vacation to Europe, and this is what he wanted to discuss?

"How did you even find out?"

He shoots me another look. This time, his amber eyes are telling. *Do you even need to ask?*

"Parker should keep his mouth shut," I grumble.

Hayden's lip curls. "You're stalling."

"What have you heard exactly?"

"You got in a fight."

I sigh. "It was *so* stupid. I was just trying to defend Henry."

"I don't think he needs defending."

"Well, he did. One of our cousins said something... something stupid. And he had been annoying the entire week, stealing my pens and hiding them so I couldn't draw, mocking me about my hair."

Hayden's eyes steal up to my braid. *"Your hair?"*

"Yeah. He said some stupid things about gingers. We're not even that redhaired—Mom calls it auburn!"

"Idiot."

"Exactly. So I punched him."

Hayden's grin is savage. "Nice, Lils."

"Well, I thought so too. He deserved it. But I got in a lot of trouble."

"I heard," Hayden says, still grinning. He looks a bit wild, like he did when I saw him the first time, with too long hair and a too big T-shirt. Like he's actually from some other place, where rules don't apply to him. "Was it worth it?"

I think about it for a moment. "Yes. But it hurt like hell."

Hayden sets the bucket down carefully, making sure to anchor it between two rocks. "Show me."

I make a fist. He shakes his head immediately. "No, Lily, like this... you have to tuck your thumb in."

"I do?"

"Yes. You'll break it otherwise. Like this..." He reaches out and shows me how to place my thumb and to clench tight, but not so tightly that my little finger folds inwards. "See?"

"Ah. That feels better."

"And when you aim, aim here," he says, tapping against his cheekbone. "If you aim for the nose, you might break it. That's good but it will hurt your hand more."

"You know a lot about this."

He smiles again, crookedly. "I had a life before Paradise, Lils."

I shake my head at him, smiling too. It seems impossible that he did. My life feels like it started the day he arrived. He never talks about his former life, either—and when he does, it's only like this, with little hints and comments.

"Thanks," I tell him. "I'll remember this the next time I have to punch someone."

"I doubt you'll have to," he says, slowly releasing my hand. "You have a lot of people who would protect you."

"Yeah, yeah," I say, rolling my eyes. The overprotectiveness had been with me my entire life. "The brother blockade."

Hayden looks down, grabbing the bucket. "Exactly," he says.

I sneak glances at him while we pick mussels. Marissa Briggs had told me in school the other day that she thought he was cute. *In that foreign kind of way,* she'd said. I had no idea what she meant by that. Hayden is as American as they come.

But he does have really beautiful hair. I'd always thought so. Cute?

Hayden is so much more than *cute.* Plus, he's my friend.

One of my best friends, even, if you don't count Jamie.

But... maybe he's a little cute.

Friends can be cute, right?

6

LILY

The present

I pause on Parker's doorstep.

Hayden's inside.

Am I crazy, coming here to see him again? Knowing he's inside?

My first response was a complete no. Who was he to show up in Paradise Shores? To tell *Parker* and not me? After ten long years?

After what he did, leaving without so much as a note, I couldn't bear it. I couldn't see him. No, nope, finito. Conversation over.

Except, of course it wasn't. Every cell in my body reacted to the possibility of seeing him again. I need it, to see what he looks like now, what changes the years have wrought.

Parker had texted me the plans. They were going to dinner on Friday night, but before that they were sharing a few beers at his.

Do you want to join?

A simple question, but without a simple answer.

In the end, I'd found myself driving over to my brother's

in a daze. Curiosity killed the cat, they said, and I was about to be one dead feline.

I knock.

Parker shoots me a grin when he opens the door. "Lils, you made it. Did you park on the driveway?"

"Yes, like always."

"Good. The street parking here is awful."

"I know," I say distantly, walking into his house. "I've been here many times before." Hayden isn't in the living room. Maybe he hasn't arrived yet?

Parker grins at me. "Still, one day you might forget… And you'd blame me for the ticket."

"Sure." I follow him into the kitchen. And there, leaning against the counter, is Hayden.

My mind goes momentarily blank.

He's filled out. That's my first thought. In my mind, he'd still been the same young man I remembered, but coming face to face with Hayden now, I realize that he was a boy before.

He's a man now.

His button-down stretches over broad shoulders and the cut of his trousers reveals strong thighs. There's a faint shadow of stubble across his cheeks and jaw. He never had that before.

The way he holds himself makes me think of the young man in the photograph. The military has changed him, from the shorter cut of his hair to the thick, corded muscles hiding beneath his clothes.

But his eyes are familiar, staring straight at me. They're the same dark amber I remember from my childhood, the eyes that once held so much feeling. There's no expression on his face now, and for the first time, I don't have the faintest clue how to read him.

What is he thinking?

"Hi, Lily," he says. His voice has deepened, too. It sends shivers through me. For years, I'd begged and begged for that voice to be on the other side of the phone. I'd answered every single out-of-state and hidden number that called me, just in case. It had nearly always been phone salesmen.

I put my bag down on the hall table. "Hello."

"Here you go." Parker slaps Hayden on the back and offers him a beer. "It's good to have you back, man."

"Thanks. It feels good to be back, too."

"It's been a while," I say, and I wonder if he's the only one who hears the acid behind my quiet voice. If I ever thought I was over the anger of him leaving, I'm now proven completely wrong.

His gaze on mine is steady, and I'm not sure if I'm imagining it or if there's a faint trace of embarrassment in his eyes. "Too long."

"Where have you been?"

"Many places. Wisconsin, first. Then a base down in Utah before I joined the Navy. I spent five years patrolling the Bering Straits. Then I returned to military school, before becoming a commander."

Parker shoots me a massive grin. "He's a lieutenant now."

"Oh," I say. My voice sounds hollow. "Congratulations."

"Thank you."

The man in front of me looks like a more mature version of my Hayden, and he talks like him, but the words are entirely unfamiliar to me. Since when was he interested in the military?

"Are you here on leave?"

"Yes."

"Where are you staying, man?" Parker takes a seat on the edge of the couch. "You know you can have one of the guest rooms over at the house. I'm sure Mom would love to see you."

Hayden's expression is carefully schooled. "Thanks, but I'm staying in a house over on Elm Street."

"Nice. Renting?"

"Mhm."

I frown. "Have you seen Gary yet?"

"Yes."

Okay, then. The silence between the three of us isn't comfortable, and I wonder if Parker is noticing. He takes a sip of his beer and shoots me his trademark grin. Nope, it sure doesn't seem that way.

Hayden glances away from me toward my purse. It isn't until he glances at my leg that I realize he's looking for a cane. My anger flares up again, familiar and acrid. *Of course* he's wondering. He left before I was fully healed from the accident.

"Just a faint limp," I say. "It's minor."

He gives a sharp nod but doesn't say anything. The Hayden I remembered was silent when he was uncomfortable or overwhelmed by emotion, but I have no idea what it means for the new military Hayden, who disappeared for a decade without so much as a goodbye.

Parker smiles at me. "You're joining us for dinner tonight, right, Lils? I'm taking Hayden out to the Yacht Club tonight to celebrate his return." He slaps Hayden on the shoulder again. "The prodigal son has returned!"

It takes me forever to gather my thoughts, but when I do, they're laser sharp. Dinner with my brothers—with Hayden just across the table—is more than I can bear. I can't feign civility for that long, not around the people who know me best. Not when the only thing I want to do is ask Hayden *why*.

Why did he break my heart? Why didn't he call?

And why on earth has he suddenly come back?

"No," I say, grabbing my bag. "I actually have something planned, and just came by to say hi. Enjoy your dinner."

And then I flee, running from the troubled, amber eyes that I've never been able to forget.

———

I wake up late the next morning, the sun streaming in through my curtains. It's a beautiful spring day in Paradise Shores, it's a Saturday, and I have a sort-of kind-of date with Turner.

The Maze Party.

Hayden.

Ugh.

I put the pillow over my face and take ten deep calming breaths. Some of the anxiety goes away, but not fully.

I swing my legs over the side of my bed and open the curtains. Seeing the ocean in the morning is my favorite thing in the world, watching as the soft rippling waves kiss the horizon. Some days I take a walk in the morning before work, nearly making it all the way up to the family house before looping back.

But today my view is marred. Standing beside my gate is a tall man with a head of shockingly black hair. He's dressed in casual clothing, a hammer in his hand. He turns, lining up a nail carefully on the gate in my fence.

Oh no, he doesn't.

I pull my silk robe on and tie it, hiding my pajama shorts and top, and stick my feet into the first pair of shoes in the hallway. I fly out the door and down the steps.

"What do you think you're doing?"

Hayden doesn't even blink. "Your gate is broken. I'm fixing it."

"*I know* it's broken," I fret. "But why are *you* here fixing it?"

"Because broken things should be mended, Lily," he says slowly, like he's talking to a toddler. The spark in his eyes makes it clear he knows it'll drive me mad.

"Argh!"

A smile breaks across his features. "Deep breaths."

"Stop being so damn infuriating."

"It's a beautiful day," he says. "The sun is shining. The sea is calm. It's a Saturday, and there's free labor on your doorstep. What's not to like?"

"How did you know where I live?"

"Your brother."

"I'll kill him."

"Fratricide is still illegal in the state of Maine, the last time I checked."

"Stop arguing with me. Why are you here, Hayden?"

He bends to pick up another nail, looking for all the world like the definition of calm. "I heard you had a problem to solve, so I'm solving it."

"But I didn't ask you to. And by standing on this side of the fence, you're technically trespassing, you know."

He steps through the gate and continues his work from the sidewalk. "I'm on neutral ground now."

"You can't do this. You can't be gone for a decade and then just show up to fix things!"

"I'll be done soon," he says calmly. "So, you work in project development now?"

I pull my robe tighter around me, caught off guard by his question. "Yeah. But that doesn't—"

"Tell me about it."

"It's not... I help with some of the projects. Managing contractors, overseeing sketches. I handle nearly all of the styling and decor choices before they go on the market." I swallow, uncomfortable with his earnest gaze. He's looking at me like we're still friends, like we still have that childhood connection.

"Sounds challenging."

"Not very. I mean, sometimes it really is, when we have deadlines..." I shake my head. "We are *not* having this conversation. Not until you tell me where you've been."

"I told you yesterday."

"Yeah, 'the military.' It's too short of an answer."

He looks away from me, calmly picking up another nail. He's wearing a gray T-shirt and for a moment I'm distracted by his arm when he swings the hammer. Hayden had always been bulky, somehow; well-built. But now his muscles are the strong, well-defined ones of a man who uses his body regularly.

He feels like a stranger.

"Like I said yesterday, I was at a training base in Utah for a while. Then I served in the Bering Straits for five years in the Navy. I helped train new recruits for a few years after that. Now I'm here."

"I never knew you had an interest in the military," I say. "You never told me."

He pauses in his movements, a hand hovering just above one of the broken hinges. He's not looking at me, eyes focused on his work. "Well," he finally says, bending down to take a closer look. "It was a good option for me. I had been thinking about it for a while."

"*Sure* you had."

He looks up at me, eyes turning playful again as he looks me over, taking in my pajamas and my bathrobe. "Were you in bed, Lily? At ten o'clock?"

"It's a Saturday!"

Hayden's gaze snags at my feet, and then he bursts out laughing. I haven't heard that laugh in ten years, and even back then, it was a rare thing. Goose bumps race along my arms.

"No way," he says.

I glance down. My feet are stuck in the stupid bunny slippers I had as a teenager. They're ratty and ugly and must have fallen out of the back of my shoe rack somehow.

"You still have those?"

I wrap my robe tighter around myself and ignore the

blush that heats my cheeks. "Shut up, Hay. How long will you be?"

"About an hour," he says, eyes still sparkling with laughter. "Going to invite me in for tea?"

"Absolutely not. I have to get ready."

"Maze Party?"

"Yeah," I say, heading toward my front door. This absurd situation needs to end, and I need to get out of these terrible slippers.

He's a soldier, he's travelled the world, and he's returned to Paradise Shores as a man. A man with muscles and a deep voice and amazing hair. And I'm not exactly making a good impression.

Look at your childhood crush! She's a mess!

"I'll see you there!" Hayden calls behind me.

I slam the front door shut and slowly sink to the ground.

What have I gotten myself into?

7

HAYDEN

Hayden, 17

I loosen the tie of my uniform and nod at Turner. "Hand me a smoke."

He passes it to me with a nod to Parker. "Are you sure Hayden can handle it?"

"Fuck off, Turner."

He grins at me. "That's the spirit."

Parker hands me the lighter. "Of course he can handle it. Hell, Cole is my cover-up."

I nod. "And what an honor that is."

"Your cover-up?"

Parker leans back on the bleachers. "Mom would kill me if she knew I smoked. So I tell her my clothes only smell because of Hayden. Problem solved."

I take another drag and look out across the football field. The junior girls have lacrosse practice, chasing one another across the field with high ponytails and short skirts. It only takes me a few seconds before my eyes find the girl I'm looking for.

Her auburn hair is longer, and she put in some highlights

over break, but it doesn't change a thing. I could pick her out from a crowd blindfolded.

She's hanging back, playing it safe as part of the defense. I know it's not a strategic decision. She'd rather not play at all.

"Hayden, are you even listening, man?"

I slide my gaze back to Turner. "Yeah. You're hoping to score with Clarice Winthrop at homecoming. News flash—you won't."

Parker guffaws and punches Turner in the shoulder. "That's what I've been telling you for ages. Give it up."

I take another drag. "She's dating someone from Rexfield."

"A university guy?" Turner scowls. "How the fuck do you know?"

"I hear things."

"What is he, a psychic?"

I snort and look back out over the field. No, but I have a rather good connection with Rhys Marchand, who dumped her before he left for college a few months back. I knew for a fact she was using this guy in the hopes that it would get back to him. I also knew Rhys didn't care in the slightest.

Parker takes another long drag of his cigarette. The one flaw in his long, decorated career as a high school athlete. "I'm going to ask Tilly Davis."

"Of course you are." Turner says. "You Marchands, you're not giving the rest of us a fair shot."

"Not about to start now, either."

I feel my phone buzz in my pocket, but I ignore it. My dad had been trying to get in contact for weeks now. This time around I'm not going to tell Gary about it. There's no point anymore.

"That's it," Turner says. "If I can't beat you, I'll just have to join you."

Parker frowns. "What exactly do you mean by that?"

"I could ask your little sister, right? Lily?"

Oh, *fuck* no.

The response wells up inside me immediately, but before I can express myself, Parker shakes his head. "You do that, and I'll beat you up myself."

With my help.

"You're not good enough for her," I say and tip my head back, letting out a plume of smoke. Turner is a player and a cheat. Damn good at poker, though, and he has a hell of a right hook. But that doesn't mean he's good enough for Lily Marchand.

I know that firsthand.

Turner grins at us. "You're like fucking gatekeepers, you boys. Don't worry. I know the rules. I bet little Adam Bateman is about to find that out, too."

"What?"

He grins at me. "What, something I know that you don't? This rarely happens, Cole."

"What about Adam?"

"Nah, I think I'll gloat for a little while longer. I might—"

Parker leans forward. "Stop shitting around."

Thank God he is here, too. I can't act more protective of Lily than her own brothers, or it would be suspicious. I couldn't risk her family finding out about my impossible feelings. It would be even worse than Lily finding out about them herself.

I'd be out on my ass by daybreak.

"Yeah, Bateman asked her out earlier this week," Turner says, his face smug.

She hadn't told me that.

Unease and nerves roll around in my stomach. Since Henry and Rhys left Paradise Shores, Lily and I had grown even closer. Parker was often away at practice or gone for a tournament, and there would be no one but me and Lily. Her feet on the wooden staircase leading up to the beach house had become my favorite sound.

Lily told me most things. I was fairly certain she'd never lied to me in her life. But she hadn't shared this… which meant something.

Parker snorts. "Bateman? I think just sending a look in his direction would make him bolt."

I can't for the life of me remember what Adam Bateman looks like. He's probably a normal, unassuming kid. Someone with a trust fund and well-known parents.

Turner shakes his head. "You're too protective, my friends. The girl's gotta live her life on her own terms sometime."

"Yeah, but not with the likes of you."

"What, so I'm good enough to be your friend but not your sister's date?" He clutches a hand to his heart, a hurt expression on his face. "You wound me."

I force my clenched teeth to relax. It's a joke to him, perhaps, but what he described was my reality. "Madison would go with you."

"I know she would. Guess I'll have to revisit that." He throws me a grin. "Aren't you going to ask someone?"

"To homecoming? No."

Parker aims a kick at Turner's shin, which he neatly evades. "Hayden's too cool for school events."

I nod. "It's a reputation thing."

It's not.

I don't fit in and have no desire to spend another night with the shiny Paradise Shore kids. They never let me forget that I wasn't one of them—that my mother didn't drink tea with theirs at the country club, that I didn't return from winter break with a tan from a trip to the Bahamas—so I made it obvious I wasn't trying to fit in.

If they wouldn't let me win their game, I made damn sure they knew I wasn't playing at all.

Seeing the hard expression on my face, Turner backtracks. "It's kinda lame, in a way. I get you."

"Yeah."

Parker jerks beside me. "Shit."

"What?"

He grabs his backpack and hurriedly snubs out his cigarette. "*Shit.* I forgot. I have an emergency swim session that started... five minutes ago. I was supposed to drive Lily home today after she was done here, but then Coach texted me... I was going to let Mom know." He shoots me a look I recognize well. "Hayden?"

"I'll drive her home."

"You're a lifesaver, man. I owe you." He bumps my knuckles before heading off down the bleachers. Turner and I watch him go in silence. Parker's just as blond as he always was, but he's cut like a swimmer now. He doesn't owe me a damn thing.

If anything, I'm the one in his debt. Every moment I spent alone with Lily Marchand is sorted and filed into my own mental archives, treasured and valued. My memories with her were some of the best of my life.

Once practice is over, I park right by the entrance to the girl's locker rooms and lean against the car. I fiddle with the packet of smokes in my pocket, but I know better than to pull one out. Lily has never seen me smoke.

My body hums with the familiar mixture of energy and excitement that she produces. Time alone with just her, no brothers or family in sight, isn't always easy to come by.

The girls start to file out. A few shoot me speculating looks, but it brushes off me like smoke on water. The whole school knows I'm with the Marchands. I've heard the descriptions—a cuckoo in the nest, their charity case—whispered behind my back. The thing is, rumors don't sting when they're true.

Lily's hair is a mess when she emerges, a sweaty gym bag in her hand. A soft calm overwhelms me at the sight of her. I would never need another cigarette in my life if she was by my side daily.

Her green eyes glitter with a smile. "What's this?"

"I volunteered for chauffeur duty."

"You mean Parker forgot?"

I shrug. "His loss."

"My win."

"That's not a phrase."

She throws her bag into the trunk and skips over to the passenger seat. "Yes, it is. I just invented it."

I put the car in drive and pull out of the parking lot. It's not the first time I've driven one of the Marchand cars. The engine purrs smoothly under my hands.

"Nicely played today, by the way. I saw your game."

"Hayden!"

"It wasn't intentional."

"Sure it wasn't."

I keep the smile off my face. "You got some good passes in today."

"No, I didn't. Don't lie to make me feel better."

"Well, I'm not about to lie to make you feel *worse.*"

I can't see her, but I know she's rolling her eyes. "Don't lie at all, silly."

"Ohhh."

"Yes, *ohhh*. What were you doing on the bleachers anyway?"

"Hanging out."

"*Right.*"

"What's that supposed to mean?"

"With a certain blonde, perhaps?"

I have to focus on the road to hide my surprise. There's a rumor about me and Belinda Richards, yes. But it's nearly entirely false. I didn't think it had reached any of the other classes, and certainly not Lily. I'm not into blondes.

"No."

"Mhm."

She shifts, and her skirt rides up a bit, showing smooth,

tanned skin. I grip the steering wheel tighter. No, blondes hold absolutely no appeal for me.

Not when the girl next to me owns my heart and my soul.

I turn the tables on her.

"Adam Bateman, huh?"

Lily groans. "How did you find out?"

"Turner."

"Of course. He can't keep a secret to save his life."

"So Adam is a secret?" I try to keep the edge out of my voice. I would have probably fooled anyone else.

"No," she says softly. "But I didn't want Parker to find out."

"The brother blockade."

"Exactly."

If she's trying to avoid her brothers' interference, she probably wants to go out with him. Hell, it probably means she'd said yes when he asked. My hands grip the wheel tighter still.

"When are you going out with him?"

"I'm not," she says. "I said no."

"What?"

"What do you mean, what? Do you think I should have accepted him?"

"No."

"Then why the what?"

"Why would you be worried about your brothers finding out?"

Lily sighs like I'm being slow, and twists in her seat. "Their reaction will scare others away."

"Which others?" I haven't heard of any lately, but if there was someone I'd missed...

Her voice is tight when she answers me. "I don't know. I'm not exactly swimming in offers, Hayden. But, you know... if *someone* were to ask me, I'd want to be able to say yes."

If she only knew how many of the good-for-nothing boys have the hots for beautiful, sweet, fierce Lily Marchand. I would know. I'm the president of that particular fan club.

"I see. Clever."

She leans back against the seat and begins to unbraid her hair. I can see it from my peripheral view, thick and heavy around her shoulders. That fucking hair. It will haunt me, through this life and the next.

She sighs. "You were my first kiss, you know?"

My heart stops for what feels like an eternity. She has never brought that up before.

That kiss had been the scariest decision of my life, and it had hardly even been a decision at all. It had been instinct. She'd been sitting across from me outside the beach house, eating freshly picked blueberries, and I'd just leaned over and pressed my lips to hers. It was years ago.

There had been absolutely no finesse to it.

It had also been a mistake, arguably, for the way she'd reacted. My brave, brave girl, and she'd been shell-shocked. I'd been terrified that I'd screwed everything up after that.

"Hayden?" Her voice is quiet. "Maybe you don't remember. It's fine, I was just thinking out loud."

Fucking hell.

I wish I could look her in the eyes. I need to see what she's thinking in this moment. Is she just reminiscing with an old friend?

Or is this… an opening?

"I remember," I say. "You freaked out."

"Did not."

"Did too."

I can hear the smile in her voice when she continues. "Okay, maybe I did, a little. I just didn't know what to do."

"You're cute."

"That's not what you're supposed to say, Hayden. You're

supposed to tell me that I was a perfect kisser and a veritable vixen."

Hell, I can't hide the smile on my face. "Lils, not even you were a seductress at age thirteen."

"How rude."

"*Lily.*"

"No, I'm honestly offended. Wounded, even."

I reach over and grip her thigh right above the knee, like all of her brothers used to do to one another. Only, I don't grip her as tight as they ever had. She laughs and yelps, pushing against my hand. "Fine, I'm not offended."

I let go. "Good."

"So, was I yours?"

"What?"

"Was I your first kiss?"

Did her voice sound hopeful? I turn up on Ocean Drive and consider my response. More likely than not, I'm a desperate man, begging for her scraps of affection. And how I wish I could answer yes to that question, too.

But I'd never lied to Lily.

"No."

She snorts. "A playboy by fourteen. I'm not surprised."

"It was before Paradise Shores." I park on the driveway, right next to Rhys's expensive Mustang. A statement car, he called it. I called it pretentious. "And it didn't mean anything."

Lily chuckles. "Of course not. You were a kid."

I grab her sports bag from the back. "Right. Exactly."

Maybe I should get that into my head too, one of these days.

Childhood kisses don't count.

———

A few months later, at the ripe old age of thirteen, Atlas had to be put to sleep. Eloise Marchand had tried everything she could, but the dog was too sick. Vet's orders. The dog had been sweet, and it was a shame, but I didn't take it as hard as the Marchand kids.

Henry pretended like he didn't care—it was getting hard to tell if it was even a pretense anymore. Parker was a mess.

Rhys and I, we brought out the big guns. We pulled out the sofa-bed in his room and brought up the old Nintendo. It had been years since that last got played. After my first arrival here, the boys had upgraded to newer and newer consoles. Now we regularly played the latest releases.

"Here," Rhys says. "I found a six-pack in the basement."

I grab one of the beers he tosses my way. "You sure?"

He shrugs. "Dad won't care."

Henry accepts one too. "I suppose it's as good a day for underage drinking as any other."

"To Atlas," Parker says and raises his can. We all toast.

Rhys turns on the flat-screen TV in his room. The garish symbols and the cheery music of the old game flicker back to life.

I have to give it to him, there's something nostalgic about the whole thing. It fits the mood. Maybe that's what he wanted to do—to bring the brothers together one last time.

Henry is only here for the weekend, back from New York, and Rhys has to go back to college soon. Parker and I already have one foot out the door with graduation approaching.

Henry reaches for one of the controls. "Has someone checked on Lily?"

Rhys nods. "She wants to be left alone."

"All right."

I take another sip of my beer and watch as the colorful Italian brothers race across a pixelated landscape of mushrooms and plants.

Lily has never known life without that dog. She's kind,

and she could take things hard sometimes. I'd seen it happen before—with dropped plates or mean girls at school.

It doesn't feel right that she's in her bedroom alone. I feel it in my bones, but out of all of us boys in Rhys's bedroom, I have the least reason to feel protective. I'm not Lily's brother, thank God.

But I'm not her boyfriend either. I watch as Mario gets eaten by a flesh-eating flower on screen and fully empathize.

Several hours later—and a couple of more six-packs—and we lost Henry. He mentioned an early morning and something about a remote conference call.

I glance over at Parker. He's fallen asleep, one hand still on his remote control. Never one to give up on victory.

"In it to the end, huh?"

Rhys rolls his eyes. "He's got pride, I'll give him that."

"Too much, sometimes"

I stand and stretch from side to side, my body aching. The morning runs are good for me, but maybe I've overdone it lately.

Rhys shuts off the video game and the screen goes dark.

"Keep an eye on him, will you?"

I look over at him. Rhys is tall now, the tallest of all the brothers, and just as unpredictable as always. "On Parker?"

"Yes. He's impulsive. You know that." Rhys glances over at his bedroom door, shut now to avoid bothering the rest of the family. "And Lily. Especially Lily."

I meet his gaze head-on and want to sink through the floor. If only he knew just how much I kept an eye on her. He'd never invite me into their house again.

"Sure."

"Thanks, man."

I nod goodbye and leave him to deal with his dozing brother. The house is dark and silent, but I know it by heart. I'd snuck out of the Marchands' house enough times by now to know which floorboards to avoid.

Stopping by the closed door to Lily's room is habit. I'd been inside plenty of times, but never in the dead of night. And never when she was in bed.

Her room isn't quiet. I can hear the sound of faint crying.

Hell. *She wanted to be left alone.* Of course that's what she wanted. Lily doesn't break down in front of other people—we all know that. Rhys should have forced her out to be with us. Their teasing would have made her feel better.

I pause with my hand on the doorknob.

I shouldn't enter—I know I shouldn't—but walking away from Lily in pain feels like an impossibility. If the roles were reversed, she would never have left me alone.

I turn the knob. Her room is softly lit by the fairy lights she's draped around her bed. I can faintly make her out, lying on her side, dark hair splayed across her pillow.

"Lily?"

The sound of her tears stops, but not without effort. "Hayden?"

"Yeah."

The sheets pool around her as she sits up. Her hair is a stark contrast against the white of her tank top. For a moment, she just stares at me in the darkness. The tear tracks on her cheeks break me.

"You shouldn't be alone."

She scoots over and folds the covers back. It's not what I had in mind, but… hell. It's undoubtedly a solution.

"Lily…"

She swallows hard, but doesn't say anything, just looks at me. My heart breaks a little, seeing her so sad. The need coming from her is palpable. She didn't want to be alone, either.

I kick off my sneakers and pull off my sweatshirt. Dressed in just my T-shirt and jeans, I slip into her queen-sized bed.

"You okay?"

Lily turns to me. With the soft glow from her fairy lights,

her face looks magical. Familiar and achingly new at the same time. Her long eyelashes cast shadows down her cheeks.

"No."

I smooth her hair back. "I'm sorry. So sorry, Lils."

"I know."

We just look at each other for a long moment before I stretch my arm out. She curls closer, placing her head on my chest. I can feel her breathing, the soft movements of her body tucked against mine. I've never held her like this before.

"Don't cry," I whisper. "Everything will be all right."

"I forgot," she murmurs, turning up to face me. I've never seen her so unguarded before—and never this close.

"Forgot what?"

She closes her eyes. "I hurt when you're in pain. I forgot that it goes the other way, too."

I run a hand over her long, silken hair and feel the soft rise and fall of her breath. *Oh, Lily.* If only I could stay here forever, holding her in my arms and dreaming of a world where we had a future.

It took a while, but eventually she fell into a restless slumber. I followed suit soon thereafter, letting her deep breathing drag me down. It was the first night we fell asleep together, in her bed in the Marchand house in Paradise Shores, but it wouldn't be the last.

8

LILY

The present

I pull the blinds in my living room and refuse to look at my front yard. Instead, I get ready in aggressive, fast movements. I shower with too hot water and use too much eyeliner.

"It's going to be *fine*, Lily," I tell myself firmly. A casual date with Turner, someone I have fun with at work. My brothers' best friend and someone I've known for years. A party during the middle of the day, in my hometown, with family all around. There's literally nothing that could go wrong.

Except everything.

Why had he come back and sent my entire world back into uncertainty? The butterflies in my stomach feel unworthy of the woman I am now. I'm twenty-eight, for Christ's sake, not a girl of eighteen with a childhood crush.

When I dare to peek from behind my curtains, Hayden is gone. The gate is fixed, though. He's even cleared the path of fallen leaves. The man is a complete mystery to me.

I look at myself in my floor-length mirror before I leave. A white dress with a boat-neck neckline hugs my chest, narrowing at my waist before billowing out in a flattering A-line skirt. My hair is long and loose, curled lightly at the ends. I'm wearing my favorite pair of Tommy Hilfiger wedges. A bag is slung over my shoulder, made out of woven straw and leather straps. I'd bought it in the south of France as a teenager, and it's still my favorite summer bag.

"Perfect," I murmur to myself. Much better than the pajamas and bunny slippers from this morning. If I have to face down the biggest disappointment of my life, I'm going to need some armor.

I hear Turner's car on my small driveway before I see it. He's driving the small BMW today, and the top's down.

I give him a wide smile as I step out of my little house. "Hi!"

He grins. "Hey. Looking good, Marchand."

"Same to you," I say. He wears a navy-blue suit and a pink shirt underneath. A pair of Ray-Bans are perched on his nose, the same classic Harris *douchebag* air he's had since high school.

He opens the car door for me and I slide into the low vehicle. My heart is beating rapidly already, adrenaline making my thoughts sharp and clear.

Turner backs out of the driveway. "Hey," he says. "When did you get your fence fixed?"

"Pretty recently."

"Looks good."

"Thanks," I say weakly.

The drive is short and the conversation easy, quickly turning to the upcoming Morris project. We've never had a problem talking, Turner and I, at least not about the trivial things.

The Maze Party is held on the great lawns next to the marina, right on the ocean. Marquees are set up and improvised hedges brought in. Great lemon trees flank the entrance, where dazzling golden letters spell *Paradise Shores*. A jazz band plays in the distance.

Turner hands his car keys to a valet and offers me his arm with a valiant flourish.

"This is going to make waves," I warn him, keeping my tone playful. "My brothers will be here."

His answering smile is rebellious. "They might have scared me off when I was a teenager, but I can take the Marchands now."

I spot my parents immediately, standing close to the beach. My dad looks as serenely cool as always, but my mother is wearing a wide smile. She's speaking with her hands, the way she does when she's genuinely excited.

They're talking to Parker and a tall man with his back to us, dressed impeccably in a gray suit. He says something that makes my mother burst into laughter. Only when he turns do I recognize the profile.

Hayden.

"A drink?" Turner asks, giving one of the waiters a wave.

"Yes, please."

He takes two flutes of champagne and hands me one. "Remember when our parents made us come to these parties?"

I turn my back on Hayden schmoozing with my parents and give Turner my full attention. "Yes," I snort. "Dragged us kicking and screaming."

"And now we're here voluntarily. I even looked forward to it." Turner shakes his head, looking momentarily embarrassed. "Everything comes full circle, I suppose."

I appreciate his sincerity, even if it makes me a bit uncomfortable too.

He offers me his arm again. "Shall we do the rounds? There are potential clients here, you know."

"Is that why you insisted on going together? To network?"

He smiles back at me. "Of course. Work hard, play hard. Is there any other way?"

In a small community like this, most faces are familiar.

Turner and I work our way around, talking to old school friends and grandparents of friends and Turner's aunt and many, many more. It's a task to keep all the names and relations sorted out in my head.

Parker finds us quickly. He's wearing his old merino sailor's sweater, the collar of a polo shirt peeking out from the neckline. His pants are chinos—not even suit trousers.

He grins at us. "You two have become a proper little team, haven't you?"

"Bonded in business," I say, reaching out to touch the hole on his left shoulder. "Couldn't you put on a suit, Parker?"

"Nope," he answers without looking at me. "Taking out *Catalina* this weekend?"

Turner nods. "I'm thinking about it, yes. Want to join? We could go north, make a full day out of it."

"Let's." Parker leans closer, a conspiratorial look on his face. Dread rises in my stomach. I think I know what he's going to say, and I'm not looking forward to it. "Think you have space for a third crew member?"

"I've tried, man, but your sister has staunchly refused to join me on the boat."

"Nah, not Lily," Parker says with a grin. "Guess who's back in town?" He turns around and points—my brother, the paragon of subtlety—straight to Hayden. He's talking to two women I faintly recognize from high school.

Turner's gasp is audible. "No fucking way! Cole's back?"

"Yep."

He turns to me and apologizes for swearing, as if I was a delicate flower. "No worries," I say, thinking that I said many worse things when I first heard Hayden was back.

"When?"

"Two days ago. Just rolled up like he never left. Man, he always was a wild card."

"Remember the time he got us all to spray-paint the—" Turner breaks off with a look at me. "Sorry. We were kids."

"I know you were," I say dryly. "I was there."

Hayden has seen that we're looking at him. I can see his eyes zero in on Turner's arm around me, his hand resting lightly on the dip of my back. His jaw is clenched tight.

The blonde woman in front of him is talking and Hayden nods at something she says without sparing her a glance, his eyes focused on us. His gaze flicks to mine. It's expressionless, but I can see the challenge in it.

You're here with Turner? his eyes ask.

I meet his gaze head-on. *So? I have every right to be.*

Parker and Turner break me out of our staring competition. They're discussing plans for the weekend, focused on the winds.

"Of course he should join," Turner says. "I have to go and say hi... Lily?"

I shake my head. "You guys go and catch up. I saw some friends from high school that I'm going to talk to."

Turner's confusion is short-lived. He nods and presses a small kiss to my cheek. The impulsive gesture makes me blush, knowing who's watching.

"Catch you later," he says.

I want to watch—to see how Hayden talks to him—but I turn my back to them. Losing sight of him hurts. His presence at this party feels heavy, and my body seems linked to his, like we're two planets in orbit.

Instead, I find Marissa and Leighton, two girls I've known from childhood. They're the epitome of Paradise Shores, one engaged and the other just about to become a doctor, both of them beautiful.

It's not long until the conversation turns to gossip. Who's dating who, what houses have been sold, did I know that Tyler Bates had just divorced his wife? After twenty-seven years?

Finally, Marissa turns to me. "All right, Lily, you *have* to give us the details."

"About what?"

"Turner! You're here together? What does that mean?"

"We're friends," I say. "We work together and enjoy spending time together. Nothing more than that."

"Come on," Leighton says. "There's *always* more than that."

"Not this time. Not yet, anyway."

"Only time will tell, I suppose," Marissa says with a smile. "But what about Hayden Cole's return? Did you know he was coming back?"

I shake my head. "No, I had no idea. No one in the family did."

"I remember him from high school," Leighton says thoughtfully. "Always so brooding, you know? He'd be at all the parties, right at the cool kids' table, but there was something so... aloof about him."

"Yes," Marissa says. "Understandably so, though. When did your family take him in? When he was ten?"

"Around then, yes," I say. "But he lived with his uncle. They had their own place."

Leighton looks thoughtful. "And then leaving for the military... our very own veteran. I've never known anyone who was in the Army."

"The Navy," I correct.

Marissa shakes her head. "So brave, truly. What kind of career path does that result in, though? Must be hard to give the most important years of your life to the military."

"Yes," Leighton sighs. "It's a shame, really."

My hand tightens on the champagne flute. "Sorry?"

"Lily, it's very impressive, don't get me wrong." Marissa's eyes are wide. She looks surprised that I'm not in agreement. "But it's not really an up-and-coming profession, you know. It's just unfortunate that his prospects were wasted on enlisting. You want the best for him, I'm sure. Don't you agree?"

"Hayden and others like him help keep us safe, so we can

be here and drink expensive champagne and talk about who-divorced-who." My words are coming out stronger than I intend, but I can't seem to stop them. It's the same feeling I used to get when people asked if he was the gardener. "They step up to the plate day in and day out, and occasionally pay the ultimate price for doing so. You can think what you like about the profession, but we owe people like Hayden respect."

Both Marissa and Leighton look stunned. They're silent for a moment, digesting my outburst.

"Well," Leighton finally says. "You're right about that. Supporting the troops is a very important cause, and I don't think Marissa meant to imply that it's not."

"No, no, of course I didn't. And the look suits him."

"Absolutely," Leighton says with a nod. "All that muscle? I'd love a military man. Do you know if he's single, Lily?"

"Or how long he's staying?" Marissa asks with a smile.

I swallow my discomfort and excuse myself as fast as possible. Not for the first time, I miss Jamie. But my best friend is still in New York, angry at me for returning to Paradise Shores.

She would never have expressed herself so... distastefully. According to these women, Hayden is wrong to have enlisted, because that's clearly below people from this town, but he's gotten muscular from it so it's absolutely all right to sexually objectify him. It makes me want to throw up.

The whole thing does. The people here, the expectant look on Turner's face that I'm not sure I can live up to, Hayden disappearing and reappearing without so much as an apology.

I need some space.

I set my drink down on one of the tables and walk toward the beach. The grass is soft under my wedges, the sun strong as I venture out from the marquees. People are everywhere, polite laughter and the sound of glass against glass. I've just turned behind the last pavilion when I'm stopped by a strong hand on my arm.

He drops the hand the second I turn around.

"Lily."

Along with that elegant gray suit, Hayden wears an inscrutable expression. I can't tell what he's thinking or what he's feeling. He looks entirely at home here—like he fits in, in a way he never used to. If it wasn't for his unruly hair, I'd think him a different man entirely.

"What do you want?" I hiss, knowing I'm being rude and not finding it in myself to care.

He narrows his eyes. "You're here with Turner?"

"Yes." I cross my arms over my chest. We're behind the pavilion and a hedge is hiding us from view. I don't like the intimacy. "We work together."

"You and Turner?"

"Yes."

"*Turner Harris.*"

"Yes! Why is that so hard to believe? How many times do you want me to repeat it?"

He runs a hand through his hair. It's an achingly familiar gesture. "Of all the men I was expecting to find you with, you really surprised me with him."

For a moment all I can do is stare. "What does that mean? The men you expected to find me with?"

"He's an idiot."

"No, he's not."

Hayden exhales and the sound is impatient. "Do you remember freshman year? He cut the ropes from the left side of the railings to—"

"He was *fourteen!*"

"Doesn't matter. Still an idiot."

"He was your friend, too."

Hayden looks away from me, a slight smile on his face. It's not a happy expression. "No, he really wasn't."

"Why are you here?"

"Why wouldn't I be? The Maze Party is open to anyone with an invitation. Your mother was kind enough to extend—"

"Not at the party, Hayden. Here in Paradise Shores."

Hayden looks down at me. The mask is back up over his features, the one I remember from the first time I saw him. I used to think it was to protect his thoughts—his emotions. Now I don't know anymore.

"I grew up here," he says. "I wanted to return, see if the place had changed."

I narrow my eyes at him. He might be a different man entirely, but I still know when he's lying. "For *ten years*, you've been gone, and now it's convenient to check in?"

He ignores me. "How's your gate?"

"In perfect condition."

"Feel free to thank me whenever," he says, flashing a smile. "I know you were raised to be polite, Lils."

"In your dreams, Cole."

"Oh, if you only knew what I dream of where you're concerned."

Hot tears pierce my eyes and I blink them away angrily. I'm furious, I'm not sad, and I'll be damned if he thinks I am. "No," I tell him. My voice is unrecognizable. "Who are you? I don't recognize the boy I knew in this slickly suited up, snarky person. Who do you think you are, to make innuendos at me? *You left, Hayden.*"

His face falls, and for a moment, I see the person I remember. Someone I used to consider my best friend, who I thought knew everything about me. His eyes blaze and this time it's with sincerity. Hayden reaches out and wraps his hand around my wrist. His fingers scorch me with their heat.

"Don't leave with him," he tells me. "Take a walk with me. Stay here with me, Lily."

"Why?"

"Because you don't care about him."

"That's not a good enough reason."

His voice turned dark, almost hoarse. "Because I've missed you."

No. No no no. Hayden Cole doesn't get to do this. To show up and transfix me again. My teenage heart had broken so hard because of him, and it's only now starting to mend. There's no chance I'm falling back into this pit.

"You have no right," I whisper, closing my eyes. "You have no right to an opinion. Not about who I date, or their presumed intelligence, none of it. You walked out of my life, Hayden Cole, and only I can decide if I want you back in it or not."

His amber eyes, the ones I used to dream about, look back at me. There's pain in them. "Lily…"

"Bye, Hayden."

I leave him behind the hedge without another word, dabbing at the tears in my eyes and plastering a smile on my face.

9

HAYDEN

Hayden, 18

Mrs. Abrams raps her fingers across her desk. "You know why we're here, don't you, Hayden?"

I glance at the clock on the wall. Fifteen minutes of this, that's all I need to live through.

"Yes."

"College counseling is mandatory for seniors, and yet you didn't sign up to the program. We had to call you in. Why is that?" Mrs. Abrams leans forward, a deceptively pleasant smile on her features.

Because I already know where I'm going, and it's not to an ivy-and-brick institution.

"I don't plan on going to college. At least not right away."

She glances down at the papers on her desk. I recognize them: my transcripts. "You could be a B-student if you tried, Hayden. You have a few Cs, but nothing major. You could go to college. Maybe not Ivy League, but you could certainly get into some of the better public schools in the country."

Is she going to make me spell it out? I shove my hands into my pockets.

"I don't have the money for that."

"There are good community colleges around here. And there are scholarships. Although..." Her smile is apologetic. "Unfortunately, with your grades, we probably couldn't make an academic scholarship work. And your extracurriculars are..."

"Nonexistent."

"Well, yes. But there are plenty of colleges that give out grants for students from less-than-ideal backgrounds."

"Grants, but not full rides. I know how the situation is."

She flushes and fiddles with the papers. I wonder if she's ever met a student she can't help. The Paradise Shores kids here, even the ones with terrible grades and an addiction to coke, have prospects. Trust funds, legacy status... the right sports interests.

I take pity on her. "I'm going to enlist."

"Really? Hayden, are you certain?"

I'm not. Not at all, actually. But it sounds like the best option for me, and on the best of days, the idea of leaving this place behind and becoming someone new is more than a little tempting. I've always enjoyed the gym. Boot camp doesn't sound that bad.

"Why not?" I shrug. "They pay for your college after, too. Or so I've heard."

Mrs. Abrams looks at me for a very long while. It makes me uncomfortable, this level of scrutiny, before she finally sighs. It sounds resigned.

"I can't argue with your logic, Hayden. Serving your country is a noble thing. I don't think many of your peers would give it a second thought."

I lean back in the chair, uncomfortable with the praise. "Yeah."

"There's some information I can give you, of course. You'll have to give me a few days to look into the military colleges. I want to make sure that you get the best possible outcome from this if you do decide to go down this route."

"Thank you."

"Don't mention it." She gathers up my papers and slips them back into the file with my name on it. *Case closed.* I wonder what it says in Parker's file, and what advice he got. "I'll be in touch."

"All right."

"Take care, Hayden."

I grab my backpack and move to leave when a thought strikes me. "Is this kind of thing confidential?"

She gives me a nod, and I'm not sure if I'm imagining things or if she looks a bit sad. "Yes. Yes, it is."

"Awesome. Bye."

"Bye for now, Hayden."

———

Lily, 17

"That one looks like a penguin."

Hayden snorts. "It absolutely does not."

"You have to have some imagination. Like the one over there. It looks exactly like Henry's hair, when he slicks it back."

"You're actually right about that." Hayden glances over at me, lying next to him on the lawn. "Have you spoken to him lately?"

"No. I guess he's too busy in the big city and all, setting up shop."

"He obsesses over things. You know how he gets."

"I know. He was itching to get out of Paradise, too."

"Yeah." Hayden turns over, arms under his head. They bulge against the fabric of his gray T-shirt. He'd been pale when I first met him, pale and thin and with a head of too much hair. He wore the same Paradise Shores tan now that the rest of us did. He'd filled out.

But he'd never been able to shake the hair.

I long to reach out and run my fingers through it, but he only lets me do that when his guard is down completely—when he's tired or upset and pretending not to be.

"How does it feel?"

"How does what feel?"

"Having graduated from Paradise Shores High."

He snorts. "Amazing."

I raise myself up on my elbows. The sea is a glittering blanket in the distance, close enough to the edge of our lawn that I can almost make out the sound of waves against the shore.

"Are you going to Turner's graduation party?"

"Probably."

"With Parker?" There would be girls there. Plenty of girls —and I know what they think of Hayden. I wonder what he thinks of them.

I wonder if he would ever think of me like that.

"You know, you're very chatty for someone with a headache."

"The headache was caused by the prospect of my aunt's dinner to celebrate Parker."

"My point exactly."

I raise an eyebrow at him. "It's infinitely better to stay home."

"Mhm."

He scoots closer, resting his head right next to my hand. His eyes are still closed and he looks completely relaxed for the first time in months.

"Have you decided?"

He sighs. "Must you?"

"Yeah." I reach out and put a hand on his back, warm from the summer sun. The muscles tense beneath my touch before he relaxes again. I run my nails up and down, the way I know he likes. I'd discovered it completely by accident, but now I exploited it whenever I could.

"I've spoken to the college counselor. The community college has a solid amount of grants. I'm eligible for several."

His voice is tight. I know he doesn't like admitting anything that has to do with his prospects or finances, but these things are important. Plus, we're friends, aren't we?

"That's great."

"Yeah. *Splendid*."

I sigh. "It is. Rexfield is great. You can do a three-year track, if you want. You'll be close by…

He glances over at me. "Yeah, there's that."

I run my hand down his shoulder blades, pressing into the muscles, and smile when his eyes close again. "You could even work for your uncle on the weekends or evenings."

Hayden sighs. "I could. Hey, maybe I should skip the college counselor and just use you instead."

"Well, I *do* know you better."

He doesn't have a response to that, but I can see the faint twitch in his lips.

Hayden isn't really a big talker. He rarely, if ever, speaks about his family. He doesn't talk about his future plans or about things that bother him. I know that if you want information out of him, you have to push. I also think it's good for him—the pushing.

And I'm pretty sure I'm the only person who dares.

"Things will work out, you'll see." I rest my hand on his neck. He looks relaxed enough, now. I slide my hand into his hair and smile when he sighs, this time in pleasure.

Things will work out.

How could they not?

10

HAYDEN

The present

Returning to Paradise Shores hadn't been an easy decision to make. I understood well enough that showing up here would open old wounds, reawaken things that I'd fought so hard to keep under cover. But my uncle was getting older, and I wanted to talk things out with him face to face. I wanted to see the place where I spent so many years.

I wanted to see Parker and Rhys.

And I really wanted to see Lily.

Parker throws me one of the downhauls. "Fasten this, will you?"

I tie a quick, familiar knot. It's been a long time since I was on a sailing boat, a vessel made for speed and fun as opposed to defense and war.

He flashes me a grin. "Been a while since we did this, brother."

"It's good to be back out here."

"We've missed you around here."

I nod, not knowing what to answer. Parker was always liberal with his words, his offhand comments made in good nature but often meaning far more than he intended them to.

"You entertained Mom real good yesterday," Parker continues, jumping down to sit on deck. "She was talking all evening about how glad she was to see you again."

That strikes me as unlikely, even if I'd tried to lay the charm on pretty thick at the party. The older I get, the more gratitude I feel toward the Marchands. They'd paid my tuition at Paradise Shores Prep for seven full years. Uncle Gary's handiwork was good, but it was definitely not worth the thousands upon thousands of dollars in perks.

Talking with them reminded me rather uncomfortably of the huge debt I owed them.

"Thanks," I say.

"Sorry about Lily acting weird, by the way."

My head snaps up. Parker's not looking at me—his gaze is fixed on Turner. He's standing at the bow of the boat, a hand on the wheel and his eye on the horizon.

"What do you mean?"

Parker shrugs. "I think she was taken aback by you returning. She was... well, she was pretty shook about you leaving so abruptly. You know, back in the day."

"I can imagine," I say, because I truly can. Familiar feelings of guilt and shame ripple through me. Leaving her felt like cutting off a limb, like relinquishing the most valuable and treasured part of me.

"She'll come around. But you might have to grovel a bit."

"I intend to."

Parker shoots me a sideways grin. "Don't tell her I said this, but she was very fond of you, you know. I think she saw you as an extra brother."

Unexpectedly, I feel like laughing. It takes a bit of effort to school my expression into a neutral smile. "Thanks."

"Don't mention it."

The sight of Turner, serene look on his face at the back of

the boat, wipes any mirth away. "She's working with Turner now, huh?"

"Yeah. Property development." Parker shakes his head. "Dad is thrilled she's following in his footsteps. Not just Henry, but Lily too. Puts Rhys and me to shame."

"It never seemed like her kind of thing," I venture, hoping to get more out of him. I know I should just ask Lily, but we'll start arguing again, and I'll get distracted by her flashing eyes or her pretty mouth, and I'll learn nothing at all.

Parker shrugs again. "I suppose not. But it's a bit artistic, you know, with those models and all? And I know she handles all of the decor decisions."

"And dating the boss?" I ask, nodding toward Turner. It takes effort to make my voice dry, to shape the very serious question into a joke.

"Yeah, isn't that a mindfuck?" Parker shakes his head. "I think it's a new thing, though. Nothing serious or anything."

"Yeah."

When I first made the decision to return to Paradise Shores, I'd known there was a high chance that she was taken. I was keeping myself well-informed enough to know that she wasn't engaged or married, but that left a wealth of possible boyfriends.

If her relationship with Turner wasn't serious, was it more of a…casual arrangement? The need to find out was like an itch I couldn't scratch. Parker was an exhausted source of information, and I couldn't very well ask Turner. The man had pined after her in high school, had likely never stopped. I recognized a fellow spirit when I saw one.

But she'd gone to the party with him.

I had watched them arrive from a distance, her hand tucked under his arm. Her beauty had struck me again, like it had a few days prior, with the force of a physical blow. She'd been a cute teenager and had grown into a gorgeous woman.

Her auburn hair was still long, but it wasn't the same wild

mass I'd been used to. It was shaped and softened, framing a face as freckled and opinionated now as it ever was. The body under the white, form-fitting dress was slightly fuller, too. Shapely curves that I ached to explore—to learn the ways she was different and rediscover all the ways she was the same.

It had driven me half-mad to see her angle her face up toward Turner and give him her pretty smiles.

I know you, I wanted to say. We might have been apart, but she wasn't fooling me. *I know you inside and out, and you know me, better than anybody. And not time, not distance, not all the Turners in the world can change that.*

And I'm going to remind you of that.

————

The house on Elm Street is modest for Paradise Shores. It's close to the ocean, but not within view. It's two stories, but it doesn't have a pool.

Still, it's leaps and bounds above anything I ever dreamed of when I used to live in this area. It has a large kitchen, a large living room, and a guest bedroom.

It's late on Saturday evening when I finally close the door to my house and get in my car. There's a chance she'll say no. Actually, the odds are probably overwhelming.

But I have to try.

I know her, and I know there are things she wants to say to me. Things she *has* to say, if there's any possibility to mend what we once had.

And I had been a coward once, running from what I wanted, toward what I thought I needed.

But never again.

Despite myself, my heart is in my throat as I park outside her house. She might not be home. She might even have guests.

Turner might be visiting. The idea makes my stomach turn. I know I have no leg to stand on—no reason to be jealous—but damned if I'm not regardless.

I open the gate, now in pristine condition, and walk up to her front door. It takes Lily three excruciating minutes to open the front door, and when she does, she looks at me like I'm her least favorite person.

I'm pretty sure she's debating whether she should hit me or hug me.

"Hello," I say.

She studies me suspiciously. "What are you here to fix today? My mailbox?"

"Not today, no. But I noticed that it could use another coat of paint."

Lily narrows her eyes. "Hayden, I don't think—"

"I came to ask you to take a walk with me. Along the beach." I gesture behind me, where the sound of the waves beckons. It's a melody I had missed.

I can see the fight in her eyes. She's angry with me, and she's hesitant, but a part of her wants to. *Say yes,* I beg her internally. Let me make things right.

"Or have you become too comfortable in your old age? I once remember a girl who dared me to climb trees and dive to the bottom of the pier."

Her eyes flash, just like I expected them to, like I've seen so many times before. "Oh, shut up, Hayden," she hisses. "Give me a minute."

When she returns, she's pulled on an oversize sweater and stuck her feet in a pair of loafers. The summer dress she's wearing underneath leaves her legs, lightly freckled and tan from the summer sun, bare.

"Did you go out on the *Catalina* today?" she asks as soon as we step out onto the beach. The sand is hard packed below our feet, making for a pleasant walk. With the sun about to set, I know we're going to have a view for the ages.

"Yes. It's a beautiful boat."

She nods, and I wonder if she's been on Turner's boat before. The thought turns my stomach to lead. If he regularly takes her out and kisses her under the open sky, with waves all around them, alone for all the world.

I know I would.

Silence settles between us again. It's not heavy, but it's not exactly comfortable, either. Once upon a time she was the only thing in my world that made sense—the only person I was comfortable with. My anchor and my wings, all in one.

"I've missed this," I say. "The beach and the sailing. I never knew I'd love the ocean before I came to Paradise Shores."

"You took to it fast," she says. "Do you still know how to shuck oysters? How to eat lobster?"

"Of course. I had a great teacher."

"Well, I couldn't exactly let you embarrass yourself."

"Thank you. Your pity is duly noted."

She smiles faintly, shaking her head. "I never pitied you, dumbass."

"No, of course not."

"And if I did, it was only because you were too brooding for your own good. 'Oh, look how cool I am with my dark hoodies and my refusal of organized sports.'"

"You're right," I say, a smile hovering around my lips. "As opposed to your incredible prowess in lacrosse."

Lily punches me softly. The motion rocks through me, sending shivers down my arm. The setting sun has set her hair on fire, and it's a beautiful halo around her face. The smile on her face is everything I've dreamed of for years.

"That's a low blow, Cole. You know exactly why I barred you from ever watching me practice."

"Well, you know I've never been one for rules."

"No, clearly."

"You don't play anymore, I take it? Never went pro?"

Lily pushes me firmly this time, sending me two steps

away. I dance back, trying to keep the smile off my own face. I can't believe I'm with her again like this. "Are you still thirteen?" I ask her. "What's next, will you splash me?"

Lily laughs. "Only if you pull on my ponytail."

She means it in a teasing way, but my mind is suddenly filled with the vision of my hands in her hair. Wrapped around my wrist, tugging, or slipping through my fingers as she moans my name.

"You wish," I say. My voice is just a little breathless.

"I'd forgotten just how much of a pain you were, Hay."

"I'd forgotten how prickly you could be. And just how fun it is to provoke you."

She shoots me a small smile, but it turns thoughtful. When she speaks again, all the playfulness is gone from her voice. The reprieve—the time we could be our fun selves—is over.

Lily's voice sharpens. "Ten years is a long time."

"It is," I agree, gazing down at her bare legs, at the faint trace of a limp as she walks. Seeing it never fails to bring the guilt to the surface. "Did you need a lot of physical therapy? After the accident?"

She whimpers, shielding her face from view, and I'm struck dumb. Is she crying? I shouldn't have brought it up. I'd hoped she would be okay with it. She didn't remember much from the incident itself, after all.

But then she breaks into laughter. It's not entirely a happy sound. "Is that your solution? Hayden, are we going to rehash everything that happened after you left? Month for month, year for year?"

"Well, no. We'd need a longer beach, for one. And I don't plan on keeping you out all night."

"Good. I have work tomorrow."

"I need to know, though. Will you tell me?"

She sighs, and shakes her head, but humors me. "It took three months of daily sessions. I continued with it in college. I did a lot of yoga the years following, some one-on-one work with a personal trainer. The leg hasn't bothered me for years now."

Something squeezes inside me with every word. She talks about it casually, as if it's not the greatest single mistake of my life. As if I don't owe the universe or God or *anything* my own life in thanks for not taking hers that night.

"You had to put in a lot of work," I say.

"I'm alive, and I'm fully mobile. We both know we got lucky that night. There's no need to dwell on it for my sake."

"What did you—"

Lily shakes her head so vigorously that her hair flies. "No. If we're doing this, we have to do it question by question. I have... I have waited a very long time to ask you some things, Hay. You can't deny me that."

I knew this was coming, and still, unease and guilt settle like a stone into my stomach. There's no way to explain it to her so that she'll understand. I've always known that. As much as she feels like the only one for me, we come from different worlds.

"All right."

"Why the Navy? You never told me you were interested in enlisting before you left."

Am I imagining the trace of betrayal in her voice?

"It was a good option for me. I spoke about it with the college counselor at Paradise, actually, the year before graduation. The Navy and the Army have programs for kids like I was. There was no tuition to pay, a career path laid out for me." I shrug. "I had no money for college."

Lily is quiet, her arms wrapped around her torso. "I see," she says. "I figured. It was a good option. You're right about that. I just didn't know you were... well, interested in it."

Ah, Lily.

Interest doesn't matter when you're poor and running from your mistakes.

"It's given me a home and a purpose. I might not have

been ecstatic when I started, but I have nothing but gratitude now. It's my profession," I say, and I mean it. The military taught me what it was to be a man—to have discipline and responsibility. To pick up a load and to bear it, and bear it well. It was something my parents had never managed. I'd seen it in Gary, but I hadn't understood it myself until it was placed on my own two shoulders.

She's quiet. There are a million things I want to ask her. I want to know what happened after I left. I want to know about Yale, about New York. If she still paints.

I want to know if she thought about me, like I did about her.

If her heart still aches too.

Lily stops, turning to me completely. A tear glistens on her cheek. The sight stops me cold in my tracks. If seeing her limp hurts me, her sadness and anger shames me.

"How could you leave without saying goodbye, Hayden? I loved you, you know. And you just *left*. How could you?"

I swallow at her anger. It's well-deserved. "I had to," I say. "I hate goodbyes. The thought of telling you bye, knowing you'd try to convince me to stay... It was more than I could handle. I'm not sure I would do the same today. It was a coward's way out, and I'm sorry."

It's the truth. If she would have asked me to stay, begged me, I don't know if I would've been strong enough to leave anyway.

And we would have had to live with the consequences of me staying, and I'm sure that would have been so much worse. There's more I want her to know. About my crushing guilt, about conversations in the dark, about one-way tickets and her father's voice. *It's time for you to leave, son.*

But there's no way I can make her see—there's no way to ask for her forgiveness. I know I don't deserve it.

Lily wipes away a tear. I can see it, the way she puts steel in her spine and straightens her shoulders. She doesn't want my excuses.

Her voice is furious when she speaks. "All right, then. Thanks for your wonderful explanation. I always wondered."

"I can imagine," I murmur. Because I can. Because I would have gone out of my mind if she had suddenly left me.

Her eyes are still angry, and her tone is too, despite the overly kind words. "It wouldn't be fair for a teenage crush to hold you back from a great opportunity, of course. You clearly made the right decision, Hayden."

The angry description slices through me. *Teenage crush.* I don't know what hurts the most—that she sees me that way, or that she thinks I saw her like that.

"All right," I say. "Thanks."

Her eyes narrow. The tears, brief and heartbreaking, have stopped. She's the steely girl I remember, turned into a strong-willed young woman. "How could you not have left anything as an explanation? A text. A letter. *Something.*"

I frown. "I wrote you a letter, Lils. I left it in the mailbox."

"No, you didn't. There was *nothing.*"

"I did," I say quietly, remembering the scribbled words I'd penned, right before heading to the bus stop. It had felt like cutting out my own heart.

"I didn't get a letter," Lily says. Her voice is less forceful now—more uncertain. I can see it in her eyes as she thinks back, running through the events of a decade ago.

"Damn. I'm sorry. I thought you'd... I always thought you read it." I run my hand through my hair and watch as Lily wraps her sweater tighter around herself. She looks as miserable as I feel.

I want to hold her—to warm her against my chest, to smooth my fingers down her back and tell her everything's going to be all right.

That I'm sorry and I'm back now and that I have never, not for one second, stopped caring about her.

But she doesn't want me to. She knows me better than anyone else, and still, the three feet between us might as well be worlds apart.

"Someone must have taken it," she says. "The letter. And I'm pretty sure I know who."

"Who? Lily, I… I'm sorry. What can I do? I know I've been gone for a long time, and I have no right to ask for your friendship back. But I have to ask anyway. You know I do."

Lily starts to back away from me. There's urgency in her body now, the kind I remember well. She's about to start running.

I take a step to follow, but she shakes her head.

"*Friends*. I'll think about it, Hayden. But for now… I have to find out what happened to that letter."

I watch as she takes off at a run down the beach. She disappears on the boardwalk up to the road, back to her house, the girl I've loved and lost and maybe, just maybe, found again.

She never got my letter. Had never known I'd written one.

It doesn't excuse anything, of course. But for a moment, the relief I feel is so heady, it makes me lightheaded.

I might still stand a chance.

11

LILY

Lily, 17

Jamie grins at me from her seat in my reading nook. "You're really going all out."

I smooth a hand over the miniskirt. "Yeah. Is it too much?"

"Not at all! It's not every day you get invited to a senior party." She puts on another coat of lip gloss. "Are you sure we're invited, though?"

"Of course." Truth is, I'm not sure at all. I'd only met Turner when he came by to hang out with Parker, and we weren't exactly friends. But he wouldn't turn away his best friend's little sister, would he?

I hope not. Not if my plan is to work, anyway.

"You never straighten your hair. It looks good."

I unplug the iron and look at myself in the mirror. My hair is really, really long when the waves are straightened. My legs are on full display and I'd put on a pair of white sneakers. Heels are still beyond me.

"I do look pretty good."

She laughs and comes up behind me. With her spiky hair

and glossed lips, she looks like a cute pixie. Jamie has never followed the rules, of fashion or otherwise.

"You do. Now, we stick together at this party, right?"

"Yeah. And we're not going to be home late."

"And no accepting drinks from strangers."

We nod at each other in the mirror. The senior parties at Paradise Shores are legendary. I've never been interested in going—mostly because I know I wouldn't really fit in. My last name gives me certain cred in these circles—thanks to my brothers' actions before me—but I wasn't the person people wanted at parties, usually.

"Then let's go."

I didn't lie to Jamie about my reasons, either. I do want to see what the parties are like, and I'm tired of sitting at home in the evenings, pen in hand. But more than that, I want to stop being seen as someone's little sister. In the eyes of everyone… yes. But particularly in Hayden's eyes

Jamie's mom—who has always been cooler than my parents—drops us off outside of Turner's and tells us to have fun and call her if we need her. I open my mouth to tell Jamie how lucky she is, but she just rolls her eyes at me.

"I know, I know," she says.

"She's just *so* cool."

"Let's go, dork."

We shouldn't have been nervous—no one checks us by the door. The bass is so loud it can be heard a mile away. Jamie grabs my hand and pulls me into Turner's kitchen. Guys in board shorts are standing around the keg, laughing loudly as someone attempts to do a keg stand. I don't recognize any of them. How many guests had Turner invited?

I pour myself a glass and raise it high with Jamie.

"To staying out late," I say.

She grins. "To being where we're not supposed to be."

"Let's go have a look around."

"You've been here before, right?"

"Once, for a thing with our parents."

"Show the way."

We pass two teenagers making out so furiously against a wall that the painting above slips and hangs crookedly. It looks terrible—all tongues and teeth. Was that what they had done at parties like this? My brothers?

Hayden?

"Ew," Jamie whispers in my ear. "Get a room."

Turner's living room is as massive as I remember. An L-shaped sofa stands in the middle, wrapped around an expensive-looking coffee table. Empty cans of beer are stacked in the fireplace.

My eyes find the occupants of the couch right away.

Parker, his arms moving animatedly as he speaks to a brunette, Turner next to him. I can tell he's drunk even from this distance.

Hayden sits next to him.

He's tucked a cigarette behind his ear and his arm is draped over the back of the couch, behind a blonde girl with a deep-necked dress.

Blair Davids.

Parker spots us first. He flies up from his spot on the couch mid-sentence. It would have been comical, if his friends didn't all fall quiet. Ten heads all turn my way.

I try out a little wave. "Umm, hey."

"What are you doing here?"

"I'm here to have fun."

Parker shakes his head as if to clear it. "Do Mom and Dad know you're here?"

"Yeah, I called them beforehand to inform them of our underage drinking. Don't worry, I mentioned you too."

"You did *what?*"

Jamie chuckles. "Honestly, Parker, don't believe everything you hear."

His bloodshot eyes flick to her. "Stay out of this, Moraine."

"Bite me."

I roll my eyes at them both. "There's no reason why I can't be here, Parker."

"Because I say so, that's why." I can see the decision in his eyes—it's already made: he's going to send me home. I can't bear it, not in front of his friends. In front of Hayden.

"You partied when you were my age."

"Doesn't matter. I'm gonna drive you home."

Behind him, Hayden extricates himself from Blair's tentacle-like arm. He puts a hand on Parker's shoulder, dark eyes meeting mine. For the first time, I can't decipher what I see in them.

"I'm driving her home," Parker says.

"You've had too much to drink."

"Fuck. Right. Well, I'll call a cab then."

Hayden's eyes slide back to mine. "You should have told us you were coming."

"Why, because I owe you two my itinerary?"

His jaw clenches. It's a slight movement, but I see it. He isn't happy I'm here either.

My heart sinks.

I feel silly. The elaborate eyeliner, the short skirt I'd bought for this occasion. Straightening my hair. I feel small.

And I don't know if Hayden sees that in my eyes, sees what my own brother can't, but he gives a short nod. "She should stay, Parker. Let her have some fun."

"Shit. I don't... *Fine*. But Mom and Dad can't know about this."

"I'm not an imbecile, you jerk."

"Yeah." He runs a hand through his hair. "And... don't tell Henry, either."

"It's not like I have a chance to."

"Stay with Jamie or me. Or Hayden."

"Yes, yes, yes, I know, behave myself, etcetera."

"We're not children," Jamie says, her voice sharp.

"I know," Parker says. "Come on, have a seat."

The people on the couch part like the Red Sea when we return, Parker leading the way. I knew that the guys had sway in the school, surrounded by adoring fans, but I've never seen it this clearly before.

Blair shoots me an annoyed glance as Hayden takes a seat next to me. He smells like smoke and soap.

Parker peers into my cup. "Did you at least get something good to drink?"

"Beer."

"From the keg?"

"Yeah."

He shoots me a sideways grin and reaches over, grabbing a bottle of whiskey from the coffee table. I recognize the expensive label. "If you want the good stuff, you come to me."

"I will. What's up with the cans in the fireplace?"

"A game. Think you can hit them?"

"What do I get if I get them all down?"

"Everyone has to do a shot. Want to try?" He hands me a tightly coiled ball of tinfoil, the same mischievous grin on his face that I remember from childhood.

I nod.

"All right. Shut up, everyone! My little sister is going to have a go. Get ready to drink, you miserable motherfuckers."

Parker's back on my side. There was nothing quite like having his burly, good-for-nothing grin in your life.

I aim and throw. Half of the cans topple.

"Damn."

"No worries, no worries. You get to choose who has to take a shot."

"One person?"

"Yeah."

I slide my gaze from Turner's smug appearance, to the proud gleam in Jamie's, to Parker's laughing eyes—to

Hayden's impassivity. He hasn't said another word to me since I arrived.

"Hayden."

Parker grins. "Drink up, brother."

Hayden reaches for the whiskey. Not taking his eyes off of mine, he takes a long sip straight from the bottle. His hand grips it tight—long, broad fingers, tan from time spent in the sun. I've never noticed them before. Somewhere along the line, they'd become a man's hands.

He puts the bottle down with a sharp sound. His eyes say one thing. *Happy?*

I spend the next hour laughing with Parker and flirting with Turner. My short skirt must have worked better than I thought, because I see Turner looking at my legs more than once.

And maybe it's the beer, or the two shots I've done, but I'm enjoying myself—despite Hayden's sullen silence by my side. I hear Blair try to talk to him, but he barely says a word, and she disappears in a huff.

Parker challenges Jamie to beer pong. Turner asks me to join, and I start to rise, but a glance back at Hayden stops me. He looks… well. I know that look.

"I'll sit this one out," I tell Turner.

"You sure?"

"Yeah. I'll join the next one, though."

Hayden has one leg over the other, eyes only on me. We're alone on the couch now. I see as part of his defenses come down, slowly. He isn't entirely the Hayden he is when it's just me around, but the mask he'd worn with the others is gone.

"Don't stop on my account," he says. "If you want to go with Turner."

"What's up with you?"

His eyes narrow. "Nothing."

"Right." I tap my fingers against the back of the sofa and feel far braver than I should. "You don't want me here."

"Not true."

I inch closer, made braver by drink and attention. "Did I ruin your game with the blonde?"

He's annoyed, but he's surprised, too. "Don't be ridiculous."

It's been ages since he's been this standoffish with me. It used to be more often, when we were younger. When I pried too much or I got too close. But it hasn't happened in a long while.

"Good God," I say, letting my hand trail closer to where his rests on the couch between us. "Not even Parker was this hard to charm."

"Of course not. You have your brothers wrapped around your little finger."

I glance back at him. He looks exasperated, his amber eyes glittering.

"But not you?"

"No," he says. "I like to think I have a bit more willpower."

"An illusion," I tease.

"Most likely."

His eyes fall to my hair. It's a curtain of dark red silk around me, none of the usual waves and bobs it carries.

"You don't look like you," he says. A hand reaches up and traces a long strand of my sleek hair.

"Do you like it?"

"No." A long pause. "Yes."

"I'm still me," I say. "And you're still you. Even if we're at a party."

His eyes find mine again, his hand still lost in my hair. I watch as they shutter. Slowly, he withdraws his hand. "Yeah. Why did you come, Lily?"

"I wanted to party."

"You've never been interested before."

"I'm not allowed to change my mind?"

"Of course you are." He takes a sip of his beer and looks out over the crowd. "But you're too good for this sort of thing. For *Turner*."

Oh, not this. "*Don't*."

"What?"

"I'm tired of being put on some pedestal. I can take it from my brothers, but not from you."

His eyes slide back to mine. "But not from me?"

"No." Maybe it's the drink, or the tight dress I'm wearing, or the way he's looking at me—but I feel brave. "I don't want you to see me as a little girl in need of protecting."

Hayden's eyes darken, and for just a moment, I can read them clear as day. He's my Hayden again. "I don't see you that way. You know I don't, Lils."

"Good."

He glances away, out over the crowd of people. I can see his jaw working, clenching and unclenching. Whatever is eating at him, it's deep.

His voice is low when he finally speaks. "But... maybe I should."

Whatever hope I'd harbored before is now a flame, a wildfire, and I can barely get the words out. "Why?" I breathe. "We can be whatever we want to be."

"*We?*"

I meet his gaze head-on. He's being evasive, and we both know it. There's been a *we* since we were eleven and twelve, with bruised knees and dirt under our fingernails.

"Yes," I repeat. "We."

An odd emotion flickers through his eyes. It looks like regret and longing and something else, something soft and fragile that I've never seen before.

But when he speaks, his voice is hard like a whip. "We'll never be a we."

Fine.

I know when I'm not wanted—and I can't handle any

more humiliation doled out by Hayden Cole. I've reached my limit.

Grabbing the bottle of whiskey, I brush my straightened hair back and get up from the couch. I should find Jamie and make sure she's all right.

"Suit yourself," I tell him.

Hayden's hand reaches out and grabs my wrist, quick as a snake. "Where are you going?"

I shake off his touch. "To dance. To drink. Isn't that what you do at these parties?"

He runs a hand through his hair. I don't see the Hayden I used to know—not here in this smoke-filled house. "Fuck, Lily, do you have to be here? Can't you just go home? I get if you don't want to do it for Parker, but would you do it for me?"

The request hurts.

"If I won't do it for my brother, why would I do it for you?"

Hayden doesn't respond, just staring at me with those dark, judging eyes.

"I'll go find Parker. Go have fun with your girl. Blair, was it? Or Belinda?"

Not waiting for his response, I hurry from the living room and into the crowd of moving bodies.

———

"That's not true."

"Of course it is," Jamie scoffs. "How else do you think the water polo team gets all that funding?"

Parker shakes his head. "Because we're a good team. A great one, even."

"Great enough to score forty percent of all the school's funding for high school athletics?"

I roll my eyes at them. Jamie has gotten deep into investigative journalism mode—which I usually adore—and Parker is deep into his umpteenth beer. It's not a good combination. They've been arguing for half an hour.

Turner slings his arm around me casually and leans in to whisper something. "It's like Ali vs. Frazier all over again."

"Are we placing bets?"

He chuckles. "We should. Or we could get out of here."

Nerves flicker in my stomach. I understand the implication well enough—what he's really asking. There would be kissing involved at the very least, if not more, given his reputation. Do I want that?

He's nice enough.

He's not Hayden.

What am I doing here?

I shoot him a smile and pull away. "Let's dance instead."

Turner nods good-naturedly. "Lead the way."

We join the other people on Turner's makeshift dance floor. Music is pounding from the speakers, the bass heady and strong. We dance opposite each other, smiling, being silly. Turner throws an arm around my waist and I smile at him, trying to decide whether I like the feeling of it or not. This kind of environment... Everything is new to me.

Turner turns me around, and I see Hayden. He's cutting through the dance floor. He's using his shoulders to get ahead, pushing people out of the way without so much as a second glance.

I sway closer to Turner and meet Hayden's eyes head-on. I'm not doing anything wrong. He was the one who said we couldn't be a *we*.

He reaches us.

"Hey," Turner says, a smile on his features. "We were—"

Hayden puts a heavy hand on Turner's shoulder and leans in to whisper something in his ear. I try to make out what it is, but the music is too loud and the whispers too low. The only thing I hear is the word *brother*.

Turner shoots me a sheepish smile. "Sorry," he says, giving me a wink. "Can't blame a guy for trying."

I give him a wan nod and watch as he retreats through the crowd. Hayden is left, looking at me, eyes faintly narrowed.

"What did you just tell him?"

"Nothing he didn't already know."

"What's that supposed to mean?"

"Just that he knows your brothers wouldn't be happy with him if he messed with you."

I cross my arms. "And you're what, their enforcer? The attack dog?"

His jaw works. "Something like that, I guess."

There's tension in him, but it's in me, too. I don't have the energy to be thoughtful or understanding. I'm pissed off and I'm tired and I don't know who he is at the moment.

"You didn't do that for Parker. You did that for you, and you're a damn hypocrite."

Hayden's eyes narrow, but he doesn't respond.

"Nothing to say for yourself?" I'm vaguely aware that I'm talking too loudly, but there's no stopping me now. "You've been nothing but rude to me since I came tonight. For no clear reason, either."

Hayden glances at the people around us, jaw still working.

"Do you know what I think the real reason is? You're afraid, Hayden. Afraid that I might go off and—"

He grabs my hand and I'm pulled through the throng of people, toward the back of Turner's house. Hayden turns a corner and ushers me into a dark hallway.

"Stop it."

"Stop what? Asking you to explain yourself?"

"Yes, god damn it." He reaches out and puts a hand on the wall behind me. I catch a whiff of his body spray, of beer and ocean and sweat. His breath is coming faster than normal.

So is mine. The storminess in his eyes feels reflected in my heart, every beat reminding me how close he is but how far away.

"You were the one who said we can't be a we," I say, voice low.

"I did."

"So why would you care if I was with Turner?"

Hayden doesn't answer. Our bodies sway closer, until our chests very nearly touch. He passed me in height a long time ago, but it isn't until we're this close that it's noticeable. I have to tilt my head back to meet his steely gaze.

Only it's not steely anymore.

It's crumbling, and the longing I see there is the same I've harbored for months.

I reach up and press my lips against his.

Hayden hesitates—I can feel it in his body—before his lips move against mine. They're warm and soft.

He opens his mouth to say something, but I don't let him. I kiss him again, desperate, pressing my body against his.

Respond, I'm begging. *I want you so bad.*

My hand gets lost in his hair and I'm tugging him closer, his lips gently pressing against mine.

And then the dam breaks for him too.

Strong arms wrap around me. I'm forced closer until there's no space between our bodies, until his heart and mine beat in tandem through the thin fabric of our clothes.

Hayden's lips are insistent on mine, soft and warm and tender in a way he so rarely is. I can't believe he's kissing me, or that I'm kissing him.

Hayden—my Hayden—is fisting his hands in my shirt as if he wants me close enough that we'll become one. His shoulders are taut under my hands, the skin of his back warm through his shirt. I want to touch him everywhere, my hands roaming as far as I can.

His hands skim my waist, fingers dancing over the faint display of skin where my shirt's lifted. The touch is electric.

I'm suddenly aware of everywhere we're touching. My breasts, pressed flat against his chest. His thighs, strong against mine. The heat of his breath against my mouth.

His lips skim my jaw and trail down toward my neck. He flicks my hair back impatiently and presses kisses to my skin.

Kissing Hayden was better than I could imagine, but the feeling of his hot mouth on my neck undoes me. It spreads down my body, the fire, making my limbs languorous and heavy. I wrap my arms around him and bury my face in his thick hair. I never want him to stop touching me. I never want him to let me go. I surrender to his imploring tongue, to the heat and the fire and the flames.

I lean back, pressing my forehead to his. He smells like salt and home. Like boy-on-the-cusp-of-man and all I'd ever want.

"Are you ever going to ask me out?"

His breath is coming hard. "You know you can't date."

"That's not an answer, Hay."

"I can't, Lily." His voice is hoarse. "I can't." He pushes me away and takes a step back. A hand in his hair, his chest heaving and eyes wild.

I put a hand over my own beating heart. "Hayden."

He closes his eyes and takes a deep breath. "Let's get you home."

"*What?*" My lips still ache from his, body tingling.

"We can't do this, not here, not... this shouldn't be happening. Let me drive you home, Lily."

Anger courses through me, just as suddenly as the desire. "You've had as much to drink as Parker. Why would you be able to drive when he can't?"

"Damn it. Fine, I'll walk you home." He bends to grab my bag from the floor. I must have dropped it, completely absorbed in him.

"No."

"Lily."

"No." I snatch my clutch back. "I'll walk home alone, thank you very much."

He follows me out through the living room. "It's not safe."

"When was the last time anything bad happened in Paradise Shores? Besides, I'd rather be alone than with you right now."

Hayden steps in front of me, hindering my progress toward the front door. The music is a loud beat in the distance, the hallway deserted. "That's fine. I can be quiet."

Such a Hayden answer. "You know that's not what I meant."

"I'm sorry about what happened. I didn't mean it to." He rubs his neck. "It was a mistake."

A mistake?

The pain and the hurt lash through me. As high as he brought me with his touches, he can bring me just as low with his words.

For a second, all I can do is stare at him. When I finally answer him my voice vibrates with angry tears.

"If kissing me was a mistake, what does that make the rest of this?" I gesture toward the living room, the writhing bodies and alcohol and party drugs. "Spending your time with these people, with Belindas and Blairs and… people who couldn't care less about you. I don't for a second think that was the first time you've made out with a girl half-drunk in a hallway."

He looks shocked, eyes wide. "That's not true."

"So what makes tonight a mistake, exactly? That it was *me?*"

"Lily, that's not what I meant."

"No? Explain it to me then."

Hayden swallows, amber eyes locked on me. I can see him struggling for words, and for the first time, I don't have patience with him.

"Never mind. I'm going home. Have fun without me here,

bringing you down." I head down the fancy glass steps from Turner's porch and try to stop the tears from falling.

"Lily!"

I stop, a hand on the railing, and wait for the apology—the explanation.

It doesn't come.

"Take Jamie with you, at least."

A tear rolls down my cheek.

"I'll text her."

12

LILY

The present

I'm reeling from Hayden's words.

Did he really write me a letter? If he did, it never got to me. It's been ten years, but I'm flung back into the same state of anguish as when I was eighteen, waking up one morning to discover he had left. My heart is pounding with beat after painful beat. I had thought that the old fracture was more or less healed, but it hurts like it had been broken just yesterday.

I grab my jacket and my keys, hurrying out of the house and into my car. I'm filled with urgency—just like a decade ago.

When I'd called everyone to ask where he was.

When the days passed and there were no answers.

When I finally gathered the courage to hobble to the beach house on my crutches, to knock on the door, and to ask Gary where his nephew was. *He's gone, girl. I'm sorry.*

The kind pity in his eyes had nearly made my knees buckle, as if he could guess just how hopelessly in love I was with Hayden. Hayden, who'd left, without a care or concern for me.

It's late when I park at Ocean Drive 12, but I know my mom will be awake. Dad's away on business, and for once, I'm happy about that.

I have never once spoken to Mom about Hayden. When I was younger, there had been times when I suspected... but she never let on that she knew about us. But she must have known—and known all along, because there's only one person in this household who empties the mailbox.

I find her sitting on the porch with the light on. She's reading a magazine, her hair—the same color as mine— braided down her back. It's hard, sometimes, to realize that we look so similar but are so different. She's never understood my love of art, for example, or Rhys's rebellion against status and prestige.

"Sweetheart? I didn't know you were coming today."

My hand clenches and unclenches at my side in anger and fear, fear of what I'll find out tonight. When I speak, I don't recognize my own voice. "Ten years ago, Hayden left to join the Navy."

Mom puts down her magazine. Her gaze is curious. "Yes, I suppose."

"He put a goodbye letter in our mailbox, addressed to me. You took it."

"Oh, Lily," she says with a soft sigh, turning to look out across the ocean. "Yes, I did."

I sink into the chair next to her. "*Why?*"

"He wasn't right for you."

"That was for me to decide. I spent *years* wondering why he left. Years! And you knew the whole time? How could you keep that from me?"

She's quiet for a long time—so quiet that I wonder if she'll even deign to answer me. But when she does, her voice is low and thoughtful.

"I had someone like that once, sweetheart. Someone who

wasn't good for me. Who couldn't give me the future I wanted, but who I loved more than anything."

I just blink at her. "In France?"

"Yes. We went to the same high school."

I've never heard this before. To the best of anyone's knowledge, Mom's life started when she met Dad on one of his business trips, just the way she wanted it. She rarely mentions her life before.

"He would disappear for months and then return, asking me to take him back… asking me to give him another chance. He was charming, and tortured, and I loved him very much." Her voice grows hard. "He kept saying that he would change, but he never did. It was always the same story with him. And there was no ambition. He would have ended up a bum, and me right there along with him."

"That wasn't Hayden."

"It looked like it. I escaped that fate, and I'd be damned if my own daughter fell victim to it."

"But I wasn't you, and Hayden wasn't him. History wasn't repeating itself."

Her frown deepens. "He had just *crashed* a car with you in it. You were considering going to community college and breaking your father's heart over this boy."

"The truck driver was driving drunk! The police confirmed it!" I can't believe this conversation. For ten years, she had known, and never said a word. "And what university I chose was *my* choice. Hayden broke my heart when he left, and you're saying you're happy he did?"

"Happy? I'd just listened to a doctor tell me that he was unsure my daughter would ever walk again. Yes, I was happy when he left. I was relieved. I only wanted the best for you."

"So why take the letter? Why not let me have an explanation?"

Her eyes soften. "A clean break, sweetie. You were healing physically. I wanted you to heal from him, too. And you did."

It hurts. It hurts like it had when he left, when I cried into my pillow for weeks, when Mom checked in and pretended as if I was only sad because of the accident. She'd known exactly what I'd been upset about—and she'd never let on, never helped me through it.

"Did you read the letter?"

"No."

"Do you still have it?"

Mom looks at me for a long moment. It's like she's evaluating if she can say no—if I'm still eighteen and impressionable.

I'm not.

"Yes," she says finally. "Are you sure you want it?"

"*Yes.*"

I follow her into the house, as she walks up the stairs and into the master bedroom, heading straight into the adjoining walk-in closet. I'd played there as a child before I accidentally ruined one of her shoes. It feels like an age ago, a different time.

Mom rummages through the wooden dresser. "I know I put it in the back here somewhere…"

I watch, arms crossed, as she runs her hand along the back of each drawer. Beneath my anger I can feel the hurt, running deep, threatening to consume me whole.

"Ah, here it is." She fishes out a yellowed envelope from the back of her sock drawer. One word is scribbled on it—my name—in messy handwriting. My eyes burn suddenly with the threat of tears as I take it from her. For a long moment, both of us are quiet, just staring at the envelope in my hands.

Mom clears her throat. "He's back now."

"Yes."

"And he's made something of himself." There's a faint pause, and then she looks away. "Served in the military."

"The Navy," I correct softly, still staring down at the envelope.

"Lily, *ma chérie*, I'm sorry. Genuinely. I never wanted to hurt you."

I grip the envelope hard and swallow against the lump in my throat. "But you did."

"Yes." Green eyes search my own. "Can you forgive me?"

"Tell me something. Do you still think you made the right call? Would you do it again?"

Mom looks at me, her gaze sad. "Yes," she says finally. "I didn't make him leave, but I tried to make sure you moved on. You were too young to throw away college for a boy."

"All right. Then I can understand why you did it, but I can't forgive you."

"Lily, I—"

"No. I'm done for tonight."

I turn on my heel and walk away from her, down the hall, the stairs, out into the warm evening air. Away from that beautiful house, with its memories, beautiful and painful alike. The envelope feels red-hot, lying on the passenger seat as I drive the short distance home.

When I've parked on the driveway, I rest my head against the steering wheel and take a few deep breaths. It's too much —all of it. Mom's decision. That she'd known all along.

That Hayden *didn't* leave without a trace, after all.

I grab the letter and cross the deserted street out to the beach. The waves are soft in the distance—the sound usually soothing—but nothing can soothe me now.

Sitting down on the beach, I open the envelope with trembling hands and pull out the letter inside.

Lily,

I've decided to join the Navy. They have a great program for college, after you've served. You know that I never had a real shot at getting into any college around here, not to mention the great ones that you're headed to, so this is my best option. You have always wanted more for me, and more from me. I promise to do my best to live up to that faith.

I want you to go to Yale, Lily. I want you to take so many art classes that you piss off your dad. I want you to wear the black nail polish that your mom hates. I want you to never be in another car accident for the rest of your life. I want all of that for you, and I know I can't be a part of it.

You always believed in me, and you always believed in us, that we were stronger than the world around us. So I know this won't make sense to you right away. Maybe it never will. I'm sorry for that. I'm sorry for a lot of things, but most of all, I'm sorry for that, for breaking your belief in me. I have never wanted to hurt you, and knowing that I have cuts deeper than I imagined.

And I'm sorry for leaving when you're still healing from the accident. That night will haunt me for the rest of my life, but I hope it never haunts you. You deserve better than that. Your future is bright, Lily. Always has been.

My world is infinitely better because you've been in it. Thank you for everything. I hope you can forgive me one day, even if I don't deserve it.

Hayden

I read it once, and then I read it twice, having to stop when tears blur my view entirely.

The ten years that have passed might as well have been a week, for all the strength I have left. I cry for myself—for how crushed I'd been when he left and broke my heart without a word, while the explanation was hidden somewhere in the very house I lived in.

I cry for young Hayden—for thinking he had no other choice, for leaving the one place that was home because of me, and the one person he trusted failing to see how intensely guilty he felt after the accident.

I cry for the ten years that feel wasted in longing. For how I've seen him everywhere, in everything, even when I desperately wanted nothing more than to forget him. For how I heard his encouraging words in my head during difficult times. For how I could curse his very existence and at the same time wish he was right there alongside me.

He had been honest. He had left because he wanted to pursue college.

But the words written here, in a strong, sprawled hand, speak of anguish and desperation. Of guilt and fear. And somehow, I'd failed to see that entirely, or even consider the possibility that he felt that way.

So I cry for that, too, for good measure. For my own blindness, and for clarity and insight that comes too little, too late.

13

HAYDEN

Hayden, 18

Gary rolls his neck and shoots me a look I know well. I put down my cup of coffee. I'm not going to like what's coming next.

"Your dad called again."

My breakfast turns to unease in my stomach. "You answered?"

Gary sighs. "Yes. And I told him the same thing I've said before—that you don't want him in your life. I didn't tell him where we are."

"Good."

"He mentioned that he's been texting you." Gary bends down to tie his shoelace, the picture of studied ease. "That true?"

Damn. "Yeah. I haven't been answering, though."

"How'd he get your number?"

"Through Aunt Ella, I think."

"Of course. That woman couldn't keep a secret to save her own life." Gary sighs. "You know it's your decision whether to talk to him or not. I can't decide that, kid, even if you know where I stand regarding that man."

"I know."

"Just… be careful. Don't give him any clues about where we are, okay?"

"I haven't. I won't." I haven't seen my father in nearly six years and I have no intention of changing that. There's only so many times he can lure me in with the promise of an apology before I know to leave well enough alone.

The years I'd spent with Dad, after Mom died, were the worst of my life. I had been lucky that Gary had taken custody of me instead. He'd come to see how his nephew was doing, blissfully unaware of his brother-in-law's addictions and violence. He'd taken one look at the situation and called social services. Without him, I would have been in my tenth foster home by now.

Plus, the absolute last thing I need is that man here, in Paradise Shores. The Marchands can never cross paths with that part of our past.

There's just some filth that stains, never to be washed out.

Gary throws me an apple. "Don't forget your lunch box."

"Funny."

"I'm a straight-up comedian." He grabs his jacket from the hook on the wall. Another day as the handyman. "Won't you be late if you hang around here?"

"Yeah, yeah."

"Don't think I haven't noticed that you're not hanging out with the other kiddos as often lately, by the way."

I zip up my leather jacket and ignore him.

"I'm not gonna meddle. But Hayden… You've got a good job at the docks. A good place to stay. Don't screw this up."

"I won't."

He pulls on his cap and shoots me a warning glare. If I thought I was too old for guilt, I'm not. The familiar feeling creeps through me. I know this job is solid for him—I can't be the one to fuck that up.

"I know," I tell him, one hand on the door. "You don't have to say it."

"Good. And about the girl, Lily... Be careful, kid. Be very careful."

The sea is gray and so is the sky. On days like this, there's nothing charming about living right next to the ocean—it's cold and miserable. I take the long route toward the garage, avoiding the back lawn and the Marchands' wrap-around porch. Gary's right.

I have been riding with the Marchand kids less likely.

I've also been feeling intensely guilty, all on my own.

It's hard to avoid thinking about the reason why. *Lily.* Beautiful, strong-willed, sweet, soft Lily. Lily-with-the-wild-dreams, Lily-with-the-shy-smile.

Lily, who my own uncle warned me to stay away from.

She thought I'd been angry when she arrived at Turner's party, when that couldn't be further from the truth. Seeing her was amazing—it always was—but it drove me to despair. How could we act within the finely set parameters of our friendship in that kind of environment?

She was too good for the good-for-nothings who went to those parties, with the alcohol and drugs and the closed bedroom doors. They were for people who wanted to escape, not for people with things worth fighting for.

Turner had always joked around about Lily, and Parker had taken it good-naturedly, but I knew he wasn't just kidding. Any man with half a brain cell would see what a catch Lily Marchand was. And as for Turner, half a brain cell was exactly what he had.

Lily had been angry with me for pushing him away, angry at me treating her the way I know she hated to be treated. And then...

I try to stop my mind from going back there, to that hallway, to her body against mine, but it's pointless. The feeling of her lips is imprinted in my memory. I wake to feel them against my own, dreams receding like the high tide, too fast for me to catch.

She'd been a living flame in my arms.

Auburn hair soft through my fingers, her body soft and inviting. It had been easy, far too easy, to be swept up in her sweetness. I could still feel the sigh she'd given against my lips, the soft sound of surrender, her trusting hands around my neck.

Hayden, she'd whispered.

I knew I couldn't go there. Couldn't be what she wanted, give her what she needed. She might have a crush on me, but that would pass with time. All it would take was one good look at what I had to offer compared with everyone around her, and the illusion would shatter. She'd break my heart, and I'd break hers by not being *more.*

I had to save us both from that if I was to have any hope of keeping her in my life, even from a distance.

I cut through the garage to where Parker's BMW is parked. The trunk is already open, his sports bag thrown in there. The engine is running and the driver's door is open. I roll my eyes at his predictability and get into the passenger seat.

A minute later he comes running into the garage with a protein shake in hand.

He shoots me a grin as he gets into the driver's seat. "Forgot breakfast."

"I figured."

"I've got to say, you've got the timing thing nailed down." He presses the controller and we both watch as the garage door opens slowly. "It's a bit creaky, by the way."

"Oh."

"The door, I mean."

"Yeah."

Parker looks sheepish. "Sorry. I meant… never mind."

"I'll ask Gary about it."

"Thanks, man."

"Don't mention it."

He cranks some old-school rock as we roll through the broad, tree-lined streets of Paradise Shores toward the marina. Working on one of the fishing boats that left from the marina, I was at sea for days at a time. It was hard work, but it paid well. Parker taught sailing at the yacht club, so we caught a ride together most days. It was a good summer job.

It also meant I didn't have to see Lily.

Not that she hadn't avoided me too, since the party. I'd tried nothing more than to catch her eye that first week, taking any opportunity to be where she might see me. Playing video games with Parker, just across the hall from her? Check. But she made it clear that she wanted space and I wanted her happy, so I left her alone.

It's just that I figured she'd wanted a few days, a week tops. Not over *a month.* The sudden lack of her in my life feels like a black hole inside, swallowing all light.

Parker's discussing the intricacies of fly-fishing when he suddenly goes quiet. "You're not listening, are you?"

"Of course I am," I say. "Place bait on the hook. Let it fly. Catch fish. See?"

He huffs out a laugh. "Sorry. I know this is boring. I just have to… Dad's taking me next weekend and I've sort of become obsessed in preparation."

"No worries," I say. Each of the Marchand kids has their own complicated relationship with their dad. In some ways, Mr. Marchand is larger than life itself, with his cold eyes and calm, measured words. He invests millions at a time in building projects and is rarely home. And when he is… I know he's impossible to impress.

So I know Parker wants to make a good impression. Must be a nice feeling, to have standards to live up to.

"Is something wrong between you and Lily, by the way?"

"*What?*"

"Look, I can't say I haven't noticed that the two of you barely speak anymore. That's cool, you know. You've never exactly been friends, but I just wanted to check in."

Despite myself, I want to laugh. Trust Parker to be a month late to the party, not to mention completely wrong in his assessment.

"No, we're cool. Everything's good. Don't worry about it."

"I'm not, mostly because I already spoke to her."

"Oh?"

He shoots me an amused sideway glance, long enough that I feel like telling him to keep his eyes on the road. "Yeah. And she said the same thing. So I know you've had an argument or something. Your stories are too similar."

"Maybe."

Parker sighs. "Look, she's my baby sister. Just watch yourself, all right? Even if she gets cranky or annoying, which she can be sometimes, you still have to be nice."

I grit my teeth. "Sure. Noted."

"Good." He turns up the volume and starts whistling, brotherly duty done. Not for the first time, I hate him a little bit. For his privilege and ignorance and thoughtlessness. But it passes, as it always does. I owe him more than he can fathom for his friendship and acceptance. Not to mention, he's right on the money, too.

I do have to watch myself around Lily. Even if the way things are looking, I might not be around her much at all.

I walk home from the marina later that day. It's a long walk, and my body aches from the day spent hauling nets, but Parker finished early and already drove home. Besides, I don't want him around for what I want to do next.

Lily's eighteenth birthday party is in a week. It's the massive event of the summer—the highlight of the Marchands' social calendar. Eloise Marchand has rented a marquee, waiters, catering… the whole thing. Henry and Rhys are both coming back home for the summer and the house will be full.

Lily has been dreading it and looking forward to it in equal parts.

I've only dreaded it—the house filled to the brim with snobby family friends and relatives—but I know it's important to her. To the family.

Paradise Shores doesn't have much of a shopping center, but it does have a small jewelers store. Nothing too fancy, but I'd seen them sell bracelets with charms, everything from seashells to unicorns to little Eiffel Towers. I'm sure it's something her mom or grandmother would call tacky.

But I think, if I manage to find the right combination of charms, it might just say the things I can't bring myself to.

14

LILY

The present

I look in the mirror. A casual skirt that reaches just above my knees. A blouse in soft blue silk smooths down my arms and leaves just a little bit of cleavage free. It's a perfectly respectable outfit for seeing an old friend.

Because that's what he'd asked for, on the beach, after revealing that he had left me a letter. *Friendship*.

And in honor of what we once had, I decide that I'm going to give it a try. Even if being friends with Hayden—who had meant everything to me—feels like dancing with danger.

But I would have to overcome that. We might have been childhood sweethearts, but we're grown now. A lot has happened in those ten years. Lord knows I've been on my fair share of bad dates, and no doubt he has as well.

We should be able to be friends. And popping by an old friend with a pie is a perfectly ordinary thing to do. A welcome to the neighborhood. I'd done it for people in the past—why should Hayden be different?

But as I park outside of the big red brick house on Elm Street, I'm suddenly overcome with nerves. My heart is beating a steady, cacophonous rhythm in my chest. After reading his goodbye letter, I'd felt raw, like I was still eighteen years old. The days that had passed since then hadn't made that any easier.

"Friendship," I whisper to myself. "*Friendship.*"

I'd missed him so much, and here I was, with another chance to have him in my life. Even if it hurt a little bit—even if it wasn't exactly what I'd once envisioned—could I really deny myself the opportunity?

I ring the doorbell. It's a little past seven in the evening and he might very well be having dinner or be out with friends. Maybe I should have texted, but I wanted the opportunity to chicken out at the last second if I wanted to.

Hayden opens the door. Thick, dark hair falls across his forehead. It's wet—and so is the towel he's slung over his shoulder. Dressed only in a pair of slacks and a gray T-shirt, it's clear he's just come out of the shower. His feet are bare.

Amber eyes widen in surprise at seeing me. They flick down to the pie in my hands, my skirt, my small studded ballerina shoes.

"Hello. Sorry to drop by like this, unannounced. I was curious about this place you're renting and I made tarte tatin. I know you used to like Mom's, so I thought… well, it's like a welcome present." I hand it over to him, my stupid mouth still going.

"Thank you."

"No worries. And no need to return the pan. I have plenty. You'd actually be doing me a favor if you took it off my hands."

This time he actually smiles, and when he does, he completely takes my breath away. The T-shirt stretches tight over his chest and around large, muscular arms. There's a faint scar around his left bicep, the hair on his forearms more pronounced than it was years ago. He's a man—and an extremely handsome one at that.

"Do you want to come in?"

"Me? Oh… If it isn't a bother."

"It's not. Come on." Hayden pushes the front door wide and steps back to let me pass. As I do, I breathe in the scent of him. Shower soap, male deodorant, and just a hint of cologne. The scent does odd things to me. He never used to wear cologne.

"Thanks."

"Let me just put this in the kitchen."

He walks past me, but I stay in the hallway, peering into the living room. The house is big, I can tell that much already. There's a massive fireplace. A dining-room table that fits eight people. Peering in the other direction, I see a white-and-blue kitchen with state-of-the-art appliances. This is a really nice house. There's a wide staircase that no doubt leads up to his bedroom.

"My mother hid the letter," I say to no one in particular, heart still pounding in my chest. "So that's why I never got it."

Hayden is back in an instant, a hand braced against the doorframe. "She admitted it?"

"Yes," I say thickly. "She'd even saved it."

His amber eyes hold the question—I can see it clearly—but his voice is tentative when he finally asks. "Did you read it, Lils?"

"Yes."

We look at each other. I can tell that he wants me to continue—to tell him what I think—but I feel too hot, all over, like I'm exposed. He's always been able to see far too much of me.

His words in the letter brought up my own feelings, and I'd found that they weren't gone at all. They were just buried. *My world is infinitely better because you've been in it.*

I want to ask him if he still thinks that. If he thinks about kissing me, the same way I remember his lips on mine. If, staring at me now, he feels the same pull between us that I do.

But he had asked for friendship.

And he'd left, letter or no letter. And I haven't forgiven him for that yet.

So I turn my back on him—and the silent question in his eyes—and walk into the living room instead. It's cozy, with two couches arranged around a flat-screen TV. It's way too big for one person.

"This is a great place, Hay."

"Thank you," he says quietly. "I was lucky when I found it."

"Renting it with furniture and all?" I run my hand over the back of a couch. It's a soft linen fabric, very much the vogue at the moment. It's expertly decorated, if a bit bland with the colors. No personal touches. It looks almost like the sort of decor I do for Harris Properties when we stage houses.

"Yeah, it came furnished."

"This is excellent," I murmur, looking at a driftwood lamp in the corner. It's understated but works perfectly with the Paradise Shores aesthetic.

Hayden returns, coming to stand beside me. The scent of man washes over me again. "You work with this stuff now, right?"

I nod. "Yes, I do most of the decor and staging for the new properties before they go on market."

"With Turner? At Harris Properties, right?"

"Yeah. I help out a bit with the architectural plans, too. It's very fun."

"Huh." Hayden runs his hand over the back of the couch. It's a thoughtful gesture, and combined with the sound, I can practically hear what he's thinking.

"Just say it."

He sighs. "I would have thought you'd work with art. In a

gallery, or painting... It was always your dream. Not getting into the same sort of thing as your father."

"I still paint," I say, although it's not technically true. I haven't for months. Whenever I pick up the paintbrush, all I can think about are my shortcomings. It's not fun anymore. But I miss it. I miss it like a missing limb.

"Good," he says. "You're too talented to stop."

"Well, I'm not *that* talented."

"Yes, you are."

I roll my eyes and take a seat on one of the couches. Hayden follows me, sitting on the opposite one and stretching out his long legs. *Friends,* I remind myself.

"Tell me about the galleries you worked at in New York."

"You've never liked all that artsy stuff."

"I've always liked yours," he says, voice entirely sincere.

I rub the back of my neck. "Thanks. Well... I worked in a place in Soho before switching to two on the Upper West Side. It was a lot of fun, that world. Seeing new artists come in and help curate exhibitions. I loved it. But everything has its time, you know? I missed the ocean, and I missed doing something practical with my hands. It was so conceptual all the time. I wanted to actually *create*, not just curate."

"So you came back here."

I nod. "I wanted to come back here and paint. To see the ocean every day, to be closer to my family. It was good to be away for a while, but it was even better to be back."

Hayden nods. "I can imagine."

"How about you? How does it feel to be back?"

"Weird." He's quiet for a moment. "Good."

"How's Gary doing?"

"Oh, you know him. He's doing the same old things he's always been doing. He's talking about trimming the lawn mower for your parents' place, getting it to go faster. I asked why speed was necessary, but he just laughed me off."

Hayden's uncle had always been one for tinkering.

"Remember when he made us homemade rockets for New Year's one year?"

"Yep. I was pretty sure he was going to get fired for that."

"What? My parents would never fire him."

His eyebrows rise. "If they found out about those rockets, I'm pretty sure they would've."

I don't believe that. "Well, he became my brother's hero after that."

Hayden snorts. "That's true."

"Anything Parker knows about cars today, he's learned from Gary. He still goes there sometimes, you know, just to ask for advice."

"Yeah, he told me something about that," Hayden says.

There's something I want to ask. Something that's been nagging at me for years, in the back of my mind. About being a fish out of water—dropped into a strange new place.

"How was it, growing up with us? Truly?"

His smile flashes again. "Truly?"

"Yes."

Hayden shakes his head, still smiling.

"What's funny?"

"You," he says.

"Why?"

"You just are. All right, I'll try to answer your question." He looks away, running a hand through his hair, the smile still playing around his lips. He's arrestingly handsome like that, sitting casually in his own home, freshly showered and shaved.

"It was great. You four, you were... well, I think it's something you only see from the outside. But you have each other. And as intensely jealous as I was of that, I also loved being close to it. Seeing what a family was supposed to look like."

It's more than he's ever told me. I run my hand over the throw on the couch, thinking about all the times we were together, all of us. "Everyone missed you, you know. After you left."

"They did?"

"Yes. Henry tried to hide it, but I could tell he was rattled. He was the one who kept us all updated on your military achievements."

Hayden's eyes are wide. "He did?"

"Yes. I'm sure it took meticulous research, but you know how he is. He has to have control over everything."

"Yeah. Yeah, that's true."

"Rhys wasn't surprised, though I don't know why. Parker missed you the most, I think."

Hayden nods, but not like he believes me. More like he's humoring me.

I frown. "They did, you know. I know things were complicated at times. But they did."

He nods and stands, stretching lightly from side to side. His gaze is softer, and I don't know if it's because of what I said or because he thinks it's cute that I tried. I never know what really gets through to him.

"I've been a bad host," he says. "Do you want something to drink? A piece of the tarte?"

"I can't eat my own gift."

"Of course you can. I'll be right back, Lils."

I sit in silence on his couch, hearing the rustle and bustle in the kitchen as he prepares plates. It's oddly domestic in a way we haven't been for years, perhaps ever. As children, we mostly spent time together with my brothers. Any moments for just him and me had to be stolen, to be carved out and guarded. They were some of my favorite memories.

My gaze snags on something on the mantlepiece. A large, pinkish cone shell, with a painted landscape on the side. *No way.*

He kept it?

I want to look at it—at the scribbled handwriting I know is

on the other side—but Hayden returns. He hands me a glass of white wine and a paper plate with the tarte on it. "Sorry," he says. "I don't have plates and all that stuff yet."

"Just wineglasses?"

"I found some in the back cupboard."

He takes a seat next to me on the couch, his big body so much closer than it was before. His arm drapes on the back of the sofa. My mind instantly wants to race ahead, thinking about the cone shell and what it could mean. I take a sip of my wine and try to ignore it completely.

Hayden smiles after he takes a bite. "Well, I've definitely missed this. Your family pretty much spoiled me for anything but French food."

"You know I don't do this half as well as my mom, not to mention my grandma."

A shadow briefly crosses his face. "No," he says. "Yours is the best."

I laugh. "Thanks, but now I know you're lying."

"Not a lie." He takes another bite of the tarte. He'd cut himself a huge slice, but it's already halfway gone. It doesn't surprise me. Together with my brothers, he always had a huge appetite. I guess it had to go somewhere—and now I know where. Straight into broadening his chest and strengthening those muscles.

I take off my shoes and curl up on his couch, legs crossed, turning to face him. "Let me guess what you didn't miss about Paradise Shores. The people. The organized parties. The water polo team."

He rolls his eyes. "Oh, Lily, don't mention the water polo team. I've missed them the most, I think. Not to mention their shaved chests."

"The school uniform?"

"Every day in the Navy, I just kept thinking, *this uniform would look so much better in the colors of Paradise High.*"

My smile is wide now. "Mandatory classes in Latin."

"*Non sibi sed patriae,*" he says, the pronunciation flawless. "You don't know how often that's come in handy. I might be the only sailor in the Navy who can actually conjugate our motto."

"Hanging on the bleachers."

"My great pastime."

"Smoking?"

Hayden narrows his eyes at me. "Smoking?"

"You used to smoke in high school, remember? I figured you'd stopped."

He puts the empty plate on the coffee table, turning to face me. There's an expression on his face that I can't quite place. I don't know if he's uncomfortable or embarrassed, but then he runs a hand through his hair and I know it's the former.

"You knew I smoked, Lils?"

I grin. "Of course I knew."

"I made sure to never smoke when you were around."

"Yeah, well, I figured it out."

"Hmm," he says. "A real Sherlock."

"That's me."

"You never called me on it?" He shifts closer, moving so that our knees almost touch on the couch. I don't know if it's a conscious movement or not, but his body has turned to face me too. It's hard to stop my pulse from increasing, or the painful tear in my chest. *Friends,* I remind myself. *He wants to be friends.*

But I can't stop the faint protest. *He kept the cone shell.*

"No. I figured it was important to you that I didn't know."

"I didn't want to be a bad influence."

"My own brothers wouldn't even swear in front of me. You were the one who taught me."

His smile is crooked. "That's right."

"And how to punch someone."

"Have you had to do that?"

"No," I answer honestly. "But I still remember. Look." I

raise my hand and make a fist, just like he taught me. Thumb on the outside of the fist, not inside, or it'll get broken instantly from the impact. Make sure you're not clenching so tight that your little finger starts collapsing inwards.

"Hmm," he murmurs, taking my hand in both of his. He twists it around, looks at the placement of my thumb. "Very good."

"I didn't forget," I murmur. His eyes are warm this close, the same amber color I remember. His skin is tan, and there are small, faint lines around his eyes now. He's seen things—done things, things I can't begin to comprehend. He's lived a whole life in the decade we've been apart. So have I.

But his hand on mine feels as familiar to me as my own. And while his hair might be shorter, it still curves over his forehead the way I remember.

"Good." Hayden lowers my hand slowly, until it's resting in both of his, in the open space between us. His thumb rubs a slow circle on the inside of my palm. The touch sends shivers up my arm and warmth through my chest. "What about you?"

"What about me?"

"You told me that your brothers missed me. Were they the only ones?"

My breath is coming fast. What he's asking...

"I'm sure your uncle did too," I tease softly, and he laughs. The throaty sound makes me lean in closer.

"*Lily*," he complains.

"I know, I know." I look down at where my hand rests in his. "I missed you too," I whisper. "You know I did."

He doesn't say anything for a long time, just sits there with my hand in his. They're warm and bigger than I remember, the skin dry and slightly calloused. I wonder what they'd feel like on my cheek, cupping my chin, sliding down along my neck and further down still.

My heart feels like it might beat out of my chest. Isn't he

going to respond? My heart aches for his words and my body for his touch.

His hand drifts to my knee, resting easily there. There's barely any pressure but my body still curves toward the touch. It's an automatic reaction where he's concerned.

"Lily," he murmurs, close enough that I can feel his warm breath against my mouth. "I'm sorry."

"Me too."

He bends his head and slowly, giving me more than enough time to pull back, presses his lips against mine. They're warm and soft and strong, kissing me with a powerful restraint. It's a test, I realize.

He's testing the waters.

His hand on my knee tightens slightly, fingers slipping under the skirt to softly caress my leg. I deepen the kiss—how can I not? His taste and warmth is everything I need. Everything I've missed, for years and years. Kissing Hayden was never *just* kissing. It's life-giving.

Warm lips coax my mouth open and I welcome his tongue inside. He's kissing me sweetly, our bodies barely touching. I can feel my heart opening.

Hayden…

For so long, I've dreamed of this. Of him, back in my arms. Of his lips against mine and the soft, warm gaze of his eyes that only I get to see. How hands that are hard and calloused can become tender, the feeling of his body when he's close to release but fighting it. Fighting it like he does everything in life.

Except he left.

I break the kiss and put a hand on his chest. "Hayden, we can't."

He leans back. There's fire in his eyes, and I realize just how tightly leashed he kept himself, to kiss me so gently for so long. "Why not?"

"I just can't." I shake my head and stand up. I struggle to

get my shoes on and try to close my heart. It can't open to him again—I can't handle the pain. It would kill me this time.

"Lily, I didn't mean to push you away."

"I know. And we're friends. We still will be. Thanks for the wine, and for the... for the dessert."

"Yes, of course. Anytime." Hayden's eyes search mine. I can tell he's curious as to the sudden change in me, but I can't explain it. I just know I'm in dangerous territory.

"I'm sorry," he says again, and I don't know for what. For kissing me? For leaving? For coming back?

Who was I kidding, thinking I could handle being just "friends" with him?

"I'll see you around," I say, and practically run for the door.

15

LILY

Lily, 18

Rhys is sprawled on my bed. His head is in a book, which is nothing new, but his hair is. He's shaved it short, all the long tresses gone. Something changed in him after he left for university.

"Can you explain to me again why the cousins from Maine are invited?" I ask him.

"Why, because it's Lily Marchand's eighteenth birthday party, of course!" I know he's not mocking me—he's mocking Mom.

"But I haven't seen them since I was thirteen."

"It's to humor Aunt Elaine. You know her and Dad don't see eye-to-eye."

"I know. But why use my birthday party for it?"

He flips a page. "Family politics."

"I hate it." I put the final pearl pin in my hair. It's in a massive updo, the way I know my grandmothers—both of them—prefer. But I've let some soft curls fall down, framing my face and my neck. A small act of rebellion.

My dress is gorgeous, though. Deep blue, with a low back

and a twirling A-line skirt. It took me nearly five months to sew.

I hear Rhys flip yet another page. His ability to read and simultaneously keep up a conversation has never stopped making me envious. "I haven't seen Hayden around," he says.

"Yeah," I say, fiddling with my zipper. "He's working at the docks this summer, on the fishing boats."

"Well, he can't be at work all the time."

I shrug. "I don't know his schedule."

That's not entirely true. I see him leaving the beach house in the mornings sometimes, and I occasionally catch him returning. It's the only glimpse I have of him, now.

It's been over a month since the graduation party and we still haven't properly spoken. I felt silly, a girl who threw herself at him at a party, dressed up to the nines, only to be reprimanded and turned away.

But as much as his rejection hurt, not talking to him might almost be worse. In the beginning, I'd avoided him because of my own hurt pride. I'd put myself out there and he'd turned me down, plain and simple. And when he'd tried to talk to me... Well, I'd turned away. The idea of him explaining it to me again—how we couldn't be together—hurt too much.

So I know it's on me now, to start a conversation—but how do you begin? If there is a roadmap back to our casual friendship, I certainly don't have it.

"Is he coming tonight?" Rhys asks.

I smooth a hand over the silk of my dress. "I think so."

In truth, I have no idea at all. He might stay away entirely. But I hope he doesn't.

———

"A drink?"

I shoot the well-meaning waiter a small smile. "Can't. I'm not twenty-one."

He looks sheepish. "Sorry, miss."

"No worries." I'd like nothing more than a cool sip of the champagne my dad's serving tonight, but I know that the approximately sixty guests would crucify me for it.

The bad thing about being the guest of honor? Everyone has their eyes on you.

Jamie threads her arm through mine. "Come on, Lils. You don't have to stand by the front door the whole night. Let someone else welcome the guests."

We walk through the house to the backyard, where soft music drifts from the live band my mom hired. They're good, I have to give it to her. Canapés are served, and I manage to nab one of the small quiches with tomato relish on top.

Jamie grins at me. "Thank God your mom hired the same caterers as for their wedding anniversary. Remember their desserts?"

"Are you kidding? I still dream about them." I pretend to swoon. "Oh, you fair chocolate eclair."

"That's why I came, you know," she says, eyes glittering with humor. "For the desserts. Sorry, Lily."

"I should be offended, but that's why I came, too," I say with a grin.

A strong arm wraps around my shoulder, and I look up to see Henry. He's freshly shaven, hair pushed back neatly. He looks older every time I see him—the kind of person who was never really meant to be a child in the first place.

"Hey, Lilypad."

"You made it!"

"Of course." He gives me a sideways hug. "How could I miss this? My baby sister is finally grown up."

Parker joins us, shooting Henry a grin as they bump fists. "Glad you're here, man."

"Likewise. Sorry I couldn't make it to your graduation."

"No worries," Parker says, eyes happy and open—although I know he's not entirely over it. "Have you seen Mom and Dad yet?"

"Yes, I spoke with them before. Is Rhys around?"

I nod to where Rhys is engaged in a discussion with our grandmother, Evelyn. I wouldn't be surprised if she's berating him about his new haircut and he's countering her with metaphysical arguments or a Nietzsche quote, the weirdo.

"I saw Hayden earlier," Parker says. "He'll join in a bit."

"Good, good," Henry nods. "Is he still living out in the beach house with his uncle?"

"Yeah."

"I wonder how much longer Dad will let him stay."

Parker frowns, echoing my own expression. "What do you mean?"

"Well, he's an adult now. The deal was surely that he'd be taken care of as long as he was a child and under Gary's guardianship." Henry's words, so matter of fact, feel like daggers.

"Henry, you can't say stuff like that," I say. "Stop being an ass."

He looks both amused and affronted, eyebrows raised high. "What? It's just the truth."

"Nah, man, Hayden's been like a brother to us," Parker says. He looks just as insulted as me. "That place is his home. He can stay with Gary as long as he likes."

"Sure, sure. Let's get a glass of champagne and enjoy Lily's birthday. We don't need to discuss this now."

Or ever, I want to add. I already know that Hayden will have to leave one day, and just imagining it breaks my heart.

The evening is a blur of names and faces and laughter. As much as I thought I'd hate it, I find that I actually don't. A few of my girlfriends from school are here, and so are Parker's and Rhys's friends. The Maine cousins are nice.

The only one missing is Hayden. I keep glancing over at the beach house, but it looks deserted and distant. No dark-haired, brooding boy in sight.

I'm taking a break from dancing when Turner shows up, a small smile on his face. "Hey."

"Hi. Parker's somewhere around here, I think."

He laughs. "I know, but I wanted to say happy birthday to you."

"Oh. Thank you."

"This party's really something."

"Yeah, you could say that again." I glance out over the marquee, the hanging lights, the smell of lilies from the many bouquets. "Mom sort of went all in."

"How about a dance?" He nods toward the dance floor.

The music is soft and soothing, and I want to say yes. But the memory of the graduation party holds me back. "And what if someone interrupts us?"

"I won't back off so easily this time, I promise."

"Good," I say. "Because *all* my brothers are here this time."

Turner shoots me a grin. "Let them do their worst."

Turner's a good dancer. He leads well, and I don't step on his feet, not once. He's taken the same classes at Paradise Shores that the rest of us have, but unlike most of my brothers, he seems to have actually paid attention.

My parents are dancing, too. I watch as they glide gracefully around us and feel the familiar ache in my chest. There's so much pressure to be like them. Beautiful. Successful. Universally adored. Even this party, which my mother threw out of love for me, reminds me of it. The expectations have nearly suffocated the joy out of Henry. I don't want them to do the same to Rhys or Parker. Or to me.

As if he can read my mind, Turner nods. "It's a lot, isn't it?"

"Yeah."

He leans in. "Parker has grabbed some of the champagne bottles. There's a sub-party going on in the basement."

"There's a *what*?"

"A sub-party. Come on, let's escape for a bit."

He's right. Rhys is already in the basement, opening a bottle. He hands me a flute of sparkling champagne. "Glad you could make it, my dear."

I sink down onto one of the large sofas and bend down to undo my painful high-heeled shoes. "Thank God for this."

Turner laughs and sits down next to me. "All we need is some food, now."

"Parker's on it," Rhys says. "I think he's gonna get Jamie and the girls too."

"Really?"

"We want you to enjoy yourself, Lils." He reaches over and tweaks my nose in a way he hasn't for years. "Soon enough you'll be on your own here for senior year, with all of us gone for college. Let us spoil you a little longer."

And they do. There's music and games and drinks, not to mention an entire tray of roast lamb vol-au-vent that Parker somehow managed to score. I have to filter in and out, to mingle with the guests, but together the whole thing feels a lot less lonely.

There's only one person missing. I had hoped he would come, but as the hours wear on, I don't think he will. This isn't his scene on the best of days, and especially not with me this dolled up... with the house filled with strangers. Strangers with trust funds and upturned noses.

Still, I had hoped.

It's many hours later when I've finally said goodbye to all the guests. Turner is in the basement with Parker, both of them passed out. My parents said goodnight ages ago, and the caterers have all packed up and left. I'm officially eighteen.

It's still warm outside, though. I stand in the backyard and take a few deep breaths. Salt and ocean spray hangs in the air, and the stars stretch out in a glittering blanket above me. The lights are still lit under the marquee, and without any guests, the place looks magical. The only music still playing is the sound of waves against the beach. I close my eyes and breathe in the salty air.

A familiar laugh, soft and low, rings out in front of me. My eyes snap open, only to see the one person I thought would never show.

He's wearing a dark suit, the one I know he bought for his graduation. It's a little short in the sleeves and snug over the chest, which only makes him look manlier. His dark hair hangs over eyes that dance with laughter.

Hayden looks so handsome that I think my heart might break from the sight. I know I've been in love with him for a long time, but it strikes me then just how far I've fallen. There's just no one else for me.

There never will be.

His lips curl, just slightly. "What are you doing out here, Lily?"

"I'm enjoying the night," I say. "The stars."

"More than your party?"

"It was nice, too," I say. "A bit boring at times."

"Did Henry show up?" he asks, taking a step closer.

"Yes, he's here. We had a sub-party."

"A sub-party?"

I step closer to him, too, and realize that I'm not wearing my shoes anymore. The grass is cold between my toes. "With champagne and games."

He nods. "And you had some?"

"Just a bit."

He lifts an eyebrow, in that way he's always been able to, and I can't help but smile. "All right. Maybe a few glasses. But not too much."

"I'm glad you enjoyed yourself."

We're quiet, just watching each other. I wonder what he's thinking, if he's missed me as much as I've missed him. If he feels like I do—filled with electricity from his nearness.

"Why didn't you come?"

"I'm here now."

"Yes, but…" I gesture at the empty tables. "Earlier."

Hayden frowns, like he's not sure if he should tell me the truth or not. The little crease between his brows makes my hand ache. I want to reach out and smooth it away, to run my fingers over his cheek. "To tell you the truth, I wasn't sure if you wanted me here."

"I always want you around."

He looks away, as if he's shocked by my admission. As if he doesn't already know how much I want him. "Yes, well, I screwed up last time. I can only say sorry so many times."

"I don't want you to say sorry," I say, shaking my head. Not that—anything but that. I want him to say what I'm feeling, that our kiss was *everything*, that he wants me as much as I want him.

He doesn't say that. He just smiles, small and true, and hands me a golden box. "Happy birthday, Lily."

"You shouldn't've."

"Open it."

I unwrap it slowly, looking from him to the gift. I hope he didn't spend a lot of money on it, knowing how hard he works for his keep. But I know better than to bring that up.

"It's just something small," he says with a shrug. "But I… well."

I open the lid to a reveal a gold bracelet resting on tissue paper. Small charms hang from it at evenly spaced distances. There's a seashell, shaped like a cone. A little painter's palette. There's a large tree—the one we used to climb in, I imagine. A tiny golden dog.

Shivers race across my arms as my eyes flicker between

the shooting star and the dog, wondering how he captured my heart in such small icons.

"Lily?"

"It's beautiful," I whisper. "Thank you."

Fastening it around my wrist is tricky one-handed, so Hayden helps me. I can smell the faint trace of soap and sea wafting from him.

"There," he murmurs, letting his hand linger at my wrist for a second longer. A calloused thumb smooths over my palm before he takes a step back. "It suits you."

"Thank you again." I touch a finger to the small dog, for Atlas.

"Don't mention it."

"Do you want to come in?"

He nods, eyes glued to mine. "Yes."

I lead him up the stairs to the porch and through the kitchen door. The rooms downstairs are dark and empty. Abandoned cups and glasses are everywhere, and in the corner, the rest of the food is packed up in one of the caterer's big cooling boxes.

"Are you hungry?"

Hayden's eyes are still glued to me. "No."

I swallow. The way he's looking... he looks hungry. "All right."

We walk up the stairs as silently as we can. Both of us know which floorboards to avoid, which part of the old railing creaks. I gently shut my bedroom door behind us.

The air between us feels heavy with things unsaid. I sit down on my couch, motioning for him to sit beside me. He doesn't join me.

"Lily, I..." He trails off and shakes his head. His eyes stop at the photos I have on my wall. Parker, Dad and me on a sailing boat. Riding on Rhys's back in front of the Eiffel Tower. Mom and I by the Colosseum.

"I missed you," I say. "I'm sorry for pushing you away."

Hayden's eyes snap back to mine. "That's all right. You were right to be angry."

"No, I don't think I was." I touch a finger to my bracelet again. "This is amazing."

He has his hands in his pockets, eyes dark. He doesn't say anything. He never has, really, about what we are. Neighbors? Friends?

Something more?

His gift makes it feel like we're something more. Something I've dreamed about for longer than I can remember. An us. A tangible unit.

I can see the same storm in his eyes, too. He can hide many things, but not from me.

My lips tingle at the memory of his touch. I'd felt like I was close to combusting under his insistent mouth. His hands on me… I thought I had been so familiar with them. Having held hands with him as a kid or seen them working, skillfully shucking oysters together in the summer.

But they had felt entirely new when they were wrapped around my waist.

"Hayden…"

He reaches out and grips the doorpost. To a stranger, he might have looked unbothered. But I can see how hard he's struggling to keep his expression neutral.

"Lily, we can't."

"You keep saying that. Don't I deserve to know *why?*"

He shakes his head, but it doesn't feel like a no. It feels like despair.

I don't understand why. He had been so responsive last time—he'd kissed me with reckless abandon. I know what I'd felt in those touches.

I know he wanted me too.

"It wouldn't be right."

I get up from the sofa. Hayden looks good in a suit.

Unusual. Different, even though the scowl on his face is the same. "Because we grew up together?"

"Yeah."

Reaching out, I run my hands up his lapels. The chest underneath is solid to the touch. "But I don't see you as a brother."

His low exhale of breath washes across my lips. "Thank God for that."

Putting a hand on his neck, I bury it in his dark hair, the way I've seen girls do before. My breasts are pushed against his chest—I made sure of that. Last time, he'd groaned into my mouth when he skimmed them with his hands.

"And you don't see me as a sister," I murmur.

"Absolutely not."

His pupils are massive, the heart underneath my palm beating fast. "*Hayden,*" I beg.

He closes the distance between us. The kiss is bruising in its intensity. My lips mold to his obediently, savoring the warmth.

Hayden sighs into my mouth and wraps his arms around me, pulling me closer against his body until there is no air at all. I don't want there to be, pressing closer still, my arms around his neck. We kiss like we've never done anything else and never want anything else.

He nips at my lower lip with his teeth and laughs when I draw back in surprise. "Can't help it," he whispers.

I smile and do the same to him. I'm rewarded with another bruising kiss, his tongue slowly finding its way into my mouth. I kiss him back, my hand lost in his hair and my nipples hard against his chest.

I've never felt anything like this before.

We end up on my sofa, somehow, both of us pulling down the other. I land on his lap, a thigh on either side of him, my dress riding high. Hayden presses kisses along my jaw and neck, down across my collarbone, setting my body on fire. Everything feels hot—too hot.

His hands cup my breasts, reverently, and I gasp as he smooths his thumbs over my nipples. His lips travel upwards again, back to my jaw and my ear.

I reach down to the zipper at the side of my dress, feeling brave. This is going to happen. I want him, and he wants me, and I have him here with me. I want to feel his skin against mine. Nerves race through my system as I grab ahold of the zipper.

Long fingers circle my wrists. "No."

"No?"

Hayden shakes his head. "No. We're not going further than this, not right now."

I frown at him. This burning feeling, the one I'm falling in love with, pulses throughout my body. I don't want to stop touching him, and I don't want him to stop touching me.

"Why?"

"Because it would be too fast."

"But—"

He leans in closer, putting his lips right next to my ear. "You have nothing to prove, Lily."

I sigh, relaxing against him. "You know I hate it when you say no to me."

"I know," he says, laughter in his voice. "But I'm not pulling rank. Just slowing things down."

"Fine. You're too moral for your own good."

"Only for your good."

"If people knew," I say darkly, pressing a kiss to his neck, "just *how* moral you are."

"I'd never be able to show my face in these parts again," he murmurs against my cheek. His voice is husky, the warmth between us still there. Just because we've stopped doesn't mean our bodies have stopped desiring. And I can feel his arousal, thick underneath me.

Hayden Cole is hard because of me. The simple fact makes my mouth dry. He wants me.

I move off his lap, sitting to the side of him, and press my lips to his neck. "But you want me?"

Hayden swallows. "You know I do, Lils."

My hand creeps across his thigh. I'm so nervous I can barely get the words out, but there's pleasure in that, too. In knowing that I'm the reason his breath comes fast. That he's as lost to this as I am.

"Lily…"

I pause, my hand by his zipper. "We don't have to go further than this. I just want to…" I can't say it. He's silent, hanging on to my words, amber eyes gazing into my own. It takes me a minute to find the courage. "I just want to see how much you want me."

Hayden swears, and I take it as encouragement. I run my hand over the hardness in his jeans and his head falls back against the couch. "Shit."

"Do you want me to stop?"

He swallows. "You should, baby."

"That's not an answer." I lean forward and press a kiss to his lips again. They're soft against mine, moving insistently. His hips buck lightly against my hand and I feel giddy with power.

I tug the zipper down and reach inside.

There's a bit of fumbling at first before I manage to close my hand around the hot skin. Hayden lets out a faint groan. "Lily…"

I try to pull his jeans down. He helps me, tugging at them with harsh movements, until they're tucked underneath his hardness. I glance from his face, nearly pained with need, to the clear evidence of it.

He's big against his stomach. Swollen and red, the head lightly glistening. It makes my stomach ache with want. What would it feel like to have that inside of me? Would it even fit?

As I watch, it throbs.

"Fuck. Lily, just knowing you're watching me…"

I run my hands down his abdomen and trace the happy trail. Looking him in the eyes, I wrap my fingers around his shaft. It's hot to the touch, the skin soft but so hard underneath. "Do you like that I'm seeing you?"

His response is through clenched teeth. "Yes."

I start to stroke, up and down, like I've heard about. Like I've seen. He's so big that I'm tempted to use two hands.

"Tell me," I whisper to him. "Tell me what to do."

Hayden reaches down and puts his hand around mine. He squeezes, showing me how much pressure he prefers. "Like that," he murmurs.

"Wont it hurt you? If I grip you this hard?"

He shakes his head once. "No."

But he looks like he's in pain. His head falls back against the edge of the sofa, and I can see the muscles in his throat work as he swallows. I feel too warm, too aware, too needy. Knowing I'm the one making him feel this way… it's intoxicating. I've only had one glass of wine but I feel high off this feeling.

I grip him tightly and stroke slowly. Hayden's breath is coming fast. He's watching me through hooded eyes and I love the glazed, adoring gaze. I feel powerful. For once, I can make Hayden as unsettled as he makes me, and just as vulnerable.

I let my other hand travel further down. There's so much of him I want to explore, but I don't know how much he'll let me.

I tug his boxers down further to free the heavy weights below, cupping them in my hand.

Hayden's eyes widen in surprise and I quickly release them. "Sorry."

"No, no…" He finds my free hand and gently puts it back.

I cup them again, tugging lightly. "Fuck, Lily... how do you know how to do this?"

"I don't."

"You do," he breathes, reaching over to smooth my hair back behind my ear.

I smile at him. "As long as I'm making you feel good..."

"Oh, you are."

I nestle closer to him and begin to stroke in earnest. Hayden's breath is coming fast, and his eyes are half-closed. It's like I've bewitched him.

"Faster," he murmurs, eyes closing entirely.

So I speed up. I'm gripping him tight, pumping away, my own desire rising in time with his. I want to know what happens at the finish line. I want to hear him.

His hardness is throbbing in my hand, and the heavy balls I'm cupping contract suddenly.

"Shit." His hand covers mine, his hips jerking. "I'm close. Lily, I don't—"

"I want you to," I whisper. I want him to lose control entirely. I want to be the one who causes it.

Almost involuntarily, his hips buck once, as if he's thrusting into my hand. I feel electrocuted by the sight—of him so completely undone. I've never seen him like that before. I stroke with both my hands, fast and hard. Hayden's hand creeps up around my waist, pulling me closer, almost by reflex.

Hayden lets out a muffled groan. "Lily..."

"Yes," I murmur, hoping I'm encouraging. "Come for me."

He erupts in my hand and I watch, transfixed, as he spills across his stomach. Hayden groans, low and dark.

I keep stroking, watching his face in awe. He looks raw, naked and undone and so painfully beautiful.

He pulls my hand away softly. "Sensitive," he murmurs.

"Sorry."

"Don't be, Lily."

I lean against his shoulder and peer up at him. He looks exhausted and spent, a faint smile playing on the edges of his lips. He wraps an arm around me without looking and I rest my hand on his chest, feeling the beating heart below.

"I feel pretty proud of myself," I say.

"You should. Lily… that was amazing." He lets out a tired chuckle and reaches to run a hand over the bracelet at my wrist.

"Just wait till I do that to you," he murmurs.

Nerves and heat chase one another inside of me at the words. His smile is wicked, face close to mine. I can't help but kiss him again—and for a few minutes, both of us get lost in each other once more.

Finally, I rest my forehead against his.

"Does this mean we stop avoiding each other now? And the inevitable?"

Hayden shudders against me. "I couldn't even if I tried, Lils. And trust me, I've tried."

HAYDEN

The present

The wide desk feels unfamiliar under my hands. Grown-up. Different.

My laptop is familiar—as is the work I was doing. Ones and zeroes flash before me. I don't do this often anymore, but when I do, I have to make sure it's perfect. My former brother-in-arms, now turned business partner, is an absolute genius with computers. Me... not so much.

"Concentrate," Finn says on the phone. "You're slipping."

I swear at him. "No, I'm not."

"You've been out of the game for too long."

"No, I haven't."

"All I hear are excuses." I watch as he completes a loop, finishing off the coding with an eloquent flourish. The screen goes black for a moment before it returns to the graphs and numbers I'm more familiar with.

"All right. Now this I know what to do with."

He laughs. "Maybe it's good that we have our respective fields, huh?"

"Yes. Let's stick to that," I say, finding the numbers I need.

"We're pulling in considerable capital from the East Coast now. You saw that I got Hornby Defense involved, too. With their backing, we don't need to take in any more outside investors."

"Yep, I read that email."

I shake my head at Finn through the webcam. "You could respond to them once in a while, you know. So I know you've actually read them."

"Yeah, yeah." In the silence, I hear the clacking of his fingers against the keyboard. "So, how's home treating you?"

"Good." I pause for a moment. "Weird."

"Being back?"

"Yeah."

"That's why I never go back. Saves me the trouble."

"That's a coward's way out."

He scoffs. "That was your way out up until a month ago, so quit playing."

He's right, of course, as he is about so many things. Finn has always been a straight shooter. There's nothing he won't call you out on, no bullshit he'll tolerate. It's why he's excellent at security software. He finds flaws and points them out ruthlessly, designing systems to combat all forms of security breaches. The last system we designed together just hit the market, and it's drawing in considerable cash.

"At least I got my head out of my ass," I say, knowing it'll draw a chuckle. "If you ever feel like getting some sea breeze…"

"Yeah, yeah," he says. "I know where you live, Cole."

"Is the update complete?"

"Yes. Go play with your childhood friends."

"Fuck off, Finn."

He laughs. "Talk to you later."

"Yeah. I'll update you on the shareholder meeting next week. And please answer my emails."

"Yes, boss," he says dryly and hangs up.

I sigh and close my laptop. There's never a shortage of things to get done. Becoming an independent contractor and entrepreneur meant becoming my own boss, and there was a part of me that relished it. But it also meant I could take on as much work as I wanted. The more hours I put in, the more money I make. And my pile of cash would grow, and grow, and grow.

I might never be able to buy respectability in the eyes of the Paradise Shores elite, but I could buy wealth.

And wealth is power—in all languages.

I look around my fancy home office. I hadn't lied to Lily. The house *had* come fully furnished. Only, I wasn't renting. I bought it.

It had been a crazy decision. And nobody knows—not even Gary. I want the house to be a surprise. A place for him to retire one day. Paradise Shores had become his home as surely as it had mine, after nearly twenty years in the area and in the Marchands' service. I also know that he couldn't live in the beach house indefinitely—not once he retired.

He'd done so much for me. It had taken me a few years of adulthood to fully realize just *how* much. With a child's eye, it had sometimes seemed self-evident that he was my caretaker. My mom was dead and my dad a drunk—of course my uncle took me in.

But things aren't that simple, and I know now that a weaker man wouldn't have been as generous or as strong as he had been.

But the house would also come as a surprise to Lily and her family.

The thought of her made me groan.

Oh, Lily.

I'd screwed it up when she came to my house a few days earlier. I hadn't been able to stop myself from getting too close, from asking what I wanted to know.

She was kind to tell me her family had missed me. I'm

sure Parker had, but I couldn't for the life of me imagine Henry or her parents giving me a second thought.

Lily, though. She had. I'd suspected she would, and knowing I'd hurt her by leaving was painful. It was a wound I'd made worse rather than better by kissing her.

But damn, what a wonder kissing her was.

The sweetness of her lips, the way she'd leaned into me. The soft skin of her leg where my hand rested. The kiss was painful in its carefulness, in the way I had to hold back ten years of want and need and sorrow.

It had been an innocent kiss, but it had meant so much more. And Lily knew that too.

Hell. I knew why she'd left so abruptly—I understood it. I'd stirred up things I should have let lie. *Damn it, Cole.*

The strategy of this operation was simple: ask forgiveness. That was my goal in returning. If I could have her friendship, if I could just have her in my life, it would have to be enough. I knew well enough that I could never ask her to be mine again. I'd hurt her too badly for that.

But now I'd gone and messed up the prospect of a friendship, too. It's been two days and I haven't heard a word from her.

Everything in me tells me we need to talk. Knowing she's in this town and not seeing her, not going to find her, feels like torture. She's like a magnet to me. Always has been.

But my fear wins. Without time to think, she might push me away. And if she did… It would kill me.

At the same time, I can't just leave it, either. So I do the only thing I can think of. I drive to the large arts and crafts store just outside of Paradise Shores. Lily had said she still painted, but her eyes had betrayed her. It might not be a complete lie, but it wasn't entirely truthful, either.

And the Lily I'd known had only ever wished for one thing, every birthday and Christmas. More art supplies.

I ask one of the employees to help me pick things out, and

by the end, I leave the store with a giant basket filled to the brim with brushes, acrylics, rolled-up canvas and clay. It's an assortment of everything I know she likes. Or *liked*, once upon a time.

She's at work when I stop outside her little beach cottage, so I place the basket on her front step. I scribble something on a little card and place it on top, wedged in between a set of fan brushes and a sponge.

And then I drive away, feeling satisfied. It doesn't matter how many times I say sorry—sorry for everything, for the other night, for leaving her ten years ago, for not staying in contact. It's just words, and actions speak louder.

I just pray I didn't screw everything up by kissing her.

HAYDEN

Hayden, 18

Lily is sitting in my lap, her hair a curtain around me, her smiling lips against mine. "Just stay."

"I don't think that's a good idea."

"Hayden…" She kisses me again, and I forget what we're arguing about. That happens a lot these days. My hands trail down her back, finding anchor at her waist. She's as familiar as the back of my hand and still as stunning as the dawn. Kissing her never stopped striking me silly.

I pull back, tipping her head so I can reach her neck. It hadn't taken me long to realize that's where she was the most sensitive.

Well… the most sensitive part I could get to while she was clothed. I feel her pulse flutter under my lips.

"Your grandma hates me," I say. "If she wasn't invited for Friday night dinner… then maybe."

"That's not true."

"Lily, it's absolutely true."

Her breath is coming fast. "Okay, maybe, but so what? You're one of us."

Oh, my sweet, sweet girl. I might be accepted among the younger Marchands, and tolerated by their parents, but I was an absolute outsider among the extended family and their friends. The cuckoo in the nest.

"Come anyway," she whispers. "Come for me."

"Lily..."

"I won't enjoy myself if you're not there."

For Lily, I'd brave the wolves and the devil himself.

"I'll come by around dessert," I murmur. "Just to say hi."

She hums in pleasure against my lips. "Promise me."

"I promise."

"Good." She kisses me again, achingly soft, her hands playing with the hair at the back of my neck. "I barely see you these days. I can't spend the evening without you, too."

"Mmm." I know she dislikes my job on the fishing boat. She never says it, of course, but it took me away from Paradise Shores for hours on end, not to mention the occasional overnight trip. It sometimes got windy or stormy, too, and I knew she hated those times, imagining all the things that might happen at sea. My girl has too good of an imagination.

But it paid well. So well, in fact, that I'd more or less decided to skip the idea of the military or community college altogether. I could stay here and work for another year.

"What about Parker? Won't he suspect something?"

Lily shakes her head. "We've managed to keep it a secret for weeks and weeks. Why would he?"

"I don't hang out with him as much anymore," I whisper, shifting so I can touch my lips to her collarbone. "He's already asked me what's taking up all my time. Twice."

Lily's fingers undo the first two buttons on her blouse. "Lie."

I grin and watch as her bra is slowly revealed. White, prim cotton with a lace trim. Unbearably sexy. Her skin is tan from the summer sun, lightly sprinkled with freckles, her hair framing her beautiful neck. I kiss down the slopes of her breasts, toying with the idea of just getting the top and bra off her. But we're short on time, and I don't want her to ever feel rushed or used with me.

"I guess I'll have to," I say, thinking about Parker. It's understandable that she doesn't want him or her family knowing about us. It would only complicate things.

"Mmm." Lily bites her lip, her eyes twinkling as she leans back to pull off her shirt. "Whoops?"

I shake my head at her, but my hands are already moving to the fastening of her bra. "We have very little time, baby."

"Five more minutes."

"All right. And then I'm out of here before your parents get back."

She moves closer to me, a soft sigh of pleasure escaping her as we meet, skin to skin. "That's a deal, Cole."

In the end, I have to run, but it's worth it. The scent of her hair and skin cling to me throughout the evening, reminding me of what I've somehow gained. Lily is too good for me—that's true—but for the time being, I've decided to let myself dream that we are possible.

She wants me, just like I want her.

She likes me, just like I like her.

And for the first time in a very long time, I'm happy.

And if she wants me to show up to her family's place for dessert... well, I'll damn well try. I take a shower. I shave and get dressed, wearing the one button-down I own over my worn-out chinos. The only nicer shoes I have are my old boat shoes, inherited from Henry, but they'll have to do.

Lily's parents have always been kind to me. A reserved kindness, true, but still. I can't imagine they'd be happy if they knew... But maybe they'd come around. But her grandmother, Evelyn? The first time she met me, she had asked if I was the pool boy. I'd been thirteen years old.

And the Marchands didn't even have a pool.

She would *hate* me with Lily.

I pause on the lawn behind their house. The dining room is well-lit—I can see it from here. There has to be at least fifteen people in there. The whole clan and all of the extended relatives.

Great.

I usually go in through the back door, by the kitchen, and I head there now. The last thing I want is to open the front door and arrive smack dab in the middle of mingling Marchands in the foyer.

I reach the back door and it swings open on quiet hinges. I'd oiled them just two weeks earlier so they wouldn't make a sound when I snuck out of from Lily's bedroom.

I wipe off my shoes on the doormat and straighten the button-down. It's been a hell of a long time since I've worn something like this. The house smells like pumpkin soup and cinnamon, and I close my eyes and just breathe. This house has never felt like home to me. It's never been uncomplicated. But one day... one day, maybe I could have a home like this for myself.

"Are you sure?"

The voice is softly spoken and cultured. I recognize it immediately. Grandma Marchand herself, right in the kitchen next to me. So much for a stealthy entrance.

"Yes. I think it's been going on for a while now," Eloise says.

I push back against the door. The last thing I want to do is interrupt the two matriarchs while they're conspiring. I know very well that they hold my potential fate with Lily in their hands.

"Hmm. Not surprising, I suppose. Teenagers will be teenagers."

"Yes."

"But you're worried, you and Michael?"

There's a faint, heartbreaking pause as Eloise Marchand

deliberates. "Well, he has no real college prospects. That's a shame, too, because the boy is bright."

"I'm sure," Grandma Marchand says, in a way that implies she's not. "Lily's got a big heart and she's as stubborn as her father. Do you think she'll make a stupid decision because of this boy? Stay here just to be close to him? Go to the same community college as him? If he's captured her as thoroughly as you think…"

"She might," Eloise says.

"And give up her spot at Yale?"

"She hasn't gotten in yet, Evelyn."

An elegant snort. "But she will. She is a legacy, two times over. Of course she will. And this boy… He might stand in the way."

"That's what I'm afraid of. Still, the decision needs to be Lily's."

"Of course," Grandma Marchand says. "And in making that decision, we need to make sure that she has the proper guidance."

"I'll talk to her." I hear the slamming of pots, closer to where I'm pressed against the back door. "I'll make sure she knows that no boy is worth sacrificing her future for."

"That's right. Least of all that rogue, too. Where did you say he came from again?"

I don't need to hear anymore.

I wait for a few more moments, until I hear them leave the kitchen, before I slip out through the door.

———

The waves are soothing against the beach. A few almost make it all the way up to the stairs to the beach house. They inch closer, but I know they won't make it. They've tried for years —every night at high tide—but they never make it.

The ocean is complete blackness. I don't know how long

I've been sitting out here. It feels like I've been alone with my thoughts and the ocean for an eternity.

The dinner party will be finished up by now. Michael Marchand will drive the old lady home. Lily will stand on the grand porch, the pearls she hates to wear around her neck like a noose, and wave goodbye like the good girl they want her to be. The good girl she is.

I can see her in my mind's eye. Her hair is piled high on her head in a nod to old-fashioned customs. Her dress is perfectly ironed. All of her, one gigantic *do not touch* sign.

Eloise and Gran weren't wrong. I'm beneath her, and we all know it.

And I would rather die than let her sacrifice her future just because of my lowly prospects. Her love would turn to resentment soon enough, when she's denied the same opportunities her brothers are, because of me. Because she didn't go to Yale. Because her boyfriend doesn't drive a sports car. He currently doesn't have a car at all.

It's late when I hear the soft padding of her feet on the sand. She's barefoot, walking from the main house. The perfect dress is hitched up to give her more legroom, and she's released her hair. It tumbles wild and free down her shoulders, a river of auburn curls.

She's so beautiful it hurts.

Lily takes a seat next to me on the steps. We sit in silence for a while, watching the waves as they fight against nature's laws to make it up the beach.

I can tell that she wants me to talk. To explain myself— why I didn't show up, despite promising to. But I can't tell her what I overheard. The words won't come. Not for the first time, there's absolutely nothing I can say to make this right or to explain myself.

"Hey," I finally murmur.

"Hiya."

"How was dessert?"

"Disgusting. Liquor-infused cherries. You didn't miss a thing."

And there she goes, trying to make me feel better even though she doesn't have a clue why I'm down. Lily's kindness has always been one of the most amazing things about her. I've never understood how one person could carry so much understanding and love.

But that's also why I need to ask her something, even if the answer will break me.

"That sounds awful."

"It was." She scoots closer until we're sitting shoulder to shoulder and thigh to thigh. I can see the goose bumps on her legs.

"You're cold, Lils."

"I'm not."

I shrug out of my hoodie and wrap it around her. She nestles into my side until I'm forced to wrap an arm around her shoulders. It feels better than it should.

"Lily, have you thought more about college?"

She takes my hand and puts it on her bare knee. Her soft skin is riddled with goose bumps and I rub my thumb in little circles, trying to keep her warm and failing. "A bit. I've been reading course catalogs this week."

"Yale?"

"Yeah, and Princeton." She traces one of my knuckles. "And Rexfield College. They have some interesting courses in art design."

I feel nauseous, all of a sudden. "They do?"

Lily's voice is soft. "Yes. And I know it's not as prestigious as the others, but I don't really care about all that. What's really important is that I get a good education."

"Your parents would hate community college."

"Yes, well, they'd come around. I'm the last to go." She shoots me an exasperated glance. "After all of Henry's success, do you really think it matters what I end up doing?"

"Yes. I think it matters."

Her green eyes soften, just slightly. "I'd be close by, you know, if you continue to work at the marina. If you apply too, we'd even be going to the same college."

"You always spoke about Yale," I murmur. "It's your dad's alma mater."

She rolls her eyes. "Not you, too. Have you and my dad finally begun to see eye-to-eye?"

"Sometimes we do," I say. When it comes to her and her happiness, I figure we might be on the same page entirely. And in this regard, I know I'm not a part of the calculation.

She senses my hesitation. With a small sigh, she leans her head against my shoulder as I tighten my grip around her thigh. Lily has never been closer to me than she is now, with no brothers around, just the two of us together on the beach without secrets or pretensions.

But she has never been more out of reach.

"It's just a thought so far," she murmurs. "We can talk about it more later."

Her voice might be soft, but I can hear steel lacing her words. She would go to the mat for this if she had to. Fight with her parents over this. Turn down her legacy and an opportunity that kids like me didn't even dare to dream of.

For me.

And fuck if that didn't terrify me.

"Yeah," I say. "Let's talk about it more later."

There's no sound but her soft breathing and the waves gently crashing against the beach. I'm so used to the smell of salt by now that I barely register it anymore, but it suddenly hits me with the same force it had the first time. The sound of the ocean has become home, even if I'd never meant it to. Somewhere along the line I had forgotten that I wasn't from here.

I'd forgotten who I was, and suddenly I can't stay here for even a second longer, or it would tear me apart.

"Come on," I say and grab her hand. "Let's go."

She smiles at me as I pull her into standing. "Where to?"

"Somewhere. Anywhere. Away."

Lily pulls my hoodie tighter around her. Her eyes search mine, and I don't know what she sees in me, or if she realizes just how close to the edge I am in that moment—that there's a storm inside me that I need to let out or it would drive me mad entirely—but she just nods.

"Okay." There's a smile as dazzling as the night sky on her lips and trust in her gaze. "Let's go, Hay."

18

LILY

The present

The first thing I think is, *This must have cost him a fortune.*

The second thing is, *He got me pastels. I haven't painted with pastels in forever.*

The third thing is less complimentary. *How dare he?*

I carry the giant basket inside and put it on my dining-room table. It's filled to the brim with the very best supplies a girl can ask for. It's with shaking hands that I pull out a jar of gesso, and I can't help the smile that breaks across my face at the packet of charcoal crayons. It's been over a year since I did this—since I painted just for fun. Looking at these supplies, at the millions of possibilities… it does something to me. Tightens my chest and opens my heart. Dangerous, dangerous.

There's a note, too. His handwriting has improved, compared to the ten-year-old letter.

Sorry for the other night.
Let's give friendship another try.
I promise I'll behave. -Hay

Friendship. He comes back out of the blue, not a call or a text in ten years. He goes out of his way to be at events I'm at, fixing my damn gate without my permission. He tells me he's sorry for leaving and asks for friendship.

Okay. All right.

I can handle that.

But I can't handle him asking me, in that deep voice of his, whether or not I missed him while he was away. I can't handle Hayden kissing me like he's afraid I'm going to break, like I'm all he's ever wanted, like he wants to start something anew. It wasn't a kiss for old time's sake—it was a make-up kiss. A start-things-again-kiss.

My hands clamp into fists of their own accord. *How dare he.*

I'd worked so hard to get over him. So hard to ignore the painful beat of my heart when I thought of him, the constant comparison when I was around other men.

Why did he still have the cone shell?

I'd seen it on his mantlepiece. A large cone shell with a delicately painted landscape on it. A blazing sunset cast against trees, a full moon. I'd made it for his fourteenth birthday. I knew that if I turned it around, on the inside of the shell, I'd see the scruffy handwriting that thirteen-year-old me had worked so hard to perfect. *To Hay, love Lils*

He'd kept it.

He'd even brought it with him to his rental—a house so clinically decorated that it practically screamed bachelor pad.

Why?

I pick up the big basket and carry it to my guest room. I put it on the bed and close the door behind me. Until I figure out what to do with Hayden, I won't use a thing. I don't want his gifts until they come with a proper explanation—or when I've decided I can live without one.

As it so happens, I might just be able to get one tonight.

My mother likes Friday night dinners. It had been a

standing routine growing up. On Friday night, at seven o'clock, she'd serve some amazing dish in the main dining room. In the summers, we would barbecue on the porch and Dad would handle the grill. Sometimes we ate roasted lobster, giggling as we waved the claws around, pretending to fight one another.

Being back in Paradise Shores meant going to Mom's Friday night dinners, as often as possible, or suffer her wrath.

Sometimes it was just the family, but more often than not there were plenty of people. Friends of my parents were invited to join, as was the extended family. Sometimes the neighbors. Growing up, Hayden was often there, especially if he'd already been playing with my brothers beforehand.

After the argument I'd had with Mom—after she hid that letter for *ten* years—I hadn't planned on going this Friday. But then she told me she had invited both Gary and his nephew. *For old time's sake,* she had written in the text, but I recognized it as an attempt at an apology.

She's trying to make amends.

And while I don't forgive her... I also don't want to pass up on the opportunity. When I arrive at the family house, my parents' driveway is already filled with cars. I recognize the black Mercedes that Hayden's currently driving. Parker's Jeep is there too. I'm the last to arrive.

They're out on the porch and I hear the sounds of laughter and ice against glass. Parker spots me first. He has his sunglasses on, sitting on the settee, a beer in his hand.

"Finally!"

I shake my head right back at him and head to the barbecue. My dad is focused on the steaks, a look of supreme confidence on his face. He treats everything in life like he does his business deals. "I'm only five minutes late."

"Sure, sure," Parker says.

Dad wraps an arm around me. "Hello, sweetheart."

"Hi."

He frowns down at me. "I heard about the Anderson project from Reed Harris."

"You did?"

"Yes. He said his son was running lead on it… with help from you."

"I worked on it, yes. We just recently sold it. Turned a solid profit."

Dad nods and turns back to the grill. "That's good. Cut your teeth, sweetheart."

He doesn't say it, but I hear the implication. *And in a few years… you might work with me.* I know he doesn't consider Harris Development proper builders, not in the way he is.

"I will," I say, knowing it might be a lie. I'm not sure I want to work with this, not forever.

My dad gives a nod. "Your mom is inside."

I know when I'm dismissed.

Hayden's standing at the end of the porch. He's wearing dark-blue slacks and a button-down. It's simple clothing, but he fills them out completely. There's no doubt just how muscular he is.

His eyes meet mine. There are questions in them, questions I know he'll ask later. About the kiss. About the basket. About us.

He glances down at my dress and I see the exact moment he realizes just what I'm wearing. I have to admit, after eleven years the fit isn't quite what it used to be, but somehow, that only works to my advantage. The blue dress hugs my curves and the scalloped back shows off more skin that I usually would nowadays. Still, it's modest enough for a Friday family dinner.

His eyes flick back to mine with surprise. *Yes,* I want to tell him. *You remember this dress.* It's what I wore to my eighteenth birthday party—the night we became *us.* For a while, at least. Before he broke it.

I turn my back on him.

Gary comes up the stairs to join us. He's rarely at Friday night dinners, and I've always wondered if he feels uncomfortable with the odd mix of friendship, family and work. But Hayden's presence isn't something he'd miss.

My dad shakes Gary's hand.

"Glad you could join us tonight."

"Thanks for the invitation, sir."

"Have a seat. There's wine and beer." Dad raises his voice. "Parker, get Gary something to drink."

My good-for-nothing brother shoots out of his chair to do as Dad bids. I resist rolling my eyes and step past them into the kitchen. Mom is working on the final touches.

She stops when she sees me. "*Chérie...* I'm glad you came."

"It's tradition."

Mom nods, her eyes glinting mischievously as she looks at my dress. As if she knows exactly why I've dressed up.

She's put her hair up in a big bun and gold earrings dangle from her ears. The years have been good to her. It's vanity, but I hope I'll age like her. Like nice, aged French wine. Like a woman who gave up her home country for an American businessman. Who dedicated her life to raising four children and making this small, seaside town her home. She hasn't always been easy to please—God knows that—but... I'll forgive her eventually for the letter. I know that.

"Help me with the *haricot verts*?" Her voice is tentative, pointing at the small casserole.

"Sure."

"A bit more salt." She's quiet, both of us working in silence for a few beats, before she surprises me by talking about Hayden. "The military...it's not exactly a place for just anyone. I didn't know he had that streak, but when I think back on it, I think it was just the right place for him."

"You do?"

"Yes. Can you imagine Parker in the Army? Rhys?" Mom

takes a tray of baked potatoes out from the oven. They smell amazing, filled to the brim with herbs and seasoning and cheese. Dad might know how to grill—the only thing he knows how to do in terms of food—but Mom reigns supreme in here.

"Henry, maybe," I say.

She nods, a smile on her face at the thought of my oldest brother. The wonder child. "Yes, *Henri* would manage it. He'd probably excel. But no, I can't imagine any of you others would, apart from Hayden."

I can't tell if she's genuine in her praise of Hayden, or if she wants to get on my good side again, but I decide to not question it.

"Are we ready to sit down to dinner?"

"Yes," she says, carrying the potatoes. "Do you want to tell your dad to take the meat off the grill?"

We all take a seat around the dining table. Hayden takes the spot opposite me, and I can tell that he's searching for my gaze, but I avoid making eye contact with him. I'm feeling too much, not all of it good, and I don't trust my gaze. He's always had a way of being able to read me.

But as it turns out, it's difficult to avoid looking at someone who's the clear subject of conversation. Mom asks him repeatedly if he got hurt in the Navy. Dad asks about rankings and career prospects. Parker makes sly innuendoes about scars and women, drawing laughs from all corners of the table.

Hayden grins and bears it all.

The boy I remembered would have hated being the center of attention, had disliked praise, but now he handles it with grace. The expression on his face is one of serenity.

And when Hayden regales us with a story from his time patrolling the Bering Straits, nobody eats, hanging on to his every word. My dad and Parker can't get enough of the details.

"And you were *right* off the coast of Russia?"

Hayden nods. "We're in international waters, but the storm caught us off guard. There was no warning—nothing. We wouldn't make it to port in time, so we had to ride it out at sea. That's not unusual in the Straits in September, these storms, when the sea ice is starting to form in the Arctic. It's one of the last patrols of the year before we need to use the ice-breakers."

"The waves?"

"Over forty feet."

Parker whistles. "Shit."

"Thing is, the wind is so strong, it's pushing us closer to their border. And command knows that the closer we come, the more antsy the Russians are getting."

Mom frowns. "But you're not meaning to. It wouldn't be intentional."

"One would think that matters, but in these situations, it doesn't. A breach of naval space is a breach of naval space." Hayden shrugs. "We would be on edge too if the situation was reversed."

Dad is leaning forward. "What did you do, son?"

"The USS *Denver* is a big ship. But it's not an aircraft carrier or a destroyer, it's a cruiser. This was a regular patrol. So I had one of my lieutenants radio in to command and make sure they made contact with the Russians. That had to be step one, that they knew this wasn't intentional. And in the worst case so that they could help us if we went down."

Gary draws a breath. "Hayden…"

He shoots his uncle a small smile. "It's rare. But we didn't have cargo or ballast, only ballast water."

"What?" My father reacts immediately. Ships and boats, and you'll have his rapt attention. "You're telling me a US cruiser went to sea without proper ballast?"

"Yes. It was a tactical decision, but one that backfired given the unexpected storm. We were rolling heavily. We went from thirty degrees heeled over to one side, only to whip to the other at thirty degrees, all in the span of seconds. The crew was… well. It took its toll."

"Did you have steering-way?"

"Yes. We had to fight for every inch to make sure we met those waves head-on. But she's a well-maintained ship, and the crew is worth its weight in gold."

"What did you do?" I murmur, looking at him. It's easy to picture him in his uniform, out under a darkened sky, thousands of miles from home. The waves crashing around him, barking orders.

Hayden's gaze softens. "You do what you can. You give the right orders and you follow the ones given to you. And then you hold on, and you pray for luck, and hope you win the fight against the sea."

There's complete silence around the table. I can see the pride in Gary as he looks at Hayden. Oddly enough, it's also mirrored in my dad's eyes. Who knew?

"We're so thankful you're back," Mom says finally. "And no more active service, huh?"

"Not sure yet," Hayden says carefully, avoiding my eyes. "I'll have to see. I don't know how long I'm staying."

My mom shoots him a massive smile. "Will you come tomorrow? To the marina?"

Hayden looks confused, but nods. "Sure."

"Mom is on the organizing community for the Junior Sailing Regatta," Parker explains. "I'll be there, helping out. You should join, man."

"Sure. I'd love to."

"I'll text you the details," Parker says. "Lily will be there too, won't you?"

I grit my teeth and nod. "Yes. Yeah, I will."

Mom puts a hand on mine and I resist the urge to withdraw it. "Lily is painting children's faces, the dear. It was so popular last year that we had to get her back a second time."

Hayden looks straight at me. There are a million things in his eyes—laughter being the main one. "I can't wait to see that."

The rest of the dinner is uneventful. We make it through the main course and dessert without any mishaps or odd questions. I even manage to avoid talking directly to Hayden.

But Mom turns to me after dessert, and judging by the teasing look in her eyes, she's about to put an end to the peace. "Lily, how's Turner? Is it time we start inviting him to a few Friday night dinners?"

I can practically see Parker's grin next to me, just like I notice the sudden edge in Hayden. God, get me out of this dinner, and save me from my own meddling mother.

"No, I don't think so," I say, gritting my teeth. "We just went to an event together. It's too early for family dinners."

Avoid Hayden's gaze, avoid Hayden's gaze... It's a mantra in my head now.

"But you've known him forever," Parker points out. "It's not a stretch, exactly."

Dad comes to my rescue. His face is marred by a frown, as it so often is. "They work together. There's no denying he's a good man, like his father. But mixing business and pleasure is never a good idea."

"Yes, there's that. Thanks, Dad. I'm very concerned about what it might do to our professional life. Now, let's move on from my dating life."

But no, apparently we aren't quite done. Hayden frowns, suddenly looking like a mirror image of my father. "Not to mention, Parker and I knew Turner quite well in high school. I'm not entirely sure about some of his actions."

"Is that so?" my dad says, leaning back. "Parker, is that true?"

Parker shoots Hayden a look so filled with surprise it's almost comical. "Well, yes. Technically. But he's grown up since then."

"He has," Hayden says thoughtfully. He's leaning back in his chair too, muscled arms crossed over his chest, looking like the sole authority on the topic. "One wonders how much, though."

I'm so angry. It's a hot furnace inside me, burning and burning. *Now* he's protective? Is it the kind of protective you are of a friend? The same kind of friend you kiss—or the friend you send platonic gift baskets to with notes asking for friendship?

"Turner's a great person." It takes effort to keep my voice calm. "For the moment, I'm not interested—but if I want to date him, I will."

My emotions are like a yo-yo. One pull from Hayden and they bounce, sending me reeling again. And I'm tired of it.

I stand to clear the plates after dinner. I've barely made it to the kitchen when Hayden follows me, carrying plates of his own.

There's tension in his shoulders. They echo the same unease in mine. He puts plates down next to the dishwasher and taps his fingers along the countertop.

I fill the machine with dishes and let the silence stretch on.

He finally speaks up. "Did you get the basket I left you?"

"Yes."

"And...?"

"And what does it mean? Is it a friendship basket? Is it a sorry-I-kissed-you basket?" I ask, not saying the third option. *Is it a sorry-I-left-you basket? I-want-you-back-basket?*

"You're angry. Damn." He runs a hand through his hair. "It was both, I suppose. A sorry-for-everything basket."

"For everything? It was a good basket, Hayden, I'll admit, but still..."

"You're right," he says, leaning closer. "It's not enough."

I close the dishwasher and face him entirely. "Why did you kiss me the other night?"

He's quiet for a moment, like I've surprised him by

needing to ask. But then his eyes blaze. "Honestly? Because I wanted to."

It sets something off in me. It's anger, and it's need, and it's so many more things. *Because I wanted to.* Well, I'd wanted to as well. But now it's complicated things, and I'm no closer to getting answers. I still don't know what I am to him. A fun fling from the past? A childhood friend he remembers fondly?

Parker walks into the kitchen. "Hey, guys. Care for a drink? We could head downstairs and let the elders do their thing."

"No," I say. "I'm heading out."

Parker frowns at me. "Already? Not a single drink?"

"No. I have an early morning tomorrow." I kiss him on the cheek as I pass. "Have one for me. I'll see you tomorrow at the marina."

"Yes, of course."

I don't say goodbye to Hayden. I head straight out to my parents and Gary, kissing them goodbye and thanking them for the dinner. I can't stay around Hayden another minute, or I'll demand proper answers to my questions. And then I'll break—and it won't be pretty when I do.

I hear them talking as I leave, but I don't turn around. More *goodbyes* and *are you really leaving, too?*

Hayden is following me out, but I still don't look back. I keep walking. He's taller than me, though, and with his long legs he catches up with me easily. "Damn it, Lily. Wait a second."

I turn on my heel, taking the path behind the hedges to the greenhouse. I open the door to the smell of hydrangeas and sun-ripe tomatoes straight on the vine.

Hayden closes the door behind him. He glances around, eyes narrowing at the abundance of green. My mom had it built six years ago and it's been her pride and joy ever since. It's so filled now that once inside, you're completely concealed from view. But of course, he hasn't seen it before.

"This is new."

"Yes." I wrap my arms around my chest. "Just another thing you missed while you were gone."

He takes a step forward. His face is set in hard, rough lines, nothing at all like the charming appearance he presented at dinner. "I'm sorry about the kiss, all right? Truly."

I laugh. It's not a happy sound, not at all. It's too hot in here—balmy, even. I can already feel sweat down my back, anger making my cheeks flush. "I don't think you're sorry."

Hayden scowls. "Why are you angry, Lily?"

"How could I not be? You come back here and you fit in with the family. You joke around and make Mom laugh. You say you're back *indefinitely.*"

I must look a mess: crazed expression, arms moving. I don't stop, either. I walk up to him and shove him hard, backwards.

He takes it in stride. "Lily?"

"*Why* did you kiss me?"

"Because I wanted to," he repeats. "Because I..." He shakes his head, but doesn't try to stop the blows I'm aiming at his chest, my fists barely connecting, tears burning behind my eyes.

"You can't come back here and kiss me and act like we're friends, as if you didn't break my damn heart." There's so much inside of me—ten years' worth of anger and resentment —and it's all coming out.

"I'm sorry."

"How *could* you? You just left!"

"I'm sorry."

Hayden wraps his arms around my waist, steadying me against him. He doesn't stop me from hitting. It's like he's taking it all, offering me his flesh as payment. "I had to."

"Why?" Another hit. "*Why?*"

His voice is pained. "I *had* to, Lily. I didn't want to. It killed me to leave you."

"It killed *you?*" I tear at the buttons of his shirt, needing to get closer to him. Needing the connection of skin, my nails on him, to make him hurt like I've hurt. "You didn't even say goodbye. I spent *years* wondering if it was something I did."

Hayden's mouth is there, kissing away the hot, angry tears on my cheeks. "No. No, nothing you'd done, baby. Never anything you'd done."

I bury my hand in his hair and meet his lips with my own. It's fire and flame, the two of us, colliding without restraints. We're still arguing, just with our lips. I punish him with my lips and he responds with his tongue. It's a fiery dance.

His hands skim the side of my chest and I shiver. My nipples are taut against the fabric of my dress; I can feel it.

"You can't just come back here," I say, my hands finding the buttons on his shirt. I tear and rip and get them open.

"I know." He helps me with my own clothes, tearing at the zipper of my dress. "I know. Fuck, this dress, Lily... When I saw you... You kill me."

I get all of his buttons undone and he releases me long enough to tear the shirt off his body. My hands feast on him— on the long clean line of his shoulders, so much broader now. The smattering of hair on his chest that he never used to have. The taut muscles of his stomach. *Mine*, my mind says. *Always*.

"Here." He pulls me to a wrought-iron chair in the corner. I push him down onto it and straddle him. This is going fast, too fast, and not nearly fast enough. Ten years of anger and disappointment and resentment. Ten years of loving him from a distance.

Hayden's breath is hot against my neck. He pushes my dress down and presses kisses to my collarbones, my chest, my breasts. He kisses me like I'm a lifeline. Below me, I can feel the strength of his arousal, tearing at the fabric of his jeans. I want him inside me as badly as I want to hurt him.

The greenery around us is a beautiful backdrop to our anger, hiding us from the outside world.

"Lily," he murmurs. His hands find the clasp of my bra and snap it open in one smooth moment. He pulls it off me, baring me to his view.

"See?" I ask, though I don't know what I mean. *See what you do to me?*

But Hayden understands. His hands smooth up my waist to cup my breasts. He leans forward, closing his lips against one of my nipples. He sucks strongly, alternating with a bite that sends me gasping.

"Asshole."

He laughs around my nipple. "I know."

I pull at his hair, tug and grip as he presses bruising kisses to my skin. I missed his hair, the thick, silky blackness that's so uniquely him. Nobody else has hair like Hayden.

"You had to shave this off," I tell him. "I saw a photo."

He nods. Strong hands pull at the fabric of my dress, bunching it high on my waist. He's fighting, always fighting, but this time to get us closer together. "You had a photo of me?"

"Yes. Gary showed us." I kiss him again, a searing warmth flaring through my body. The fabric of my panties is so thin that I can feel the roughness of his jeans below, rubbing at me through the underwear.

The anger is like a kindle to my fire, to my desire, to my need to be one with him. I run my nails up the muscular grooves of his back and Hayden groans against my neck. "Fuck, Lily."

"Don't you remember?" I whisper in his ear. *"I hurt when you hurt."*

His hands move, tearing, tossing, getting fabric out of the way. He kisses me deeply as his hands grip my ass, holding me against him, against the hardness in his jeans and the strength of his chest.

It's easy to move my hips like this, to rub against him. Friction is our friend. "Siren," he groans.

"*Asshole,*" I say again.

Hayden slips his hand into my panties. The first touch of his callused fingers sends me gasping. It's been too long, too long since I've been touched. Desire throbs between my legs. Hayden finds my center easily, circling a few times.

And then, gently, he slips a finger inside me. Once, twice, he pumps it, my world changing with every delicious intrusion. I know what he's doing. He's making sure I'm ready for him.

"Yes," I groan against the curve of his ear. "*Please.*"

Hayden knows what I need. The communication between us is instinctual, natural. He undoes his fly and pulls down his briefs and there's a bit of positioning and then he's rubbing his hardness along my wetness and I can't breathe for wanting him. There are things we should discuss—things to say and confirm—but I can't find the words. Can't even think them.

"*Lily,*" he breathes, and then he pushes inside me in a single, strong thrust. The sudden force of our joining jars me and sends me off balance. I grab his shoulders for support, digging my nails in deep. I can feel him throb inside me.

Hayden releases a shaky breath and grips my waist with hard, demanding hands. I don't know how I made it ten years without him—without this.

I grip his hair. "Tell me why you still have the cone shell."

His laugh is breathless. "What?"

"I saw it on your mantlepiece." I rise on my tiptoes, feeling him inside me, before I let myself drop back down. Every inch of friction is delicious. "Don't lie."

"Because *you* gave it to me," he growls. He rolls his hips and grips my hips so hard I know I'll have bruises. Every thrust of his hips is punishing, reaching places deep inside me. He fights to fill me just as I fight to get closer to him.

I grip his hair too roughly and breathe his name, just like he used to whisper mine. "*Hayden*."

He gives me everything, and I take it, holding on to him tightly. There's no time for tenderness, both of us struggling with the strength of our emotions.

"You shouldn't have left."

Hayden thrusts into me hard, his body shuddering. "I *know* that," he groans. "Don't you think I know that? Don't you think it kills me?"

He buries his head against the crook of my neck, one of his hands working at the top of my legs. The fact that he remembers how to touch me—how to get me to the edge—makes me angrier. But as my orgasm barrels through me, as pleasure crests through my body, there's nothing but blinding ecstasy.

He groans against my neck as he comes and I hold him through it, hands in his hair, pressing him closer. He grips me just as tightly.

I cling to him through the aftershocks, through the trembling in his own body. It's too much. There's nothing left, no pretension to hide behind, no it's-nice-to-see-you-again.

We're bared entirely.

For a long time, the only sound was our heavy breathing and the feeling of him inside me, still pulsing. I rest my head against his shoulder and close my eyes. He still smells like salt and Hayden and home.

"Lily," he murmurs, wrapping his arms around me.

We sit there, just breathing together. And for a minute I let myself believe. That we're still an us. That we're still together. That he cares.

But only for a second.

And then I stand up warily, aware that we need to clean up. That we're in a greenhouse on the edge of my parents' property and we should have left fifteen minutes ago, and that I'm no closer to understanding why he left than I was a week ago.

Hayden looks up at me as he tucks himself back in and zips his pants up. He bends over to grab his shirt from the floor, and in the flash of a moment, he's back to looking respectable

I pull my dress back down and snap my bra back into place. It's enough to shove my arms back through the holes of the dress.

"Do you have a tissue?"

Hayden shakes his head. "No. But I'll go get—"

"No, it's fine. I'll just head home." Plus, I really don't want the others to know.

"I'll help you."

"No, I'm good."

"Lily—"

"It's fine." I grab my purse from where I'd tossed it, abandoned in a flower bed. It's a bit dirty, but nothing I can't fix. Hayden looks at me with a mixture of resentment and anger —his eyes betraying his own sense of confusion. There was a time when I'd give everything to solve his problems for him. But I can't, not anymore.

"Let's talk," he says, as if we haven't already tried that.

"I have to go. I have to clean up." I push the door open and hurry toward the driveway. It's not a lie—I do need a tissue. But it's more than that. Another moment in there and he would've seen the hot tears that overflow and race down my cheeks.

19

HAYDEN

Hayden, 18

Mile after mile of dark road. I take us out of Paradise Shores, in toward the country, the road guarded by the dark outlines of maple and birch. There's no one on the road except us.

I don't have a goal in mind, I just want to feel the wheels beneath me. Driving at night feels like flying. It feels like freedom.

Lily has her feet up on the dash. Her hair is splayed over her shoulders, and in the dim lighting it looks much darker than usual. She's been quiet since we left the house. I can tell she's still curious, but she's not pressing. I don't think I've ever loved her more than I do right now.

I reach over and put a hand on her smooth leg. Just to double-check that she's here—that I haven't lost her. *Yet.*

Lily threads her fingers through mine. Her skin is warm and soft, and she turns my hand over, lightly tracing each knuckle. "They're getting so rough," she murmurs. "From the fishing boats."

Hauling nets and burning rope through my hands has taken its toll. They're cracked in places, calluses sore on the inside of my palms. Against her soft skin my hands must feel like sandpaper.

I start pulling my hand away, but Lily won't let me. "You're not getting away," she says and turns my hand back over. "I can read your palm, you know."

"My future?"

Maybe she hears the tightness in my voice, or she can sense my emotions, but Lily just shakes her head. "Of course, but that's to be expected. I'm more advanced than that."

"Oh?"

"I can read your thoughts."

"Through my palm?" She's being outrageous, and I know it's to cheer me up. It makes me feel even less deserving of her love, but I can't give it up.

"Oh, yes. It's a secret, ancient practice from… Antarctica."

My lips twitch. "You learnt this from penguins?"

"Don't mock me."

"All right, all right. What am I thinking, then?"

She settles into the seat and traces a line across my palm, avoiding a sore spot. "You're thinking about the car. It runs very smoothly, because I know Parker asked Gary to change some thingamajig or add oil or something. And you're enjoying the way it feels."

She's right about that. The car is an old, beautiful Jeep, only used by the kids. I've driven it before, but only with Parker, when he's been too drunk to drive himself after a party. I've driven it when I've picked up Lily, too, after school. I know where the keys are kept in the garage.

But I'm not supposed to take it out for a spin like this.

"Yes, I did think that. That's an easy one."

Lily flicks my thumb. "You're thinking that you're going to take Sunday off work to join Parker and me when we go sailing."

"Good try, Lils." I glance over at her. She's smiling,

looking mischievous and too cute for her own good. "But you know I have to work."

"Fine, you're thinking that you *wish* you could take Sunday off."

"All right, then it's correct. And I can tell what you're doing, you know. These are obvious thoughts. Is this really the way they do it in Antarctica?"

Lily chuckles. "You're such a demanding customer."

I glance at the dashboard. It's past one in the morning. We've been driving for an hour already, and I know I should start heading back. But I don't want to end this—just her and me, and nothing but complete freedom. It doesn't matter that it's only an illusion.

"Very well. You're thinking about me." Lily's voice turns low, the way it does when she's shy and pushing through, or when she's trying to seduce me. It usually doesn't take much.

"You *are* sitting right next to me. It would be rude if I wasn't."

"Idiot. Fine, you're thinking that I'm the best, the brightest, the most incredible person you've ever met. The smartest, the funniest, the most beautiful…"

I pull my hand out of hers. "You're too good at this. It's freaky."

Lily laughs again. The sound tightens something in my chest, the feeling entirely too familiar. She grabs my hand back and presses a kiss to the back. I keep my eyes on the road, tension slowly draining from me. Things will be okay as long as we're together.

"I love you," she says softly. "You know that, right?"

My mind goes blank for a moment. Nothing else matters. No one else, nobody that's not me or her. I want to make this moment last forever. The road is straight and narrow, trees flashing by in the midnight darkness.

"I know, Lils."

She puts my hand back on her thigh, her skin warm and soft. "Good. I just wanted to make sure you did."

And I need to make sure she knows it's the same for me. That she's everything I want—everything I need—but the words won't form. If I say it, if I make it real, she could be taken from me.

"Lily…" But I can't finish the sentence. I keep my eyes glued to the road ahead and smooth a circle with my thumb on her skin.

She doesn't seem to mind my silence.

"I know too, Hayden," she says gently. "What's on your mind tonight? You know you can tell me. Or not, if you'd rather keep it to yourself. But I'll always listen."

I can't tell her what her mother and grandmother said. I know I can't.

And how do I explain my own feelings? She'd protest them right away. I know that.

Lights flash ahead. It's the first car we've met in over an hour.

"Hayden?"

It's a truck.

And it's not staying in the right lane. I watch in slow motion as the truck drifts over to my lane, until the lights blind me. A lot of things happen at once, then. I hit the horn. Lily screams and my heart leaps into my throat.

I swerve, tires screech, and then everything goes black.

———

It's adrenaline that keeps me going. Things move in flashes, an eternity passing in each heartbeat.

"Lily?" She's not responding. Her door is smashed, hit by the truck. It's buckled inwards. Her eyes are closed.

"Lily!"

There's no response. Her leg… I can't look at it. Get her

out. I need to get her out. I push open my own door, breaking the glass to do so.

And then I pull her out. The car is gone, smoke coming from the engine. Do cars explode? Someone told me they don't, but I can't take risks.

I unbuckle her seat belt and wrap my arms around her waist, pulling her out. It's hard to walk with her in my arms and I don't dare carry her far. Her leg… it looks bad. That runs on repeat in my head. *This is bad, this is bad, this is bad.*

She still hasn't opened her eyes. "Lily? Lily."

No response.

I pat my pockets and fish out my phone.

911 operators.

Beeping noises.

Flashing neon lights.

People in scrubs barking orders.

Accusing eyes and frantic yelling.

I'm next to her in the ambulance the entire way to the hospital. The ambulance staff made me lie down, but I can see well enough what they do. They stem the bleeding, but I can't be sure if it was fast enough. So much of her pretty dress is soaked through with the most garish red. *Too much.* It's too much.

She's unconscious, but I repeat her name anyway, just in case. "Lily. Lily. *Lily.*"

"Lie down," they tell me. I hear terms like *cracked ribs* and *fractured femur,* but the words don't mean anything to me. I don't feel any pain.

They roll her away from me as soon as we arrive in the emergency room, taking her to surgery. I'll never forget that, the long, barren corridor and her small frame on the hospital bed. A man pushes me back firmly when I try to follow.

"Family only," he says.

So after they've bandaged me up and given me painkillers, I sit in the waiting room outside the operating room. Every ticking hand of the clock is torturous. The scene replays over and over in my mind.

Bright lights on a dark road that I couldn't evade.

The sound of metal bending and breaking as we're rammed by a truck. Lily's weight in my arms as I drag her out of the wreckage. The car so bent I had to force my door off the frame to open it.

Lily's mother is the first to arrive at the hospital. Eloise is still in her pajama bottoms, a frantic look in her eyes. Parker is right behind her.

He looks the way I feel—hollow inside.

The questions are relentless. No, Lily wasn't conscious, and yes, I had been the one driving. No, I didn't know what happened. The truck had come out of nowhere.

Parker grabs my shoulder and shoots me a wild, bloodshot look. "Thank God you're all right, man."

"Yeah. Yeah…"

"Do you know when she'll be out?"

"No. They said family only, so they haven't told me anything…"

Mrs. Marchand's eyes narrow to slits. It's a look I've seen before, in her daughter. It's only a matter of minutes before we're escorted down to the room being prepared for Lily.

She'll be out of surgery in mere minutes, they say, and so far everything's good—but the following days will be crucial.

Crucial.

The word bounces around in my head. How did I only have a few fractured ribs and she has to fight for her life?

When Lily is finally rolled into the room, her face is pale and serene, as if she's just sleeping. Her hair frames her face, devoid of makeup or her usual teasing smile. She looks so young like that.

Like Sleeping Beauty, who only needs a kiss to be woken up. Instead, she's sedated and fighting for her life.

I choke back my fear and nausea.

Commotion in the hallway makes all of us turn our heads, Eloise most of all. Then I recognize the voice.

"Where is she?"

"Down here, sir. Sorry. Let me just—"

More words are exchanged, muffled by the thick walls, before a livid Mr. Marchand comes through the door. He's wearing a suit and carrying his overnight bag, and his expression wracks guilt through my body.

His face crumbles the second he sees his daughter.

I stand in the corner and watch as they crowd around Lily in the bed. *Please*, I pray. *Please, please, make sure she's all right.*

They ask me to explain it to them. Exactly what happened —why she's lying in that hospital bed, connected to tubes and wires.

"He was on the wrong side of the road," I say, my voice cracking. There had been a lot of smoke.

"Speak up, son."

"A truck. On the wrong side of the road." I shake my head, trying to clear it, and I'm rewarded with a thunderous ache. "I don't know why. Maybe he fell asleep at the wheel... I tried to swerve, but I couldn't get out of the way fast enough. It hit... it hit us straight on the passenger side."

Lily's mother gives me a weepy look and reaches out to rest her hand on my shoulder. It's the one that's bruised, but I know she doesn't know that.

"Are you okay, Hayden?"

I don't deserve her sympathy, not with her daughter only a few feet away and fighting for her life. "I'm fine."

She nods and turns away. I can tell that I'm forgotten the instant her eyes fall on her youngest child, her only daughter. Lily looks like a doll in the giant hospital bed.

Her father is still looking at me. "What were you doing out so late?"

"Driving." The glare of the truck's headlights flash before me. "We just wanted to... to get away for a while."

His eyes narrow, and I know exactly what he's seeing in that moment. He's seeing everything. My pathetic longing for his daughter, her sweetness being taken advantage of. Making her stay out too late.

Considering not applying to Yale.

Crashing a car with her in it.

If I could sink through the floor with shame I would.

There's a low groan from the bed and he turns away from me. Lily isn't conscious, her eyes still shut, but she's making noise. My heart feels like it might burst from the mingled fear and relief.

Over the next week, one after another, her family and friends appear. Rhys, white with worry. Parker is there daily, his shirt buttoned wrong. Henry is the picture of calm and composure, but when he thinks no one is looking, I see his jaw tense with fear. Jamie stops by with cookies but breaks down in tears at the sight of Lily. Parker consoles her, his own face drawn tight with worry.

All because of me. *I* caused all this.

So I sit by, gripping the armrest of the chair in the corner as I watch her family crowd around her in the hospital bed.

It takes a long, long time for her to wake.

But eventually she does.

20

HAYDEN

The present

After the greenhouse, I go home to my empty house, my empty bed, my empty life, filled with regrets.

Fuck.

We were doing everything in the wrong order. It didn't matter that it had been... well, the most life-changing, soul-altering sex of my life. Being with Lily again—being inside her—was nothing short of a religious experience.

But she'd run out of there like she was chased by the devil.

And I was him.

Of all the times I'd dreamed of being with Lily again—fantasizing about it—it had always been in a bed, for starters. It had been sweet and gentle, and she'd moaned my name against my lips. I would make her shatter over and over again with my mouth before I'd push inside her, making sure she was on fire and begging me to.

I had never imagined it mad and crazy in her parents' greenhouse at ten o'clock at night, and over before it had barely begun.

Sleep doesn't come easy to me that night, not when I

know deep in my bones that she should be lying next to me—
that she still cares for me too.

I go for a run the next morning along the beach, catching
the sunrise. And with each step, I formulate a plan. It's what
I've been taught to do these past years. Strategize, strategize,
strategize.

I show up at the marina that afternoon, dressed in chinos
and a white T-shirt. I don't own the kind of boat shoes that
everyone around here wears anymore, but that doesn't
matter. I've always failed to fit in to Paradise Shores. Why
should that change now?

There are sailing boats everywhere, their small white sails
like bobbing marshmallows in clear-blue water. Children of
all ages mingle around, dressed in life vests. The Junior
Regatta is a massive deal for the Sailing Club, just like it was
when I was a child here. Henry won his year; I know that
Parker did too.

Rhys, of course, didn't compete.

I scan the crowd for Lily. I'm going to find her and apologize. Properly, this time, with a plan for the future. I'm going
to clarify a few things, too. That I'm still crazy about her—and
that I want to give us another shot. Fuck all the talk about
friendship. It clearly hadn't worked last night.

I don't see her, but what I see instead puts a smile on my
face. Parker is dressed in the old sailing club jacket, the one he
wore all the time in high school. He's helping a few children get
fitted with life jackets. Some of the kids are small, way too small
to actually take part in the competition or try sailing today. But
it's not hard to imagine younger siblings wanting to wear one
as well, even if they're safe and dry on the dock the whole day.

I head over. Parker shoots me a tired look when he sees
me. "Hey, man."

"Hey. You look like you need help."

He hands me a life vest. "Please."

I crouch down next to him and help the next kid who comes up. It's a girl, no taller than my hip. She stares up at me with wide eyes and hands me her life vest.

"Here."

"Thanks." I flip it over and hold it out above her head. "Pop up in here for me."

She sticks her head through the hole, arms stick-straight. "What's your name?"

"Hayden," I say, bending to reach the straps. I tighten them around her methodically, making sure the thing can't come off. "What's yours?"

"Isabella." She can't quite pronounce her *l*s, and the name comes out scrambled. I can't help but grin.

"It's very nice to meet you."

"You too." She gives the life vest a sharp tug and then smiles, looking up at me. "I'm just like my brother now."

"Awesome. High five."

She gives me a high five before running off to join her mom, standing next to us on the dock. I see Parker struggling with finding the right size for his kid and figure I might as well keep helping him. This is what I came here for, anyway —at least outwardly.

Volunteers set up a table behind us on the dock. It doesn't take more than a glance to see what's happening. It's a face-painting booth, and Lily is manning it.

She's wearing a pair of shorts that show off her legs, tan and freckled. Her hair is in a loose bun, little tendrils of auburn hair curling around her face.

Seeing her nearly brings a blush to my face as I remember last night. She'd been... well. It had definitely taken the edge off ten years of wanting her.

She looks like my past and my future and everything I've ever wanted.

I turn back to the line of kids. There's fewer now, as most

have left to watch the start of the race. Parker shoots me a not-so-subtle thumbs-up and a grateful smile.

One of the last kids on the dock is a boy, no older than ten. He has large glasses and looks doubtfully at the life vest I hold out to him.

"It's your size," I assure him.

He nods. "Cool. Yeah…"

But as he steps closer, I can tell something's wrong. I slip it over his head and speak calmly as I crouch down. "What's your name, buddy?"

"Fredrick."

"Hi. My name is Hayden." I fasten the straps on his right side. "How are you doing?"

"Good." He pauses. "Well… I'm a bit nervous."

"About hitting the water?"

"Yes."

I sit back and look at him steadily. "You don't have to if you don't want to, you know."

"But my sister's competing today."

"And your family wants you to try sailing as well, with one of the instructors?"

"Yeah. My dad thinks it would be good for me. But I…" He looks over at one of the small dinghies resting close to us, its small sail bobbing joyfully. "They're so *small.*"

I resist the urge to smile. "I get you, buddy. It's not easy getting on a boat."

"No. Have you ever been on one?"

"I have, yes. But I'll tell you a secret."

"What?"

"I was just as scared as you were the first time."

"You were?"

"Yes. I had no idea what to do, or why people would do it for *fun.*"

"So why did you go?"

I shake my head at my own childhood stupidity, reaching

out to adjust his life vest just a tad. The boy is looking at me with rapt attention and I know I have to make this good.

"Because I wanted to impress someone."

The boy nods, like this is a perfectly valid reason. "Of course."

"But then I was hooked. I loved the wind and the waves, learning how the sea works. I even joined the Navy later."

His eyes grow wide. "You did? Like, as a soldier-sailor?"

I have to stop myself from laughing. "Yes. Exactly like that."

"Did you have to fight?"

"No, I was lucky enough to avoid that. But I patrolled for a long while."

"That's cool. And you started to learn here?"

"Yes, this was the first place I got on a boat. But," I say, crouching down again, "there's no pressure. Sometimes you're scared and it's the good kind, you know? Where you have to do it anyway to grow. But then there's the kind of scared that gives you a stomachache, and then it's important to listen to it, and say no."

The boy nods throughout my little speech, as if my words make sense. They do to me, but I've never tried to explain this to anyone before.

He pushes up his glasses. "I think it's the first kind of scared."

"All right. In that case, let's get you on a boat today, buddy. You can do it."

"Yeah. Yeah, I can." He tugs on the life vest. "But maybe not quite yet."

"That's all right. Let's see… Do you see that lady there?" I turn and point to Lily, currently painting the face of a small girl with pigtails. "You could get a tattoo. Something for luck."

"My mom would kill me if I got a tattoo."

Damn. I thought it would sound cooler than paint. "Well,

it's only temporary. Maybe an anchor on your arm, like a real sailor?"

His eyes light up. "That would be really cool."

There are only a few other kids waiting to be sized up, and I know Parker can handle it. I nod toward the face-painting table.

"Let's go."

"Is it okay if you go first?" he asks me, with perfect sincerity.

I blink. "Uh, yeah. Yeah, of course."

Lily sees us as we approach. Her eyes meet mine, and the look is laden with things unsaid. I want to know what she feels about yesterday. I need to know if she regrets it, if it was as explosive for her as for me.

"Hey," I say. "This little man wants a tattoo of an anchor on his arm, like a sailor."

Fredrick leans closer and looks curiously at Lily's brushes and face paints. I've seen how good of a painter she is, and this is nothing for her. The kids are getting a masterpiece for free.

She smiles at him. "Of course. Do you want it in any specific color?"

"Blue. But…" He looks up at me. "Hayden is going first."

I nod seriously and start to roll up my sleeve. "Yes, I am. Could I also get a blue anchor?"

Lily shoots me a delicious smile. She's enjoying this. "Really?"

"Yes." I take a seat in the chair. Fredrick is watching us, his eyes interested. He follows Lily's movements as she dips a brush in water and then swirls it around and around in the azure paint.

"Did you know he was in the Navy?"

She nods at him. "I did, yes."

Frederik narrows his eyes at me in accusation. "Do you

know this lady?" He asks it as if it's a crime. I see Lily trying and failing to hide her smile.

"I do, yes," I admit. "I've known her since I was your age."

"Oh." He looks thoughtful, watching as Lily starts on my arm. Her touch is careful, the paint is cold against my skin. "Was it scary being in the Navy?"

"Sometimes, yes."

"When you were attacked?"

"We were never attacked, buddy. But sometimes you're in situations that are tense, or you get caught in storms, or have to do drills that are pretty uncomfortable."

"What did you do? To make it through?"

I try to focus on his honest questions and not on the fact that Lily is only inches away, painting away silently and listening to my every word.

"Hmm. You take it one step at a time. Focus on what you can change and let go of what you can't."

"That makes sense," he says, nodding seriously. "Oh, that looks good."

I glance down at my arm. Lily has painted an intricate anchor, with a rope wrapped around it. She's mixed some green in with the blue and it almost looks like a proper tattoo. I've always known she's amazingly skilled with this sort of thing.

This close, I can practically count the freckles that dot her nose. It had been too dark in the greenhouse. I need to be with her again—to see her in sunlight.

"Thank you."

Lily looks up at me. "Yeah. Of course." She leans back and clears her throat, shooting Fredrick a smile. "You ready to get the same thing?"

"Yeah." He jumps into the chair I just left, legs swinging. I watch as Lily prepares the brush, as she starts to paint on his skin with smooth, skilled strokes. She could do this blindfolded.

He looks up at her. "Do you sail too?"

"Not very often, anymore. I did when I was a child, though."

"Do you like it?"

"Yes, it can be nice."

He sighs, a massive, exaggerated child-sigh. "I have to sail today."

"You do?" Lily's voice is soft. I watch as she fills in the outlines of the anchor.

"Well, I want to try. I've never tried before and there's a place over there where you can try."

"That's great. You should."

"Yeah. I was a bit nervous to, but Hayden told me not to be."

I smile. "Well, it's okay to be nervous, as long as you do it anyway. But only if it's the first kind of scared. Right?"

"Right." He looks down at his arm. "Is it done?"

Lily's voice is amused. "Almost. Is your brother or sister competing today?"

"My sister is."

"Ah. I used to be here just like you, every time my brothers competed, to watch them sail. It's fun to try what they like to do, but it's okay if you want to try something different instead."

"Yeah." He's quiet for a moment, looking down at her painting. "I think I'll try it, and then I'll tell my parents I want to play basketball instead."

She nods at him, smiling. "That sounds great. You're done."

Fredrick twists, trying to get a better view, and then breaks into a grin. "I look like a pirate," he tells me. "Pirates have these, you know?"

"You're right. And now we match."

He raises his hand to mine for a high five before he says goodbye. Lily and I watch as he runs off to join his parents, standing off to the side. Their eyes are fixed on the boats in the marina. It's getting to be time for the race proper, and spectators line the dock.

Lily is washing her brushes, carefully avoiding my eyes. "So," she says. "You were scared sometimes in the Navy?"

I resist the urge to groan. "*That's* what you got from that?"

"Well, it's either that or the fact that you're great with children."

"Hmm. Well, of course there were times that weren't that fun."

Lily nods. She's close to me, and the scent of her hair, the caramel shampoo and sunshine is intoxicating. I wish I could have her next to me forever.

"You're an amazing painter."

"I haven't painted in ages," she says bluntly. "I lied when I said I had."

I make my voice soft. "Yeah, I figured."

"Of course you did. Oh God." She covers her face. "Hayden, about yesterday—"

"Wait. Let me go first."

"I can't believe that we... that can't happen again."

"I know. I'm sorry about it happening like that, and I'm sorry about my reaction to Turner's name at the dinner. You were right to be angry with me. About all of it."

She lowers her hands, brilliant eyes staring up at me. "I still want some answers."

"I know. And I should never have asked you to be friends again," I say, shaking my head. "It was wrong of me, when I so clearly can't help myself. I can't be just friends with you, Lils."

"I can't be just friends with you either."

Hope stirs in my chest. "I know this is complicated. And I

should have said that right away, that what I really want is for us to do things right."

"Things?"

"Yeah." Damn it, I've never been good with words. She's the one who used to kill me regularly with affection. "Let me take you out on a date, Lily. Let me do this properly. Give me a chance."

Lily takes a deep breath. I know we're standing too close, bodies nearly touching, but I don't care if the entirety of Paradise Shores sees us right now—as long as she says yes.

This girl has had me wrapped around her finger since we were children, and it's never been clearer to me than right now just how much I need her to be a part of my future.

"If I say yes," she murmurs, "you have to be honest with me. Talk to me if you feel like leaving. If you want out, if you're feeling trapped, if something's not all right. Okay?"

"Okay. I can do that." Communication. It's not too big of an ask, not really.

"What would we be?"

"Whatever we want to be. It's you and me, Lils. We'll figure it out."

"Okay." She offers me a small smile, and the relief that I feel at her acceptance threatens to bring me to my knees. *Thank you, God.* "Why didn't you tell me this right away? When you got back? Instead you insisted on friendship."

Well, she wanted honesty. I glance away at the race, at the boats fighting for first place, struggling to find the words to explain myself.

"I was too afraid," I say finally.

"Afraid?"

"Yes. I was scared to death that you would throw me out on my ass, Lily. You could take one look at me and kill me with your words."

Her eyes soften slightly. "What did you just tell that sweet boy about courage and fear? About doing things even though you're nervous?"

"Yes, well, he had to try *sailing*."

"So?"

I lean in, close enough that I can feel her soft breath. She doesn't back away. "I have to beg the girl of my dreams for forgiveness. I'd rather look death in the eye than be refused by you."

Lily laughs breathlessly. "So dramatic, Hayden."

"Only with you."

"When?"

"When what?"

"When are we going on a date?"

I let my eyes wander along the brightness of her eyes, the pert nose, the full lips, the teasing smile. "I'm going to cook you dinner, and then we're going to watch a movie, and then I'm going to drive you home."

She smiles. "We've done wilder things than that. Are you losing your touch?"

I flick her nose. "We were teenagers. We're not anymore, and I'm going to do this right."

21

HAYDEN

Hayden, 18

It's over two weeks post-accident when Lily's finally discharged from the hospital. When the doctor read out the verdict, both Eloise and Rhys openly cried. *Lily would walk again.*

She would heal fully, even if she might have a slight limp and would likely have to eat painkillers for a long time. But she'd make a nearly full recovery, with a bit of work with a therapist.

Her father announces that he's taking a month off to personally look after his daughter's recovery at home. Because it's going to be a process, even if I know Lily will manage it.

The first thing she did when she opened her eyes was smile. She gave everyone in the room a tired, soft smile, and a whispered *hello.* I'd had to wipe my own eyes then, hidden in the back of her hospital room.

She was all right.

The days pass quickly after that. I want to see her alone—I need to talk to her—but she's never alone. Her large bedroom in the Marchand house is filled to the brim with flowers, friends and family. I once saw Rhys chucking some lilies out, and he shot me a sideways grin.

"She's getting a headache from the scent."

I'd nodded, biting my tongue to keep from asking how she'd been that day. She had family who cared—she had friends who cared—and she was universally adored. But it didn't stop me from glancing at her window every chance I got. Our few interactions had been brief. They were always supervised by her mother or one of her brothers.

For the first time, I'm annoyed at our own secrecy. If I had been her boyfriend, accepted and welcomed, I could have walked up to the front door with a bouquet myself. I would be let in with a smile, escorted to her bedroom and given as much time with her as I'd want.

But I'm not her official boyfriend.

And I had been the one who drove that car.

Most of our communication is via text instead. It's not the same, something Lily often writes. *I miss you* is a common text.

I feel too guilty to write the same thing back.

But there was one thing I'd underestimated, and that was Lily herself, with her iron will. I've just gotten back to the beach house after a full day at sea when my phone vibrates. *Come to the back porch. Hurry.*

She's sitting in one of the chairs, a thick afghan wrapped around her to protect her from the evening breeze. Her leg is in a thick cast all the way to her hip and crutches lean against the wall. It's not the first time I've seen her cast, but it still sends pain through me. It had been so close.

She hasn't seen me yet. A small sketchpad is resting on her lap, and she's drawing softly, biting her lower lip. The setting sun brings out the fire in her hair. Even sitting down, she looks like a living flame, and I'm as drawn to her as ever.

"Lily?"

She looks up from her drawing. Her smile nearly splits her face in half. "You came!"

"Of course. Are you okay being out here?"

"Oh, yes. Absolutely. I can't take another day in my room, or I'll go insane." She pats the chair next to her. "Come here. Please."

I sit down next to her and take her hand. She grasps mine back, strong and steady. For a long moment, she just looks at me in that way of hers. I can only gaze back, her eyes green and vibrant. To think that the world came close to losing them entirely. *Because of me.*

"It wasn't your fault, Hayden," she says softly.

I don't answer her. There's no point, is there? We're going to disagree on this.

"Did you hear me? It wasn't."

"Well, the police investigation is still ongoing. It *could* be."

"It won't. It'll be ruled an accident, and the car was insured. You're in the clear, Hay."

More guilt ripples through me. I'd crashed one of their cars. I know that Gary has been speaking to Mr. Marchand about it, though he'd waived off my offers to pay for reparations. More of a debt I would never be able to repay.

"I'm fine," she murmurs. "Are you?"

"Yeah."

"They told me you had two broken ribs and a cracked collarbone."

I shake my head. "All nearly healed."

"Okay." With a sigh, she pushes up into standing. For a moment, she looks so much like her old self, with her hair blowing in the wind and the grin on her face. She looks proud of standing with no crutches, even if it scares me.

I wrap my arm around her waist just in case. It feels good to have her close again—too good. I've missed her so much.

"Look," she says. "I'm on my feet. I can only hop so far, but as soon as my leg is mended, I'll be walking again.

Running, even. I've decided to take up lacrosse again. Do you think I can still make the varsity team?" Her eyes are glittering with sarcasm, but the smile she shoots me is hopeful.

I swallow down my emotions. "You're okay. You're truly going to be okay."

"Of course I am! Look!" She spins slowly on one foot, a hand on my arm for support. "One more week and you'll see me running. Usain Bolt better watch out."

"You don't run."

"I'll start." She reaches up and presses a small kiss to my lips. It's the first time since the accident, and she doesn't seem to care that her parents are around or that anyone might see. "I'm going to be *fine*."

Relief so heady it makes my knees weak sweeps through me.

"Thank God for that." I pull her closer. "God, Lily, I was so scared. You were unconscious. And there was so much... Damn."

"I know," she murmurs against my neck. "I know, Hay. Thank you for taking care of me."

I rest my head against her hair and close my eyes. It's a thank-you I don't deserve, but I ignore my guilt, lost in the familiar scent of her hair. She's going to be fine. The apology is dancing on my tongue. I want to go down on my knees and ask her for it, but I know she won't let me. Lily has always had an impressive track record in trying to make me feel better. But that's the last thing she should have to do at the moment.

Lily gets tired fast and I help her back up to her room, my arm still around her waist. Her parents are somewhere in the house—I can hear them talking—but we manage to avoid them.

She sits down on her bed. "I wish you could stay."

"Me too, baby."

"Kiss me again."

I do. Her lips are warm against mine, her taste sweet. I feel like I'm drowning and flying at once, afraid to touch her because of my own shame and guilt.

Lily leans back. "You're being too careful."

I shake my head at her. "Lie down, Lils. Do you need another pill?"

"No. They make my head a bit fuzzy."

I frown at the bottle of painkillers. "Is that normal?"

"Yes, you worrier, the doctor said that would happen." She burrows down in her covers and I hand her the book she's been reading. "Here I am, in bed and it's not even eight p.m."

I roll my eyes at her. "You're healing."

"My new hobby. Come closer, Hay."

I bend down obediently and close my eyes as Lily runs a hand over my cheek. Her fingers feel cool against my skin. "We're in this together, Hayden. Aren't we?"

I nod, feeling like my heart might break from the war between guilt and desire wagering inside it. "Yes, we are."

I close the door softly behind me and head down the stairs. I've nearly reached the kitchen door when Michael Marchand stops me with a single nod of his head. He has his hands in his pockets, the thick hair brushed back. I've always tried to stay out of his way—the business tycoon of Paradise Shores—but I can't hide anymore.

"We need to talk, Hayden."

The small, faint trace of hope I've harbored sinks like a stone. Of course we need to talk. I can imagine what he's going to say, the words that will cut like knives. The accusations. The betrayal of trust. The crashed car. The time has come.

"All right."

"I have great respect for your uncle," he says quietly. "He's been a fine employee all these years."

Unease makes my stomach flip. Where is he going with this?

"I've always been happy to pay for your schooling. You've been a good friend to my boys, too. Don't think I haven't noticed that." He pauses, waiting for my response. It's late and it's summer, but he's still in a button-down and slacks. I've never seen him in a T-shirt.

"Thank you," I say lamely.

He nods, like I've said the right thing. "Now, I'm going to talk to you man to man, because you're grown. The same way I talk to my sons." His voice turns glacial. "I'm not going to insult us both by asking why you were driving my car in the middle of the night with my daughter in it. I've got eyes of my own, as does my wife."

I want to sink through the floor. "Yes."

"Lily's always been a bit... wild. I'm not surprised that she's drawn to you. But I am surprised that *you* gave in. You know it's not in your best interest."

"Yes." My voice sounds weak to my own ears. I find myself agreeing with everything he's saying.

"And it's definitely not in Lily's. My daughter nearly died two weeks ago, partly because of you." He holds up a hand, as if to stop me from protesting. I wasn't about to. "Now, I know the truck was in your lane. The police have confirmed that. But she shouldn't have been out there in the first place."

"I know," I say again.

"You know where I'm going, I'm sure. You've figured it out yourself." He pauses, face impassive. "You're not welcome here anymore. Not around my daughter, and not in my house. It's time for you to go, son."

The pain laces through me at the words. I've always known this isn't home, not really. A place where you're staying thanks to someone else's mercy can never truly be home. But for years, it had been as close to one as I'd ever come.

I can't argue with him. There's no point, no point at all. Because he's right. I hurt her, and I don't deserve her. And if I stay, she'll have to fight with her parents over this. *Over me.*

"I see."

"Now, don't look sullen. We can find someplace for you to go, I'm sure. It'll be a quiet thing between the two of us. Do you need college tuition? There are good schools out West. I could make some calls. How does one of the UCs sound?"

I'd rather kill myself than accept more charity from him. "No, thank you."

"Don't turn down a good opportunity because of pride, son. I'd let you pay me back."

"No," I grind out.

"Very well. Make your arrangements soon, then." He takes a step forward and shakes my hand. "Don't be a stranger to your uncle. Make something of yourself."

"I will."

"Do you need money for bus fare? Plane tickets?"

"No," I say. "*Thanks.*"

He pauses for a second. His eyes are clinical, like we've just signed a business deal. "It's nothing personal, Hayden. It's just better this way."

"Yes, sir."

I walk back to the beach house. I pack a bag with my clothes and my belongings. I write a note for Gary, too short by far to encompass all that he's been for me. I promise to call as soon as I can.

I write a letter to Lily and slip it into the Marchand mailbox.

Then I grab the pamphlets Mrs. Abrams gave me about enlisting and military colleges and board the first Greyhound out of Paradise Shores. Because Mr. Marchand had really only told me what I already knew. It's time for me to go.

It's better this way.

22

LILY

The present

I try to focus on the blueprints in front of me. *Stop thinking about Hayden.* But it's very, very difficult. My mind keeps wandering to the past weekend, to the greenhouse and the conversation we'd had the day after.

We'd slept together again—and not in the romantic, soft way. It had been passionate and intense and everything I'd ever wanted.

And now... now he wants to give dating a chance. Tonight, after work, I'll head to his house for dinner. His idea.

Maybe I was being stupid, agreeing to the prospect of dating him. I knew I risked getting hurt again. I didn't want that. But for years, I'd lived carefully and quietly, been the good girl at every turn, and that got old, too.

My mom used to say that sometimes, the only thing a person can do is take it day by day, and that's what I'm going to do.

Blueprints... a large room with a fireplace. Dining room. Yes. I need to work on a staging theme for the new develop-ment over in Restwick. We have less than three weeks before it hits the market, and it's bound to cause a bidding war. This area of New England attracts a lot of buyers, and Harris Property is sure to take advantage of that.

As I look through our files later, my gaze gets caught on a small, abandoned storefront here in Paradise Shores. It's a tiny place, really, but it's still on the market. The location is good. As is the natural light.

It's easy to imagine paintings on the wall and the soft artificial lighting of a gallery. Or an art studio, for kids in the region. Maybe both.

Could I combine them? Showcase up-and-coming artists during the days and have classes in the evening?

Before I can stop myself, I'm pulling up all the stats I can find about the property. The year it was built, the square-footage. It's doable. The space is good, and I have the money for it. It could possibly even be discounted, having been for sale for so long. I'll basically be doing them a favor by taking it off the market.

My heart is beating fast, and for the first time in a long while, it's because of art. I'd given up even trying to combine it with my life in Paradise Shores—I'd thrown myself into family life and work and reconnecting with this place. But now, I'm realizing maybe I don't have to leave that life behind. Maybe I can have both.

I photocopy the listing and slip it into my purse.

Turner comes into my office after lunch, his trademark smile in place. "Did you get my email on the Craft house?"

"I did, yes. I've looked over it. I agree with your comments."

He breathes a sigh of relief. "Good. I usually have full faith in the architectural design team, but this time, it just seems…"

"It's too art nouveau. We're never going to get it sold with those plans."

"Exactly. I understand the virtues of design and all, but very few people want a perfectly round living room."

I chuckle. "Or a concrete shower."

"Send me any notes you might have, and I'll forward it together with my own." He stops by the door to my office, hand tapping against the frame. "Thanks for last week, by the way. For the Maze Party. It was fun."

"Yeah, it was," I say, with a smile. "And you were right. It's important to me, our friendship and our work together."

He nods. "I completely agree."

"And I don't want to jeopardize that."

"Me neither. And for the record, it wouldn't. I wouldn't." He shrugs, looking a bit uncomfortable, before shooting me another big smile. "Anything is at your pace, Lily."

"Thank you."

"Now back to work."

I smile. "Sure, sure. I'll send you the email as soon as possible."

"Fantastic."

He leaves and I'm left with my work and my thoughts. I know Turner wants more from me, but it's not fair to him to suggest another attempt at a date. Not after what happened at my parents' dinner—not knowing that what I feel toward him is nothing compared to the tangled jumble of emotions that Hayden evokes.

And there's no denying I'm excited about tonight.

The butterflies multiply in my stomach until I have a veritable garden by the time I have to leave work. For so many years, I'd missed having him in my life, and here he is now. I'll be damned if I don't take advantage of that.

I pack up work and head home with my thoughts swirling. It doesn't take me long to change into the casual dress I'd already picked out that morning, to brush my hair out and put on a bit of lip gloss. I put on upbeat music in the background, trying and failing to still my nerves.

I park outside Hayden's house on Elm Street. I wonder, not for the first time, how he affords what must be a significant rent. He's been here for nearly two weeks by now, and it can't be cheap. But his financial situation has always been a sore topic. I remember that from childhood, from asking about college prospects and jobs and getting monosyllabic answers. It used to kill me that he didn't want me to help. Now I understand that it came from pride.

I walk up the steps with a wine bottle in hand. I raise my hand to press the doorbell, but the door opens before I can ring.

Hayden is so handsome it hurts. A plain white button-down makes his dark hair stand out in contrast, the cut of his shoulders wide and imposing. It never stops hitting me just how different adult Hayden is from the teenager I once loved.

His eyes, though. He looks at me like I'm late—like he's been waiting forever, like he can't look away—even though I'm bang on time.

"I saw the car."

"I brought wine."

The house smells delicious, like something rich and cheesy. I can't stop myself from taking a deep whiff. "This smells amazing. Are you cooking?"

"I haven't changed *that* much, Lils."

"Take-out?"

"Yeah, I got food from Michelangelo's. Risotto and pizza. Figured we could share?"

"Yes. Yes, absolutely."

We grab the food as he leads me through the house and out to his backyard. It's a beautiful little place, with green grass and a deck for dining.

We take a seat opposite each other, the food in between us. For a while we do nothing but look at each other.

I smile, just a little. "So, how do we do this?"

"Dating?"

"Yes."

"I have no idea."

My smile grows bigger. "We never did, in the past."

"No. We were just… together."

"But you must have been on dates since then." I make sure to keep my voice light and ignore my unease at the idea. "The concept is fairly standard. Eat, talk, flirt. Repeat."

His smile is replaced by a faint frown. It makes him more handsome somehow, set against the square jaw and the dark hair falling across his brow. "I haven't dated a lot. It's not exactly a possibility in the military."

The answer makes me unreasonably pleased. "That's understandable."

"What about you? The Yale men must have been lining up, not to mention New York."

I shake my head. "Not exactly, no. But I have been on some dates."

"I can imagine. Flowers, candles?" Hayden's voice is light, too, but he's not meeting my eyes anymore.

"Sometimes," I say honestly, though there haven't been many. I've only dated three guys since leaving Paradise Shores for college. Since him. "There's often wine, at least."

He laughs and proceeds to open the bottle. "As you wish," he says with a flourish, pouring me a glass. He puts the bottle down afterwards.

"You're not having any?"

Hayden shakes his head. "Not tonight."

"Oh. Well, now I feel like a lush."

"Don't. It's…" He runs a hand through his hair, the telltale sign of nerves. "We're supposed to talk about happy things on our first date together. I want to know about Yale and school and rehabilitation. About New York. About your future plans."

"We can talk about that, too, if you want," I say. "Or about the first thing. You never *have* to tell me anything."

He shoots me a smile, and it's grateful and rueful at the same time. "Well, you always managed to get everything out of me in the end, anyway. Why should it be any different now?"

I smile back at him. I remember whispered confessions in the dark, over a decade ago, about things in his past. Hayden never liked opening up. He fought it tooth and nail, every time, against his own best interests.

"All right. Well, I don't drink anymore."

"Really?"

"Yeah. Stopped about five years ago."

Hayden had never been a massive drinker, although I remember him drinking at parties. I remember us in a hallway, our first kiss tasting like whiskey and danger. "What made you decide to stop? Not that it's a bad thing, of course."

He looks away, jaw working. "You know that my dad struggles with it."

"Yes, I remember," I say, although from what he's told me, *struggles with it* is a mild way to put it. I know he's always wanted to hide this part of his history from me, and always hated when it showed through. I never truly understood why. I still don't.

"It can be genetic. Addiction can, I mean. And I'm not going to be like him."

"Hayden, from what you've told me, you're nothing like him at all."

He looks at me with eyes that hold a fair amount of disbelief. His armor is still up, though, and I know better than to push. "Thanks. But that's the reason. I don't want to fall victim to the same thing. I don't trust myself enough for that." He's quiet for a beat, looking at his glass of water. "Or rather, I don't trust the part of me that's his."

"Have you spoken to him lately?"

"No, not for six years. Last I heard, he was somewhere in

New Jersey. But I'm not looking for him and I don't want him in my life."

Flashes of what he's told me run through my head. The images aren't pretty. I know there was heavy drinking; I know there was violence.

"Gary isn't in contact with him either?"

Hayden scoffs. "No. Lord knows he always hated his sister's husband. That didn't change after she died."

"You never told me how she passed."

"No," he murmurs, eyes unreadable. "I never did. And I don't think that's a topic for our first date, Lils. Even with you."

"All right." I take a deep breath and paint a smile on my face. Grabbing my wineglass by the stem, I pour it out in a nearby pot. "You know what? Who needs wine anyway."

Hayden looks completely stunned. He blinks twice before he breaks into surprised laughter. "You're crazy."

"Always was. Anyway, that plant looked a bit dry. You should take better care of this place."

"Yeah, you're right." He puts a spoonful of risotto on my plate. "You didn't have to, you know."

"I know. But I should probably cut down anyway. You're practically doing me a favor. Thanks, Hay."

He shakes his head, like he doesn't believe that at all, but doesn't comment. The small smile on his face is back and I feel warm inside. It feels unreal to sit here and share a meal with him. With Hayden, who I dreamed of every night growing up. Who wore the school uniform with such disdain. Who never teased me the way my brothers did.

"So," he says, voice deepening. "Tell me about Yale."

"Hmm, well, I was there for four years. I don't know where to start."

He gives me a look that sends shivers down my body, all the way to my toes. There's something about his gaze—there always was—that reaches all the way to my very core. "I have nothing but time."

So I tell him. I tell him about the annoying professors and the brilliant ones, about the seminar tutor who asked a student out during class and got fired, about the late nights at the library. He laughs when I talk about my crazy roommate who used to wash her socks in the sink and hang them along the heater, even when I told her repeatedly that it would cause a fire.

And he reluctantly shares things from the Navy.

He tells me about weeks spent in training, about hikes with fifty pounds worth of gear. About his journey to become a lieutenant.

"Do you want to go back?" I ask, pulling my legs up on the chair. The sun has set, and there's a faint chill in the air, despite the season. "I mean, are you here on leave at the moment?"

Hayden leans back. Even as a grown man—one without a leather jacket and a scowl—there's irreverence in his pose. I wonder if that's one of the reasons I was always drawn to him, even from the start. He was everything I wasn't.

"I meant what I said at dinner the other night. I'm here indefinitely."

"Indefinitely?"

"Yes." His eyes roam my face, as if analyzing my reaction. "Not going back to active service anytime soon."

"You've quit?"

"Not really. I'm more like a consultant at the moment, actually. I work with one of my old brothers-in-arms. We have a business, selling security solutions both to the private sector and to the military."

I'm momentarily stunned. "Wow. That's impressive."

"It pays the bills." He glances at my arms, wrapped around my waist, and frowns. "You're cold, Lils."

"No."

"Yes, you are. Quit being stubborn." He grabs the plates and nods toward the door. "Let's go inside."

I follow him with our glasses in hand. Despite myself, I'm nervous. When we're just sitting and talking, it's easy to forget that we're two adults, a man and a woman, who had sex just a few days ago. It's easy to slip back into the comfortable role of Hayden and Lily, childhood friends, and abandon the rest.

It's not so easy when he's walking in front of me, all shoulders and roughness and thick, silky hair.

Hayden holds the door open for me. "You got it?"

"Yes."

We end up on the sofa, side by side, in his impeccably decorated living room. There's nothing overly romantic about the situation—we're old friends—but my body feels taut with anticipation. I remember the feeling of his mouth on mine, of his body driving into mine just days ago. Something tells me Hayden is remembering the same thing.

He clears his throat. "Do you want to watch something, Lils?"

"On the TV?"

Hayden's low laugh feels sensual, rippling across my skin. "Yes."

"Um, yeah. Sure."

He turns it on and we scroll aimlessly through a streaming service. The room is dark, and it only adds to the hard beat of my heart.

"What do you feel like?"

Like you, I want to answer. I don't, trying to focus on the options he flits through. Documentaries, movies, TV shows… It's not long until my gaze snags on an old action film. It's a classic, one my brothers watched with Hayden before I was allowed to.

I point at it. "Remember?"

"Yes. You made me re-watch it with you later, when your mom told you you could."

"It was never as good as Henry and Rhys made it out to be."

"Nothing ever could be. They just wanted to rile you up."

"Let's watch it," I say, grabbing the blanket from off the side of the sofa.

"For old time's sake?"

"Exactly. Are you cold?" I hold up the edge of the blanket. Hayden looks from it to me, amusement dancing in his eyes.

"Yes," he says, voice serious. "*Very*."

I blush. It's obvious he isn't cold, but he still settles close to me, the blanket draped over our legs.

The movie starts and I can barely focus on a word that's being said. I'm too busy thinking about all the places we're nearly touching.

"Remember this part?" Hayden says, voice amused. "Parker tried to recreate it for that talent show."

"Yeah. And he forced Henry to make him a wooden sword."

"Right." He shakes his head, his profile achingly handsome. "And he made me fight with him on the lawn. Gave me a bruise too, smacked me right on the wrist."

"I didn't know that."

"Don't worry," he says, shooting me a sideways grin. "I smacked him right back."

I can't help but smile. "You were thick as thieves."

"Yeah, we were." Hayden moves in closer and grabs my ankles, resting by his thigh. He pulls my legs across his lap so I can lie fully stretched out. "Okay like that?"

I nod, unsure of my voice. "Yeah. Thanks."

Like old times, I feel like saying, the two of us watching something in the basement, hidden under blankets, kissing and stopping as soon as we heard footsteps.

I try to focus on the movie but his hand on my leg is infuriatingly distracting. He keeps it there, warm and rough, just resting on my calf. His thumb smooths back once, twice, three times...

Heat rises through my body. I want to be closer—I want his hand higher—and my traitorous body is remembering the night in the greenhouse. I didn't get enough of him then. I don't think I ever will.

But his hand stays right there, just below my knee, softly stroking my skin.

We watch over half the movie before I gather the courage. It's Hayden, I tell myself. It's just Hayden, even if there's ten years of distance between us. So I sit up.

He looks at me. "Everything all right?"

"Yes. Just switching around." I grab a pillow and put it squarely on his lap. Then I turn around, lying so my head is there instead. I pull the blanket over me again.

Hayden lets out a dark chuckle. "This is familiar."

It is, just like the times we pretended to watch a movie just to fool around instead. His hand is resting lightly on my hip, and I lift the blanket to pull his arm tighter around my waist. It's warm and heavy, lying there, and I let my fingers trail up the muscular forearm.

He sighs, and it sounds like surrender, before he holds me more tightly. His hand is close to the underside of my breast, thumb caressing again through the fabric of my dress.

"Lils..."

"Yes?"

He bends, so close that I can breathe in the scent of him, of man and cologne and warm skin. I want him to kiss me. His dark hair tickles my cheek as his lips brush my ear. "I'm not going to take you to bed tonight."

"Oh, damn it, Hayden."

His husky laugh sends shivers down my arms. "Disappointed?"

I turn my face into his chest, hiding my expression. It

doesn't help. His chest is rock hard. I mumble something unintelligible against the warmth. I am disappointed—just a little bit.

"We're not in a rush." Hayden's arm tightens around my waist. His fingers brush the underside of my breast. "I'm going to do this the right way."

I wiggle closer, wanting to feel his mouth on mine. "We've already had sex again."

"Yes, but that's not going to happen again for a little while."

I run my hand up his chest and curve it around his broad neck. "Why? The greenhouse was... explosive."

He closes his eyes momentarily, and when he opens them again, they burn into mine. "Yes, and then you ran from me. I'm not going to risk that happening again for a little while."

He bends down and brushes his lips against mine. I kiss him back, our lips meeting in the softest of touches. It quickly turns heated and my fingers weave their way into the thick locks of his hair.

Hayden groans into my mouth and cradles me closer. His lips open mine softly, and I nearly come apart at the first taste of his tongue. The world centers around the two of us, and nothing else matters. Not the sound of fighting armies on the TV or the years of separation. It's just the two of us again.

His hand cups my breast, a thumb flicking gently over my taut nipple. I can't help the moan that escapes me and he chuckles.

"So eager..."

"Mmm." I kiss him deeply again. "It's been a while."

"Since the greenhouse? It's been three days."

I smile against his lips. "Far, far too long."

Hayden grips my waist and pulls me closer, kissing me thoroughly. He has a way of touching me that completely undoes me—the mixture of devotion and need. Like he's gripping me tightly despite himself, fingers stroking my skin with adoration but body pulsing with want.

I want to feel his skin against mine, his body heaving, the both of us stretched out—

Hayden pulls away with a wry smile. The heat in his eyes is unmistakable, making my mouth dry. If the greenhouse was intense, the next time will be tortuously slow. I can see it in his eyes.

He puts two fingers under my chin and turns my face up. His lips trail slowly down my jaw, along the sensitive skin of my neck. I shiver when I feel them against my ear.

"It's time for you to go home now, Lily, or I'm going to break my own resolution."

"Maybe that's a good thing." My voice is only a little breathless.

"I'm not going to rush things with you."

"Where did you get so self-disciplined?" I mutter, thinking about the recklessness he often displayed as a child.

Hayden laughs and lifts me off him in one clean, strong movement, making it very clear that he is most definitely a grown man now. "The Navy is sort of big on that, Lils."

"I suppose." Despite myself, I'm glad we're taking it slowly. It feels right... proper, somehow. Like he's here to stay —like we're starting something again. And when we kiss goodbye that night, it's a sweet kiss filled with promise and hope.

23

HAYDEN

Gary looks familiar opposite me. There are more wrinkles on his face, true, and the hair he has left is pierced with gray. But he has the same laughing glint in his eyes.

It was my idea to take him out to lunch at the Yacht Club's terrace. We're by far the roughest types here, but I don't care. The food is delicious and we've wiped our plates clean.

He offers me a cigarette, but I shake my head.

"When did you stop?"

"Years ago," I say. "You haven't seen me smoke in a long time."

"Good lad. Do as I say and not as I do, and all that."

"Exactly."

He turns to look out over the waves. We're at the table furthest out on the terrace, closest to where the waves crash against the plinths beneath us. "So," he says. "How does it feel to be back? Really?"

"It's good. Weird, you know."

"I can imagine."

"I didn't think of this as a home when I lived here," I say. "But coming back now… it feels like coming home."

Gary's smile is quick, there and gone in a flash. He nods

and flicks ash off his cigarette into the tray. "This is the place you've been longest, so it's not surprising."

"Yes, I guess."

"And seeing the Marchands again?" The way he asks it, I know he'll be okay with whatever I say. If there is one thing Gary understands, it's the fine line we walk between being white trash and hired help, between friends of the family and an employed charity case.

He understands the mixed feelings it brings.

"It's been good. It's easier now, being grown and self-sufficient myself." I lean against the railing of the terrace and sigh. "Parker is as easygoing as always."

"The boy missed you," Gary says. "He would come to my garage sometimes to tinker with the cars, but I know he was just fishing for information about you."

I sigh, not knowing what to say. Gary has never asked me why I left so abruptly after the accident. I think, of all people, he was the only one who truly understood why I had to leave. I think a part of him even respected me for it.

"I hope you told him great things."

"Of course. You were the commander of the entire damn Navy by the time you were twenty-three, kid."

I chuckle. "What am I now?"

"If you had waited another few years to come back, I could have promoted you to president."

"Of the country?"

He shrugs. "Sky's the limit."

"Not for people like us," I laugh. "*President.* Holy hell."

Gary snuffs his cigarette out in the tray, his face taking on a pensive look. I might have been away for a while, but I know what it means. It means he's going to say something that's difficult for him.

"Not for you, Hay. Damn... when you told me you were promoted to lieutenant... Well done."

I focus on the horizon and keep the sudden tightness in

my chest at bay. "Thanks."

"Yeah. Yeah, of course." He clears his throat. "How was it, meeting Lily again? I know you were fond of her back in the day."

I try not to let my surprise show. I had been so cautious back then to make sure he never found out, especially not after he warned me to be careful with her. I know he hadn't wanted me to screw up our situation—the tuition, the employment.

"She's good," I say. "It's been nice to see her again, too."

"Mmhmm." There's a wealth of insinuation in the sound. "Right."

"What?"

"Nothing. I trust you to make your own decisions."

I fight the urge to roll my eyes, like I'm sixteen again. "I know, I know. Be careful with her."

"Nah, you're a grown man now. I don't want you to get hurt, but I know you can handle it."

The wind smells strongly of salt and seaweed as it blows past me, ruffling my hair. I blink a few times to get the full meaning of his words. Is he really saying what I think he's saying?

"You were warning me to be careful for my own sake?"

"Of course." He looks at me like it's obvious. "It wasn't hard to see how you looked at her growing up, kid. But people like the Marchands? They're heartbreakers."

My mouth feels dry. "They've always been good to us."

"Yes, and don't I know it." For the first time, I hear the rancor in his voice. I recognize the feeling. It's shame, and guilt, and the loss of pride that comes with having to accept charity. "Eloise and Michael are good people. But they're not easy people, and they're not *our* people."

It's not a comfortable thought—not with my hopes for Lily. "Did you think dinner was awkward on Friday night?"

"You mean apart from the looks you and Lily sent each

other?"

I'm quiet for a beat, just looking at him.

He smiles. "Come on now, don't scowl at me. I'm just pointing out the obvious. I don't think it was clear to anyone else. And besides, her brothers are oblivious, which you're damn lucky about."

"I know that."

"If you want my advice—"

"I don't."

"—then do what makes you happy. Life's too damn short, and you and I both know it can turn on a dime."

"Really? You're not warning me to avoid screwing up a good situation for us? That's a change."

He shoots me a wry smile. "You're not a child anymore. You have work, you have a future. I'm getting closer to retirement every day, and I have my savings. I say you go a bit wild again, kid."

I shake my head, but I can't stop the smile on my face. He's right about that. We're in a very different situation than we were ten years ago—not to mention twenty. We'd gone from town to town, barely surviving on the meager paychecks Gary had made from working in garages and on farms.

Things are different now.

"About that," I say, leaning forward. "I have something I want to tell you."

"You really *are* running for president."

"No."

Gary throws his hands heavenward. "What a waste."

I take a deep breath, playing with the edge of the tablecloth. "The house on Elm Street? I'm not renting it. I sort of… well, I bought it."

"You *bought* it."

"Yes. Remember what I've told you about the security business I have set up with my old buddy from the Navy?"

"Yes. Security consulting."

"Well, it's taken off."

I'm expecting congratulations, amazement—not the widened eyes of disapproval. "How much in debt are you? Your mortgage?"

"I paid half in cash," I say. "The interest rate is set over ten years. It's a financially sound decision, Uncle."

"Quit playing. I've seen what houses here go for, Hay. There's no way you could afford that. Hell, if you add up everything I've made in *life*, I couldn't afford a place in Paradise Shores. How did you get the money? I won't have you caught up with loan sharks just to impress Lily Marchand…"

"I'm not caught up with loan sharks. The security business is going *great*. We're making a lot of money. A lot of money, Uncle. You don't need to worry about me. And for the record, the house was expensive, but it's not exactly an oceanside villa."

He leans back, the red color slowly draining from his face as he processes my words. I can see when it finally sinks in.

"So what you're telling me, boy, is that you're rich now."

"I'm comfortable."

"No, don't pull that middle-class bullshit with me. Tell me like it is. Are you rich, Hayden?"

I know what he means. I know what he's referring to—the kind of stability people like us could spend their entire lives chasing and never get. The kind of safety net we'd lacked for decades.

He means *security*.

"Yes," I tell him.

Gary closes his eyes momentarily, and then he's out of his chair and his arms are around me. I can count the hugs my uncle has given me on one hand. He let me eat when he didn't have enough food for the both of us, but physical affection has never been for us.

I wrap an arm around him. Only then do I realize that his shoulders are shaking, shaking hard with laughter. He wipes a tear of mirth from his eyes.

"Holy hell, Hay. You made it. You fucking made it."

I swallow. "It's not… well. Yes."

"Yes you did, kid. God, there was a time when I didn't think you'd make it to your eighteenth damn birthday…" He reaches for a cigarette, and I can see that his hand is slightly unsteady. "If your good-for-nothing father could see you now… Sorry."

"Don't apologize to me."

"No, if only Alice could see you now," he says, and when he looks at me, I see that his eyes are glazed. I know he has the same eyes as my mother, the same hazel color. It's the only real resemblance between them. "She'd be over the moon."

"That her son got rich?"

He shakes his head. "That you made something out of yourself. That you're not going to become your father. That you were dealt a pretty shit hand of cards and you're standing tall. A fucking homeowner. My nephew's a *homeowner*. Not even your grandfather could say that."

I don't know what to say. His praise is sudden and unexpected, so much more than when I graduated from military college. He'd flown in then to see me, standing in one of the back rows, sunglasses glinting in the sun.

"You were dealt a pretty shit hand of cards, too," I say. "You were given a sullen and ungrateful seven-year-old and you decided to take him with you."

"Of course I did, kid."

"Not everyone would have made the same decision," I say. The words are hard to say—I have to force them out—but they're important. It's important that he knows this. "I didn't become rich on my own. You helped that happen."

He runs a hand along his neck, staring at the table. "Nah. You did that all on your own."

"Absolutely not. I know how much I owe you, Gary."

"You don't owe me a damn thing."

"Will you let me say thank you?"

He sighs. "Fine. Go ahead, boy."

"I don't know if I'm going to live in Paradise Shores. I don't know what lies in store in my future. But I do know that the house here is too big for just me. There's a spare wing with a guest bedroom and a kitchenette."

His eyes narrow at me, but I keep going, ignoring the look he shoots me. I know I have to phrase this offer right—and I only have one shot.

"You can't live in the Marchands' beach house after you retire. I don't know what your plans are, but if you want it, the house is yours to use."

He shakes his head but says nothing. I wonder if it feels too much like a handout—like the kind of charity I'd been to the Marchands.

"There's a large garage and toolshed that needs to be filled, and I don't have the time."

"Hmm."

"I could use someone to look after the plants."

Gary looks out across the ocean for a long time. I wonder if it's as much a part of him now as it is of me. He grew up inland, far away from the coast, from boats and marinas and the sound of seagulls. But somehow, it's become home for the both of us.

"Someone to mow the lawn," he says finally.

"Exactly. I won't have the time."

He reaches over and offers me his hand. There's a glint in his eyes I haven't seen before, and belatedly, I realize they're glazed with tears. I shake his hand.

"I accept, kid."

24

HAYDEN

The drive to Lily's house that evening doesn't take long. The streets of Paradise Shores feel as familiar to me now as they did when I left, structured and ordered, winding around a central square. Turning up on Ocean Drive to the boardwalk, the cafés, the marina in the distance. Knowing that the Marchand house is on the far north of Ocean Drive, Lily's cottage to the south.

The sun hangs low by the horizon and the ocean glitters with an orange hue. For the first time in a long while, my shoulders don't feel quite so tense. Gary had accepted my offer without much hesitation. And Lily had, while maybe not forgiven me entirely, accepted me back into her life.

I park outside her house and smile as I open the gate. It's still perfectly oiled and functioning. There are a few shingles on the roof that need to be changed too—I saw that from the start—but I know I have to start small.

Lily opens the door before I can knock. There's an apron around her waist, her cheeks pink and blooming with heat.

"Hi."

"Hello." I bend and press a soft kiss to her lips. The happiness in her eyes nearly undoes me, knowing how much I've missed it, how close I was to losing it forever. "What's that amazing smell?"

"Do you like it?" She dances over to the kitchen. A large pot is on the stove. "I'm trying to make bouillabaisse."

"The French seafood stew?"

"Yes. Remember?"

"I do. It's amazing." I follow her, standing close enough that I can smell the fresh scent of shampoo clinging to her auburn hair. It's braided along her back. I'm struck again by an image of it wrapped around my hand as she's bent, as she moans— I cut off that line of thinking. I'd decided to take things slow. I couldn't afford to mess this up again.

"The one your mom used to make."

"The very one." She stirs the pot, leaning back against my chest. "I think you liked it growing up, unless you were faking."

"I wasn't. Don't you know I'd never fake?"

Lily laughs. I run my fingertips up her bare arms and watch as goose bumps follow my touch.

"Neither do I," she says.

I brush a kiss against her neck and try to ignore the arousal her words produce. "I remember."

"The stew can handle being on its own for a bit." She turns in my arms, pressing the soft length of her body against mine. For a few minutes nothing else exists but the feel of her soft lips. I make my touch lazy, sweeping my hands slowly over her back, her hips, her shoulders. Savoring every inch of her.

Lily's the one who touches her tongue to mine first, and I can't help but smile at the intrusion. She's always hated being treated as if she couldn't keep up. My decision the other night must have felt like we were children again.

I slide my hands down and cup her bottom. It's easy to push her closer against me, against the hardness that's making it hard for me to think rationally. It always has been, where she's concerned.

Lily chuckles and starts to kiss my neck. "You really can't fake anything with me."

"Not that."

She slides her hand down and traces a finger along the bulge in my pants. It's already straining against the fabric and I hiss at the feeling of her nail, softly tracing the length.

"All this could be solved so easily, you know," she murmurs. "You know I'm willing."

"Mhm." I grab her wrist and pull it away from my groin, not without some difficulty. It's almost painful how hard her words make me. Wrapping my hands around her waist, I turn her back to the stove. "The stew is boiling."

"Shoot."

I smile against her hair and watch as she stirs. It's funny how right everything feels when she's in my arms. My fears and problems fall away, the past and the future too. As long as she's by my side, everything feels possible.

We eat by candlelight at her kitchen table. The food is delicious, and I tell her so, even going in for seconds. There's laughter in her warm eyes when I reach for another piece of bread, ready to dunk it in the stew.

"What?"

"I was just wondering where all of it goes."

"The food?"

"Yeah. But then…" She lets her eyes trail down across my chest, down my body, hidden beneath the table. "It's fairly obvious."

I quirk my lips into a smile. "Are you implying that I need to go on a diet, Lily Marchand? What a rude thing to say."

"Absolutely not. And don't you get any *more* in shape, either, or I'll never sleep with you again."

I laugh, despite myself. "Isn't that counterintuitive? Most women seem to want muscles. The more the merrier."

"Yes, well, *I'm* not exactly in your kind of shape. It's hard already to imagine taking my clothes off with all that going on."

Lily says it lightly, her eyes teasing, but I can't help but wonder if she's serious—if there's a thread of insecurity lingering under her bravado. I remember the shy girl from all those years ago, her hands courageous but trembling.

And there is nothing even *remotely* wrong about her shape. There's rather too much right about it, if parts of my anatomy have anything to say.

"Your body is insane, Lils."

She laughs, a faint blush on her cheeks. "Hayden."

"I'd want you regardless, you know. But that's the truth. There's no part of you that doesn't entice me."

"You haven't seen me naked yet," she says, voice amused. Her eyes promise pleasure, sending shocks of want through me.

"Of course I have."

"I mean, not now. Not since you came back."

"So?" I tap a finger against my temple. "Infallible memory."

"I've changed, dumbass."

I frown and pretend to look confused, letting my eyes wander over her collarbones, her smooth shoulders, the slopes of her breasts under the shirt. The curve of her waist before it dips out into hips that I remember gripping tightly.

"No," I say. "I can't see anything different. I'll suppose I'll just have to take a closer look to see."

Lily grins at me. "I suppose you have to, then."

"And when the time is right, I will."

After dinner, I walk around her small house. It's the first time I'm properly let in. The cottage might be small, but it's cozy, and every inch of it bears her imprint. Its Lily's person- ality come to life.

I pause at the framed pictures on the wall. One is Lily in

her graduation gown from Yale. She's posing in front a large brick building, her hair straight and gleaming, a cap on her head. There's an unexpected stab in my chest at the sight. Yale, one of the many reasons I left—to ensure she got the future she deserved.

She pauses at my shoulder. "Oh. It was a massive ceremony."

"Did your family come?"

"Yes, they drove up for the day. Henry came in from New York, Parker too." She's quiet for a beat. "Rhys was the only one who didn't make it."

"Rhys wasn't there?" I find that hard to believe. The Marchands' middle son had always been Lily's protector, the one person who'd championed and understood her dreams of art.

She shakes her head. "No."

I wrap an arm around her shoulders and press a kiss to her hair. There's more, I'm sure, that's happened in the years since I was last in her life on a daily basis. She'll tell me when she's ready.

"What about this?" I point at a picture of Lily in front of a gallery. She's wearing a sleek silk dress, her hair long and glorious over one shoulder. There's a glass of champagne in her hand. Looking at her makes me want to stand next to her and wrap an arm around her waist. *You can look, but not touch.*

"A gallery opening. The first exhibition I curated myself."

"In Manhattan?"

"Yes. It was modern art."

"Do you miss it? The art scene."

She shakes her head, and I'm close enough to see the freckles that smatter across her nose. "No. There was too much pretension. Art is supposed to make you feel, and it's supposed to be fun. There's skill to it as well, of course, but... I couldn't stand those environments."

I pull her toward the couch. She sinks down next to me. "And here in Paradise? There's not much art around here."

"Well... I sort of want to change that." Lily's smile is crooked, her eyes mischievous. It's a look I recognize well. It means she's about to say something to shock or tease me, or suggest we do something that will *definitely* land us in trouble.

"Tell me."

"There's a place on Porter Street. A small locale, nothing more. But it's not too expensive, and I think I can get a good deal through Harris Development."

"All right."

"I'll transform it. Art on the walls from people in the area, maybe showcasing art from further afield every now and so often. And I could host art classes."

The excitement on her face stirs something similar in me. I can see her vision, and I know she'd execute it beautifully. "I think you should, Lils."

"Really? I'd be using a fair bit of my trust to buy it. And it would be a risk. It might never make financial sense."

I shrug. "And if it doesn't, you'll sell the place a few years down the line. It's not a big deal."

Her smile broadens. "I don't know why I thought you'd caution me against this."

"Me neither. Have you forgotten?" I lean forward, nipping at her earlobe, loving the sound of her laughter. "I'm the wild one, remember. The one from the wrong side of the tracks."

"There are no tracks at all around here."

"Which just goes to show how far from home I actually am."

She smiles at me and I can't help but smile back. "Most people in my life won't approve," she says. "Parker won't understand. Mom will be cautiously optimistic, but she won't *get* it. Dad will hate it. He'll probably say I'm wasting my trust, my time and my talent."

"So fuck him."

She barks out a surprised laughter. "Hayden!"

"What? I respect the man, but it's your life, Lils. You have to live it."

Her fingers trail up my arm. "You're right. I'll see if I can start the paperwork tomorrow."

"Mmm. And let me know if you need any help."

She looks up at me. "Help?"

"Getting the place in shape. Hanging paintings. Reviewing art classes... Posing as a model."

Lily giggles. "You'd pose for me?"

"Yes. Nude would be best."

She leans in closer to my side and presses a kiss to my neck. Her lips are soft against my skin, moving gently down to the collar of my shirt. "I've drawn nude men before. It's a lot of fun."

My arm tightens around her shoulders. The response is involuntary. I picture another man, eager and college-educated, lying on a couch for her. I imagine what happened after.

Lily's voice is low against my skin. "In class. We had to learn how to sketch muscles, to draw movement."

My shoulders relax. "I want to see what you've painted in the last few years."

"It's not much."

"I'm sure that's a lie."

She turns and sits with one leg on either side of me, in my lap. Her hands find their way around my neck and for a long moment I can only stare at her, at the wonder of her long fiery hair and beautiful eyes. At the smile she's giving me. Now that I'm back in her life, I'm astonished I ever survived without her.

I lean forward and take her mouth in a kiss. It's too easy, with her, to lose myself entirely. To forget who I am and what I've done.

She presses herself closer, her breasts flattening against my chest. I let my hands slide down and cup her bottom, to fit her more tightly against me. I'm so damn aroused it's difficult to concentrate on anything but her weight against my groin.

"How long will you torture us both?" Lily murmurs, letting her hand trail across my shoulders. She rolls her hips and I have to grit my teeth against the sensations that ripple through me. "It's been over a week since the greenhouse now. We've been on three dates."

It's hard to concentrate through my desire. She's too important to me, and I need to make sure there are no regrets.

But that doesn't mean I can't give her some relief.

I kiss her again, stronger this time, and smile at the sound of her low moan. Her skin feels hot to the touch. It burns my hands and my lips, and still I want more of the fire.

Grabbing her hips, I flip us around. Lily grins as I spread her out on the couch beneath me. The fabric of her flimsy sundress bunches around her waist, taunting me with the expanse of pale, freckled thighs.

I kiss down her neck, touching my lips to her collarbone.

"All right," I murmur, letting my hand skim down her body. I flick her taut nipple and I'm rewarded by the sound of her gasp. "Let's check this…"

She pulls at my shoulders when she realizes where my hand is going. "Hayden—"

"Yes?" I ignore her faint protest as my hand lifts the hem of her dress. The skin along the waistband of her panties is soft as silk to the touch. It's easy work to slip my fingers underneath it, to reach down and tease her soft warmth.

Lily lets out a moan, and I can't help but smile at her. The blush on her cheeks is magnificent. "You weren't lying," I murmur, my fingers parting and circling. I slip a finger inside her, and I'm rewarded with another breathless moan. "You really are that eager."

She nods against my neck, wriggling and writhing. It

makes it harder for me to focus on touching her, until I realize what she's trying to get a hold of. I angle my hips away and she sighs in frustration.

"*Please.*"

It takes me a moment to respond, with her body pressed so close to me. But she's too important to me. I have to make sure there are no regrets.

And in my desire-addled mind, I say that.

"No regrets," she whispers. "None at all. Hayden, I want you."

And God knows I'd wanted her forever, from the first time I saw her, and would until my last dying day. She's everything I've ever dreamed of.

"All right, baby," I murmur, curling my finger inside of her. "Let's get you into bed and taken care of."

Lily doesn't protest when I lift her up, carrying her into her bedroom and onto the oversized bed. She just presses closer to me. "Finally."

25

LILY

Hayden lays me down on my bed and wastes no time in getting back to what he started on the couch. He folds me back and tugs my panties down my legs. Strong hands push my legs apart, fingers curling over the soft skin of my thighs.

I close my eyes at the first touch of his tongue. It's too much, what he's doing to me. But I bury my hands in his hair nonetheless. It's silky between my fingers, the thick, black hair he's had since the first day I met him, over twenty years ago.

Hayden keeps his hands on my hips to keep me in place, but I wouldn't move for the world. Every skillful motion of his tongue and fingers brings me closer, closer to an edge that threatens to undo me.

Hayden's touching me like he owns me—like all of me is his and he's reclaiming it. A very small part of me wants to object.

The rest is in complete agreement. I *am* his. I always have been, deep inside, my soul calling out to his. It's physical, but it's so much more than that, too.

Hayden breaks off momentarily to laugh softly against my

skin. He presses a kiss to my inner thigh and looks up at me. "So far, you haven't changed a bit, Lily."

He's driving me insane, the desire coursing through my body too strong to override. "Let's talk *later.*"

"So impatient." He does something with his fingers that makes me gasp, a wicked smile on his face.

He devotes himself entirely to my pleasure again and I break apart under his tongue. I can't control my movements, gasping as my back arches and toes curl. It's heavenly, this release, all with him.

Hayden rests his head on my hip and runs a hand lazily around my nipple. He's watching me through hooded eyes. "I'd forgotten how beautiful you are when you come."

My cheeks heat up. I run a hand through his hair, stopping right at the nape of his neck.

"God Lily, you're too sweet," he murmurs, pressing a kiss to my hipbone. "That was a good start."

I frown and tug at his shoulders. He crawls up my body, lying down next to me, a strong hand around my waist. I think it's meant to reassure me, but I don't feel the least bit calm.

I tug at his shirt, my hands fumbling with the buttons. It doesn't take long until Hayden catches on. He murmurs a protest against my lips, something about *slow* and *regrets,* but I'll have none of that.

He groans when my hand strokes along the bulge in his jeans. "Too tight," he murmurs, a sigh of relief escaping him when he finally tugs his jeans off.

My heart is beating so fast I'm sure he can hear it. There's an urgency to this, but it's not like the greenhouse, when all I needed was fusion.

This time I want him undone and broken in my arms. I want to watch where we join, and when I whisper it to him, Hayden lowers his forehead to my shoulder and mutters a string of curses.

"What?" I whisper, wrapping my arms around him. He's on top of me, the heavy weight of his arousal resting against my stomach.

"You'll be the death of me, Lily."

I hug him tighter, until his face is buried against my breasts. "I don't want that."

There's a faint laugh. "I'd die happy, babygirl."

He lifts himself up on strong arms and kisses me. It's deep and invasive, warning me about what's to come. If we had our guards up before, they're completely down now. There's absolute surrender with Hayden.

I should have realized that before, when I pushed and pushed for him to take me to bed properly—not the wild, emotional coupling in the greenhouse. I should have realized that once we did it slowly, I'd lose all semblance of control, both of my emotions and the situation.

This will change things. If he leaves again, I don't know if I'll emerge unscathed.

But he's worth the risk.

I kiss him back, letting his tongue sweep in and leave a trail of hot fire in its wake. His muscled back is hard under my hands, and I run my fingers along the deep grooves. I want to touch him everywhere—to relearn his body and have him catalogue mine in turn.

Hayden spreads my thighs without stopping the kisses, settling between my legs with a low groan. He rests his forehead against mine. I can feel him shaking with the effort to go slow, running the head of his hardness along me, teasing.

I put a hand on his chest to feel the beat of his heart, fast and racing. My own is doing the same.

"Feel that?" he murmurs. "All for you, Lils."

I kiss him, pouring all my longing and need and despair into it. All the years we've been apart and the nights without him.

He groans when he finally pushes into me, inch by inch,

until he's buried to the hilt. It feels so unbearably right to have our bodies intertwined like this again—my legs around his waist, his arms around me, our bodies moving in tandem.

I don't know how long we move like that, with him inside me, both of us gasping, before release finally overtakes us. It starts deep within me first. Hayden has a hand between my legs and he's circling, voice imploring in my ear.

"Again, Lily," he murmurs, and I can't hold back, breaking around him like a wave against the shore for the second time.

Hayden groans and follows me into release. I hold him, our bodies shaking with the force of it. For a long time we stay like that, wrapped around one another.

I run a hand over his back, stroking the muscled skin. He's warm and faintly sweaty. "Will you stay the night?"

There's a faint, noncommittal grunt against my neck. "I don't think I can move."

26

HAYDEN

I'm on a video call with Finn when I get Lily's excited text. She's written it in all-caps. **I GOT THE ART GALLERY!**

Finn is suspicious immediately.

"What are you smiling about, man?"

"Sorry. Got to reply to something urgent."

I type a quick congrats to her before I flip my phone over, screen down. It only took her about a week to draw up all the paperwork—courtesy of Harris Development.

Finn isn't convinced. "I know urgent, and that's not it. Does she have a name?"

I glare at him through the monitor, but my only reward is his wry laughter.

"Fine, man. Play it close to the vest."

"You should try socializing some time," I suggest, knowing it'll needle him. "I know it's shocking, but computers can't keep you warm at night."

He rolls his eyes at me. "I don't need socializing. Besides, computers generate heat, so they actually can."

"Just saying. I'm sure Boston has at least a few good women."

"I wouldn't know," he says, his tone surly, and I drop the topic.

We return to the planning of our West Coast expansion—and our plan to hire a consultant or two of our own. The business is expanding faster than either of us had anticipated.

I've been pushing for us to reach higher and higher numbers, but it still feels unreal that it's actually going as well as it is. Gary's words ring in my head. *You're rich.*

It would be hard to believe if I didn't know the ins and outs of my own finances. If this continues, I'll be able to hold my own with old Michael Marchand. Not best him, sure, but certainly be regarded as an equal.

But I'm not sure money is all it takes.

I drive over to Lily's new gallery that evening, stopping on the way to pick up a few things. She's already there—has been since she finished work.

Anticipation runs through my body as I park outside. Knowing she's close, and that I'll see her soon, never fails to put me on edge.

The front door is ajar and the wood has deep gashes from disrepair. It'll need to be sanded down and repainted entirely.

Old-school jazz hits me as I walk in. A lady croons about respect, filling the space with her voice. Lily is standing in the middle of the gallery-to-be, her back to me.

Her hair is up in a messy bun, and she has a pencil stuck behind her ear. I can see her frantically scribbling notes on a legal pad. I'm sure she sees something very different from what I do—yellowed walls in desperate need of new sheetrock, old linoleum floors. She's always been the one with the vision.

I wrap my arms around her waist and she leans into me, a small sigh escaping her. Her scent is as intoxicating as usual.

"Hey, you."

"Hey," I say. "How did you know it was me? The front door was unlocked."

"Who else could it be?" She runs a hand over my forearm absently, holding up her notes. She's sketched out an entirely different interior design. The odd half-wall is gone, as are the popcorn ceilings. "What do you think?"

It looks like a professional art studio.

"It looks great," I murmur, pressing another kiss to her neck. "Very artsy."

Lily smiles. "*Excellent* feedback."

It's been a week since I properly took her to bed, and since then, we've spent nearly every evening together. Cooking dinner, walking on the beach... and me, getting reacquainted with every nook and cranny of her body.

I rest my head atop hers and focus on her designs. She's drawn faint mosaic floors and spotlights from the ceilings. It's an art studio, sure, but it's not without character.

"Is that a pottery wheel?"

"Yes. Too crazy? Maybe. It might not be for right away. But I like the idea of being able to have classes with that, too. Maybe hire an expert, or just let people express themselves with clay."

"It's not crazy. And if you ever want to reenact that scene from the movie, you know, with the guy who comes back as a ghost? I'll volunteer."

Lily laughs, leaning back more snugly against me. "This place is going to take a lot of work. And there's absolutely no guarantee that it will pay off."

"That's the case with everything in life. As for the work, you know I'll pitch in as much as I can. I can't lay tiles, but I sure as hell know how to paint and plaster."

"Thank you," she murmurs, and there's a faint trace of shyness in her voice. It's unexpected. "I was thinking about something."

"Tell me."

"What are we, really? I mean, I feel like I know, but I was wondering in regard to our friends and family. I haven't told anyone that you and I are... well. But we're going to have to tell them eventually."

My reaction is immediate.

Lily feels the tension in my body and tries to twist, to see my face, but I can't let her. I'm too scared she'll see the panic that's written there.

I know I have to face her brothers and father eventually. Face the disapproval and the requests to leave. Her father already demanded it of me once, and when he does again, I'll refuse. But it will hurt her.

I could lose everything again if I don't do this right.

"What are we?" I force myself to relax, to stroke up her bare arms. "We're us. We always have been."

She finally turns. Reaching up, she puts a hand on my cheek, her thumb smoothing over my cheekbone.

"And you're here indefinitely," she murmurs.

"Yes."

I'm not fooling her. It's clear in her gaze, in the way she frowns slightly. It's always been impossible for me to hide anything from her.

"But you don't want our friends and family to know?"

I close my eyes, knowing it's easier for me to hide my emotions that way. "Let's just be you and me, for a little while longer."

When I open my eyes again, Lily gives me a small nod. I can tell that she doesn't understand. But she'll give me the time I need.

Guilt unfurls in my stomach, familiar and acidic. I know I don't deserve her, and this is just more proof. It'll be confirmed when her family learns of it.

Lily rises up on her tiptoes and kisses me softly before rocking back on her heels. "So, what's the first thing I need to do with this place?"

"To turn it into your sketch?"

"Yes."

"Well, for one, you should get an electrician in here right away, at the same time as your builders. If you want spotlights, planning that before you start scrubbing the ceiling and tearing down walls would be good."

"All right." She scribbles something down in her notebook. "We have a contractor at work. I'm going to ask her if she has space in her calendar for this, too. I'll obviously pay."

I nod. "But don't get them to do the small stuff. I'll paint these walls for you, Lils. Hell, Gary would probably love to be involved."

"I'm not going to exploit you for free labor just because I'm sleeping with you," she says with a small grin. It's clear that she wants to move on from the awkwardness just minutes earlier. "If you help out here I want you to bill me."

"Absolutely not." I force a wry smile, trying to match her tone. "Consider it down payment for the painting I'm going to commission from you."

"Really? Of what?"

"I want you to paint me like a gentleman of old. Something stately to hang above my mantlepiece."

Lily laughs. "A hunting rifle slung over your shoulder?"

"Yes. And there has to be at least two hounds at my feet."

"Let's make it three, for good measure."

"Good thinking. I knew you were the artist I needed."

She shakes her head at me, still smiling, and returns to her sketch. Tendrils of hair have come loose from her bun, and she has ink stains on her fingers, and she has never been more beautiful to me.

"Have you told your parents about this place yet?"

"No. I want to get my things in order before I do." She looks at me, a small smile on her face. I know she's not only thinking about the gallery when she responds. "It'll be our secret for now."

I smile back.

Our conversation stays with me the rest of the evening,

even as we get take-out and eat it back at hers. It rings in my mind as I drive home to let her get some well-needed sleep.

I know I can't put off the reveal to her family forever. Eventually, what we are is going to come out, because I'm not planning on letting her go again. Not ever.

I just need to figure out what I'm going to do when that happens.

And despite myself, I don't want her brothers to kick my ass for it. I know I can handle my own, and I think Lily will stand by me. But they're the closest thing I've ever had to brothers.

Paradise Shores is dark and quiet when I park on my driveway late that evening. The house still doesn't quite feel like home, even if the town does.

My phone rings and my uncle's name flashes across the screen. He rarely calls at all, and never this late.

"Hayden… I don't know how to say this," he begins, sending ice-cold dread through me. "But it's your dad. He passed away a few days ago."

27

LILY

"So you just bought this place?"

"Yes," I say. "It's all mine now. I'm going to turn it into an art gallery, and host art classes."

Parker shakes his head, looking around at the space. "Have you told the mothership?"

"No. I'm postponing that a little bit."

"Good. I can't imagine Dad's going to be happy, but it's your life, Lils." He throws his arm around my shoulders. He smells like ocean and tar. "You know I'm in your corner."

I grin up at him. "How come you were so annoying growing up? I like you much better as an adult."

He laughs, the deep, belly-kind. "Because that was my role. You already had a big brother in Henry and a protector in Rhys. I had to be the one who pulled on your pigtails."

"*Had* to?"

"Of course," he says, face serene. "Imagine how sheltered you would have been otherwise. Come on, let's go get ice cream. I've been craving mint chocolate chip all day."

I turn off the lights and lock up the studio. It's going to need work, but all I feel is anticipation. For the first time in a long while, I'm genuinely excited about a creative project.

I'm also very, very tired. As Parker and I walk toward Paradise Shores Gelato, I can't hide the giant yawn that escapes me.

"It's not even six p.m. yet," Parker points out. "What's going on? Has Turner been running you ragged at work?"

"No, no. I just stayed up too late last night, that's all." I'm quiet for a beat. "I was painting."

"Really?"

"Yes. I've started again. I need things to fill the gallery with, you know." The last part is more of a joke, but it had felt amazing to hold a paintbrush again. My body remembered what to do without instruction. I just *had* to finish the outlines of the scene before I could go to sleep—the sand dunes and the ocean, the horizon, the two people walking along the shoreline.

Parker grins. "You're right. Hey, have you seen Hayden around lately?"

I shake my head and focus on the ice cream menu. I know it by heart, but I'm afraid to meet Parker's gaze. Hayden has stayed away for days, ever since the night in my gallery. His reluctance to tell the others about us hurt. The uncertainty could only mean one thing.

He wasn't sure if we'd last.

"He's been AWOL all week, but these past few days he hasn't even responded to my texts." Parker clicks his tongue. "I wanted him to come out on the boat this weekend. It can't be good for the man to spend all his time working."

I frown. He hadn't responded to my texts, either, and if he was ignoring Parker too…

"Something must have come up," I say, trying to sound dismissive. "You know Hayden."

"Yeah, but he should talk to me," Parker sighs. "He always played things too close to the vest. At least the two of you seem to be getting along better now."

"Yes. Absolutely. It's all in the past."

Parker nabs the menu from my hands. "You're going to get cookie dough. You always do, so quit looking for other options."

"You're right. Two scoops."

He winks at me. "My treat today. To celebrate my little sister opening her very own art gallery."

We order, eat and laugh, and I try to push away the frustrating thoughts, but it's difficult. Worry and unease chase each other in my stomach. I call Hayden as soon as I've said goodbye to Parker. There's no response, just like the day before. It's not like him, to stay away like this, without an explanation.

But then, it's exactly like him, a voice in my head whispers. This is what he did ten years ago. Left without a word or a note. Maybe he's done it again, and I've been a fool for trusting him.

I wrap my arms around myself. I can't go down that path, not yet. There might still be a logical explanation—I just need to find him.

So I start at his house, ringing the doorbell. But it's dark inside and there's no response. I even call his name once or twice, like an idiot, but nobody answers.

Then I head to the marina. I know Parker goes there sometimes when he needs to think, and maybe Hayden does, too. He did spend a lot of time there growing up as well.

But hope soon dies in my chest. The docks are abandoned, and there's no lone figure sitting out by the pier.

There aren't many options left. I could call Gary and ask, but... that feels like giving up. And it's too likely to give me the answer I can't stand. I can almost hear Gary's kind, gravelly voice. *Sorry, girl, but he's gone.*

No. I can't bear it—him telling me that again.

So I text Hayden one last time. It's long, but at least it's heartfelt.

Hey. Is something wrong? I'm here for you if you need

**me, regardless of what's happened, or what's going through
your mind. Please let me know where your head is at. It's like
you said: we're us, Hayden. Always will be.**

I send it and sit staring at the phone's screen with my
heart in my throat. The minutes tick by, ever so slowly.
There's no response.

In the distance, the sailing boats bob softly in the water,
and I have to swallow to keep my tears at bay. Maybe I'd
pushed too far. Or it had gotten too serious too fast. I thought
we'd been good… but I'd been wrong.

My phone beeps.

Sorry. I'm at 47 Oakdale. Join me?

Relief pounds through me. I don't even respond, just put
the car in drive and head to the address. It's not until I turn
onto the street that I realize where he must be. There's really
only a couple of bars in Paradise Shores, and The Seahorse is
one of them. It's supposed to be a play on an old English
pub.

He's at a bar?

The place is nearly empty, low music pounding through it.
There's only one person sitting at the bar. There's tension in
his shoulders and his hair is messy, the kind of disheveled it
gets when he's run his hands through it too many times to
count.

There's a glass in front of him. He's staring at it with an
intensity that sends shivers down my arms. The air coming
off him…

Something's happened, and I'm suddenly very sure that it
has nothing to do with me. Not directly, anyway.

I approach Hayden slowly and slide into the seat next to
him. I can tell that he knows I'm here, but he says nothing,
just slowly spins the amber liquid in the glass around and
around. It looks untouched.

The air around him feels impenetrable.

"Whiskey?"

"Scotch." His voice sounds low and unused. "Twenty-five years old. Matured in an oak cask."

"The house best."

"According to the bartender, yes." Hayden waves a dismissive hand. "He'll be back soon, if you want something."

"I don't."

He turns to me and I can see that his amber eyes are bloodshot. He hasn't looked this way in... in a long time. It reminds me of how he'd looked in the weeks after my accident, the weeks before he left.

"Have you had some?" I ask gently. He doesn't seem drunk, not really, but he doesn't seem like himself, either.

Hayden frowns, turning back to look at the glass. "No. I've thought about it, though."

"All right."

He's quiet for a while. I don't say anything, knowing that he'll come to it when he's ready, even though my mind is going a million miles a minute, thinking about what might have happened.

He finally clears his throat. "Gary called me yesterday."

"He did?"

"Yes. Apparently, my father passed away." He spins the scotch glass around again. From the smooth motion, it looks like he's been doing it for a while. "He lived only a few towns over, actually. Had been living there for a few years."

My mind goes momentarily blank. His relationship with his father has always been something we've tiptoed around. There are too many thorns there. Approach the subject and you'll inevitably get pricked.

"I'm sorry, Hay," I say. "I know you had a complicated relationship."

He snorts. "Yes. Complicated."

"Do you want to talk about him?"

"No. I never want to think about him again." Hayden

shakes his head in frustration, focusing intently on the glass of alcohol. The tension in him hasn't abated—far from it. "But I don't think I can stop, either."

"That's all right, too. There's no manual for how to grieve." I reach out and put a hand on his forearm. He pauses in his twirling to look down at where it's resting.

"We never really talked about my life before Paradise Shores," he says finally.

"No, we rarely did," I say. I know there had been darkness. Fights. Alcohol.

He takes a deep breath. "I never wanted any of that shit to touch you. Any of you, but you in particular. It doesn't belong anywhere near you."

My heart constricts in my chest. "I can listen. I'm not fragile."

"I know. You're the strongest person I know," he says, and I know what he's thinking about. The accident. "But I'm not sure *I'm* strong enough."

My mouth feels dry. "What do you mean?"

"I couldn't handle the pity in your eyes. I can handle it from all the others, Lils, but not from you."

There's such despair in his voice—something I've never heard from him before. I'd known he'd harbored thoughts like this, but never that they ran this deep.

I grip his forearm tight and lean in closer. "Hayden, it's me. It's just me, and it's just you. I can promise you that I'm not going to pity you. I respect you too much for that. I have sympathy, but that's something different."

He shakes his head again and stares at a blank spot on the wall. One after another, the words spill out of him. "Fights. Dealers. It got ugly, Lily. If Gary hadn't fought for custody for me, I don't know what I would've become."

I run my hand gently along his arm in encouragement. I don't even think he notices.

"He was terrible to my mother, when she was alive. The

things he did sometimes… She'd send me from the room when he was in a rage, but I still heard." Hayden swallows. "After she died, there were times when I didn't eat for days. He'd leave and be gone for a week. Two, once. I started being afraid whenever the doorbell rang, because I knew it would either be his mean friends or the loan sharks."

It's not hard for me to imagine it. I can see the child he was, wide-eyed and with a dark mop of hair, hiding behind doors and pulling up the covers in his bed to muffle the sounds.

It's almost too much to bear.

"Did he ever beat you?"

Hayden's shrug is far more nonchalant than I feel. "Sometimes. Never too bad, really."

"Hayden," I murmur, struggling around the lump in my throat. It's ridiculous, but I feel like crying. Not in pity—but in empathy for the boy he once was. For the man he is now. That anyone ever treated him wrongly feels like the gravest of injustices.

He doesn't notice. He just stares at the glass in his hand, a thoughtful expression on his face. "This had such a hold on him," he says. "I don't know if he ever kicked the habit or not. I didn't speak to him for years before he died."

"Do you regret not having contact?"

"No. I didn't want him in my life." There's a faint furrow in his brow. "Although there were things I wanted to know. Things I… I don't know."

"With him gone, so is your last connection to that time?"

"Yes. But it lives in me," he says, rapping his fingers against his temple. "I wonder if the same weakness is here. If I'll go down the same path. Make the same mistakes."

"You won't."

"I've seen what a good man can be. I've seen it in Gary. But I've never seen what a good partner looks like, not to mention a—" He breaks off and glances at me, brows knitted. "Well. A father."

I grip his arm tighter. "*Gary* has showed you what a good father can look like. Has he not been that to you since he became your guardian?"

He sighs. "Yes."

"You won't make the same mistakes. You've already proven that, several times over. Besides, do you think we would let you?"

Hayden's eyes widen. "We?"

"Yes, the people in your life who love you."

"God, Lily…" He braces his hands against the bar for a moment, some unspeakable emotion coursing through him. "I shouldn't have stayed away. Forgive me."

"There's nothing to forgive." I grip his forearm tighter, strong under my fingers. His gaze runs to my hand, and then higher, to the bracelet around my wrist.

Hayden reaches out and touches a finger to one of the charms. His voice is quiet when he finally speaks. "You're wearing this?"

"Yes," I say, swallowing. "It's the one you gave me."

"I remember. I didn't… wow." He laughs, suddenly, and it's entirely unexpected. "Seeing it now, I realize how off the mark I was."

I lean back, offended for his former self. "Why? It's lovely."

"You should be in diamonds, Lils."

"I should be in things that have sentimental value. Plus, I happen to really like it."

He returns to his study of the charms. The brief amusement has faded, and his eyes look lost in thought. "Did you wear it sometimes? When we were apart?"

"Sometimes," I admit. "Though the first couple of years I buried it in my jewelry box. I couldn't look at it."

"I deserved that."

"And then, when I got older, it felt like something from my childhood. Something that connected me with you."

He nods, his finger still playing with one of the charms. "The cone shell you gave me? I brought that with me on each of my postings."

"Really?"

"Yes. It was from the ocean, from this place... from you."

I stand up and gently push the glass away from him. "You weren't planning on drinking that, were you?"

He's quiet for a beat. I can tell there's a decision being made, and I don't want to rush him.

"No," he says finally. "I wasn't."

"It's late. Come home with me?"

Hayden nods and stands, too. He leaves enough bills on the bar to settle his tab and then we walk out, side by side. He holds the door open for me and stops on the sidewalk, looking sheepish.

"I don't have my car," he says. "I walked here."

"Really? Your house isn't that close."

"I didn't want to have to drive later in case I decided to have that drink."

I can't stop myself from smiling. "You're so far from your father, Hay. Light years."

He gives me an uncertain smile back. "I suppose I am."

We drive back to mine in comfortable silence. He's deep in thought, but the tension that radiated off him is gone. I don't know if there's an easy solution to his emotions—losing a parent, even if it's an estranged one, isn't something you can work through with a manual. Everyone's experience is different.

Hayden pulls me close as soon as we shut my front door behind us. He puts his lips against my temple, his arm strong around my waist. For the first time in days I let myself fully relax.

He's here. He didn't leave.

"Thanks, Lils."

"Anytime."

"I'm sorry I didn't answer when you texted. I was…" He shakes his head, the silkiness of his hair soft against my forehead. "I can't explain it."

"Because it would become real the minute you told me?"

He shakes his head. "I didn't want to burden you with all that stuff. But it doesn't make it right."

"It's all right," I say, breathing in the salty, masculine scent of him. *He's here, he's here, he's here.*

"If you thought I'd left again, I'm sorry. I never would. Not again."

"I know." I take his hand and pull him toward my bedroom. "It's late, Hay."

We get undressed in soft, smooth caresses, both watching each other as we get into bed. He holds me tucked close to his body, silent and still. When he whispers in my ear that he needs me, I almost don't know what he means until I feel his hot arousal against my thigh.

I slide my hands around his neck and pull his face down to mine. We kiss in the dark for what feels like an eternity, heat slowly unfurling in my stomach.

"Lily…" he murmurs against my lips, my jaw, my neck. He leans down on his elbows, his body covering me entirely. His chest hair tickles against my breasts and I press myself closer still, wanting to fuse us into one.

The fiery, ecstatic passion we've shared for the past week is replaced by something much softer. But there's salvation in this too—in loving and being loved. I stretch out beneath him and keep my hands on his shoulders as he enters me. He starts to move, slowly, a shudder passing through his body.

Release finds me sooner than I expect. Hayden follows soon after, groaning my name as his body shakes in my arms.

He moves to my side and holds me close, cradling me against the strong lines of his body. I close my eyes and rest against his chest. There's a faint tickle of hair against my cheek.

Hayden runs a calloused hand over my hair and down the soft skin of my back.

"I haven't decided if I'll go the funeral yet," he whispers. "But if I do, will you come with me?"

I put my hand over his heart. "Always."

28

HAYDEN

I look down at Lily, lying in my arms. Sunlight streams in through her bedroom window. It sets her auburn hair on fire, draped across my chest. She's always gorgeous, so beautiful it hurts, but when she's sleeping... she looks like an angel.

My head hurts, despite the hours of sleep. It doesn't take a brain surgeon to figure out why. The conversation we had last night was a long time coming.

She knows everything now. Just how bad it had gotten, before I came to Paradise Shores. And she hadn't turned away in disgust or looked at me like a charity case. There had been none of her parents' kind patronization in her gaze.

My arms tighten automatically around her at the thought. I'm a lucky bastard, gaining a second chance with her.

Lily blinks her eyes open. Clear, green eyes meet mine. They warm when she sees my expression. "Good morning," she whispers.

"Morning."

"It's late, I think."

I nod, glancing over at her alarm clock. "It's past ten."

"Wow. That's late."

"Yes, but it's a Sunday." I tip her head back, wanting to

touch her lips with my own. "We have the whole day. Let me take you to the beach…"

She smiles. "It's just across the street."

"So much the better. We can swim…," another kiss, "and you can lie in the sun…," another kiss, longer this time, "and I can lie beside you and admire you."

She laughs, properly this time. "You're silly."

"Only sometimes," I murmur, "and only with you."

There's a loud knock at the front door. Her cottage is small enough that the sound is sharp and clear.

Lily struggles to sit up. "Damn."

"Do you know who it is?"

"No. I'm not expecting anyone." She gets out of bed, her lithe body naked and illuminated by the faint light from her window. It disrupts my train of thought completely.

I shake my head. "Don't open it. It's probably just a door-to-door salesman."

"In Paradise Shores? They're never here." She finds her underwear and reaches for her robe. Another sharp knock rings out.

I sigh and swing my legs out of bed. "Let me open it. Who knows who it might be."

She tosses me my underwear. "I doubt it's someone dangerous, Hay."

"You can never be too careful." I pull on my boxers.

We both freeze as we hear the unmistakable sound of a key being inserted in a lock. Whoever it is is coming in, invited or not.

"Fuck." I push her behind me and head to the bedroom door. Adrenaline courses through me. If they're here to do harm, they're about to get another thing coming.

"Hayden, the only people who have a key—"

"Good morning!" Rhys announces, standing in the middle of Lily's living room. His grin falters and disappears entirely as his gaze lands on me in the doorway of his little sister's bedroom.

"Rhys." He looks exactly like I remember. The auburn hair is disheveled, true to form. The artful leather jacket, the jeans, the old boat shoes that make it clear he belongs in Paradise... For all his attempts, he's never been able to shake the look.

"Hayden," he murmurs. His face looks set in stone, all color slowly draining away. "I heard you were back. But I wasn't expecting to find you... here."

Lily pushes past me, tugging her robe tighter around herself. Her voice is ringing with happiness. "You're here? I can't believe it!"

Rhys breaks his glare at me to shoot her a wry smile. "Hey, little one. It's been a while."

"Too long." She wraps her arms around his neck and presses a kiss to his cheek. "Don't be angry, Rhy."

He pushes her aside with a gentleness that doesn't match the cold expression on his face. Oh, Rhys isn't angry. He's fucking furious with me.

"How long have you been back?" he asks, each word spoken through clenched teeth.

"Three weeks." I'm fairly certain what this conversation is going to devolve into, and I don't want Lily to see it when it does. Rhys was always slow to anger, but when he snapped, it was like a thunderstorm. I had seen him whoop Parker too many times about some small prank played on Lily.

"Wasted no time, huh?"

"It's not like that."

"Sure it's not." He walks forward, and I force myself to hold my ground. Rhys might have an inch of height on me, but I have nearly twenty pounds of muscle and ten years of training. I'm not going to hurt him, but if he thinks I'll go down easy, he's dead wrong.

"Rhys, it's not like he—"

"No, Lily. I want to hear him say it," Rhys spits out. "Tell me how you broke my little sister's heart ten years ago, and then show up out of the blue to do the same thing again."

He must see the faint widening of my eyes, because he laughs, but it's not happy. "You think I didn't know? Oh, of course I did. I'm not clueless like Parker or distant like Henry. But I thought you were good for her. You proved me wrong."

"I didn't want to leave her."

"*Of course* not. Just like you couldn't call or text her."

Rhys's first swing comes out of nowhere, and I realize belatedly that that was always his talent. He's unpredictable as hell. Made him impossible to beat in Mario Kart once upon a time.

I duck, just narrowly avoiding the punch. "Hey man, I know it doesn't look good."

"That's because it's not."

I avoid another poorly thrown punch, only to be hit squarely in the center of my stomach by his other hand. Shit. I've forgotten that Rhys is left-handed.

"Damn it," I gasp. "Don't make me fight you."

"What, because you'd win if you did? Be a man and try."

I block another punch and grab hold of his arm. It's easy enough to twist it around, holding him still in an armlock. "You're right to be angry. So was Lils."

"I was," she adds helpfully, standing to the side with a shocked expression on her face. "Rhys, stop. *Please.*"

"No." Rhys aims a kick to my knee as I turn away, my hold on his arm loosening. He twists free and attacks me, arms around my torso.

I stagger back and narrowly avoid hitting Lily's dining-room table. If he keeps going like this, we'll destroy her house.

So I grab him and tackle him smoothly to the ground. We fall to a heap on Lily's shaggy rug, far away from any breakables.

"Asshole," he growls at me, hitting me hard on my shoulder. I grunt in pain and block another one of his punches. It's hard as hell to fight when you don't want to hurt your opponent—especially when he doesn't share the same restraint.

"Rhys! *Stop it right now."*

He doesn't listen to his sister. He struggles to sit up, pushing me down beneath him. I hold my own, but I let him rain down punches over my arms, covering my face. Rhys won't stop until his anger is burned out—and unfortunately, I think this might be the only way. I've seen it many times in the military.

"We took you in," he growls. "You were like a damn *brother* to me."

And that's when it hits me that he's not just angry for Lily's sake, although that's undoubtedly there too.

"I know, man."

"*Asshole.* You're not even trying to defend yourself. Fight, damn it."

Fuck this.

I twist around, throwing my leg over his. I've never fought in only boxers before, but it does give me a lot of room to maneuver.

I flip him over, hard, and grasp his arms in a lock. He tries to throw me off, but I'm stronger than him.

"I had just crashed a damn car with her in it," I hiss. "You think I *wanted* to leave like that? Even your own dad told me to go. I was trying to do the right thing."

Rhys stills, but his face is still etched in anger. "Fuck you," he says.

"I know."

"If you hurt her again…"

"I know," I repeat. "I won't."

He shakes his head in resignation, before he bucks up and hits my head with his. It hurts like hell, my skull ringing with pain.

"Shit."

Rhys pushes me away and crawls back. He grabs his forehead, doubtlessly hurting too. "What made you brave enough to come back?"

I wipe blood away from the corner of my mouth. "It hurt too much to stay away."

He nods, like he understands perfectly. For a long moment, we just stare at each other. The hot anger in his gaze lessens to something more like simmering resentment.

When he finally speaks, his voice is full of resignation. "Welcome back, asshole."

"Thanks."

Lily approaches us slowly. She has her hands on her hips, her expression dazed. "You're both idiots," she says. "Rhys, you should know better."

"Yes, I should have kicked his ass years ago."

Lily turns to me. Her hand smooths over my shoulder, eyes scanning me from head to toe. "Are you okay?"

"I'm fine."

She ignores her brother—who is staunchly ignoring us too —and leans down to press a kiss to my lips. "I'm sorry about my family."

"Don't be."

Lily shakes her head at me again and goes to the bathroom. I hear the sound of water running and rummaging in drawers. No doubt she's looking for things to patch us up with.

Rhys stares at me, and I stare at him.

Finally, he shakes his head. "You should be happy it wasn't Henry or Parker who came in and saw you half-naked in here. They would have killed you."

"I'm not easy to kill," I say. "Plus, I'm a better fighter than all three of you. Always was."

He shoots me a wry smile. "So we'd have to be three-on-one. Good to know."

"Think the others will object?"

"Maybe at first," he says, but then he shakes his head. "I don't know, man. There's no telling."

"Did you just get back?"

"Yes. Came here first."

I nod, running a hand through my hair. There's a lot of stuff to work out with her brothers. I left them too, ten years ago—not just Lily. And even if she claims the opposite, I know Lily could never bear to have her family disapprove of us.

So I take a chance.

"Let me just put on some clothes and let's head to the marina. I know Parker was going to sail today. Want to hit the waves?"

There's a flicker of hunger in Rhys's eyes. It's something I recognize easily: the call of the sea. It lives in Rhys as surely as it lives in me, drawing all of us back here, like driftwood caught in a current.

"Let's," he says.

Rhys accepts a Band-Aid from his sister, kisses her forehead, promises to be back for dinner, and heads to his car. He throws out a dark "I'll only wait five minutes!" to me before shutting the front door behind him.

I accept some fussing from Lily—she pads my busted front lip—before gently pushing her away.

"I have to get dressed, baby."

She puts a slim hand on my shoulder to stop me. "What did you mean earlier, about my dad telling you to leave?"

Damn.

I rub my neck. "Well, there was a conversation after the accident. We both agreed that it would be best if I left."

"You both agreed, huh." She's quiet for a beat, and when she speaks again, there's anger in her voice. "I love my father, but he's a bastard. I can't imagine he'd change that, especially not with his kid in the intensive care unit."

"It was a long time ago."

She shakes her head. "Doesn't matter. He shouldn't have ordered you away. Because that's what he did, right?"

I sigh. The conversation I'd had with Mr. Marchand feels light years away. "He told me to leave, yes," I say gently. "But I agreed. It was my decision, and it was a terrible one. One I'm sorry for."

Lily runs a hand through my hair, her touch soft despite the steel in her tone. "I know. But you were eighteen, and you were injured in that car crash too. He had no right."

"It was a long time ago," I repeat, catching her hand and pressing a kiss to the palm before releasing it. "I have to get dressed."

She watches me in silence as I pull on my shorts and a T-shirt, sticking my feet in the pair of boat shoes I'd picked up just the week prior.

An impatient honk sounds outside.

I look back at Lily. She's pulled on the same dress from yesterday. Her hair is in a high ponytail and her cheeks are flushed with intent. She looks amazing.

"Sorry about my brothers," she says. "And my father."

I shake my head at her nonsense and press a goodbye kiss to her lips. Her softness draws me in, and it's by willpower alone that I break the connection. She's a hell of a lot more enticing than the prospect of spending hours with two of her big brothers. I'm not sure if Rhys's beating will be the only one I'll have to endure today.

"Don't be. I can take care of myself."

"I'll see you tonight," she says.

"Can't wait."

29

LILY

I watch as Rhys and Hayden drive away. There's sweat beading on my forehead, and I feel a bit shaky from the interaction. The cat is really out of the bag now—and far sooner than Hayden would have preferred.

Just a week ago, he'd asked me to wait to tell the family about our relationship. And here he is, forced to endure it all in one day. All I can is hope that the pressure won't be too much.

Damn Rhys. He'd been gone without any settled return date, and of course he just *had* to make a surprise out of his return. I'll have words with him later, too. I shoot my brother a text. **Be nice.**

There's no response, but I know he'll read it, at least before they set off. And Parker... I have no idea how my youngest brother will react. He's always seen Hayden as a given member of the family.

I shake my head and reach for the car keys. I can't deal with that right now—not when I have to go fight the dragon myself. It had been hard to hide my anger in front of Hayden. I didn't want him to know just how much my dad's actions had hurt me—not until I got a chance to speak my mind.

Luckily, I know exactly where my father will be on a Sunday morning. He'll be in his study on the second floor of the family house, going over the latest housing developments and looking at investment opportunities.

My mom greets me with a smile when I arrive home. The smell of nail polish hangs heavy in the air, and she gives me an air hug to avoid ruining her freshly applied coat. I'm still angry at her too—it's going to take a while—but she seems to have accepted that.

"I didn't know you were coming today, *chérie*."

"I'm here to talk to Dad."

"All right. You seem stressed." She leans in closer, peering at my face. "And you look flushed."

"I just have something to take care of."

"Here on business?" She nods to the stairs. "He's upstairs."

I knock twice on the door to the study before I head inside. This used to be a no-go zone when I was young. No playing hide-and-seek in here, and absolutely no disrupting Dad when he was working.

Now, I hope I disrupt him completely. I'm angry for nine-teen-year-old Hayden, who had just been in a car accident, and I'm angry for eighteen-year-old me, who thought her boyfriend left on his own.

Dad looks up when I enter, his brow furrowing. "Sweetheart? I didn't know you were coming by today."

"I needed to see you."

"All right. Can it wait?"

"No."

Whatever he sees on my face stops him from arguing. He puts his reading glasses down and leans back in his chair. The gray in his hair only makes him look more distinguished, despite my mom fighting a losing battle against her own streaks.

"What's the matter?"

"What did you tell Hayden after the accident, all those years ago?"

Dad sighs and reaches up to rub the bridge of his nose. "I only gave him some advice. He hasn't had a father figure in his life, you know. I tried to guide the boy."

"He has his uncle," I say, trying to keep my voice from shaking with anger. "You told him to leave. You sent him away."

"For his own good, and for yours, sweetheart."

"The accident wasn't *his* fault. The truck driver was driving drunk."

"Yes," Dad says calmly. "I know those reports by heart. But you're always responsible to a certain extent when you're in the driver's seat. He took you out for a spin in the middle of the night, and as a consequence, you have a permanent limp. You could have died."

"Not his fault. He nearly died too, and instead of showing compassion, you told him to get out of town."

Dad's eyes flash with irritation. "He was bad news. I let him stay here because the boy had potential, but he was wasting it, spending his days on the fishing vessels and his nights panting around you. I wanted him gone and I would do the same thing again."

"It *broke* me."

"No, it made you stronger, and it made him stronger, too. He's a decorated vet now, isn't he? And you went to Yale and got to try your hand in the art world." My dad shakes his head, reaching for the papers on his desk. "You won't understand. You never could."

"No, I understand perfectly," I say coldly, standing up. "And I refuse to let you play God in my life anymore—and not in Hayden's either."

"Have you taken up with him again?"

The way he phrases it... but I won't let him make me feel

less. "We're together, and I don't think that's likely to change."

Dad stares at me, a thoughtful look on his face. It's not exactly acceptance, but he doesn't look angry, either.

"He's grown," he says finally. "I suppose you could do worse."

"Thank you for that ringing endorsement."

"Always thought you'd end up with the Harris's boy," he says, returning his gaze to his papers. "He has a good sailing boat, that kid."

I shake my head in disgust and head toward the door. Only then does it strike me that I haven't told him everything. I turn back slowly, a smile on my face, and deliver the coup de grâce.

"I bought a space in town. I'm going to turn it into an art gallery."

My dad pauses with his hand halfway to his face, about to put his reading glasses back on. I can see the exact moment the realization settles over him. He can say what he wants, but it won't bother me. Not anymore.

"All right," he says slowly. "I look forward to the opening."

I give him a nod and leave his office, closing the door firmly behind me. For a few long moments, all I can do is take deep breaths before a giant smile breaks across my face.

There's a text waiting for me when I come out of the family house. Actually, there's several.

I open Hayden's first. **Sorry about this morning. Come join us at the marina this afternoon, when we get back?**

I smile and type a quick response. **I'll be there when you get back! And please ignore my family. It's still just us, Hayden. You and me.**

Because that's all that matters in the end—love, and friendship, and family. And Hayden feels like the perfect combination of all three to me.

I love him. I always have, and I never stopped, not even in the long years spent apart. Years where we both missed each other, all because of misunderstandings and meddling. And perhaps... perhaps it's time I told him that.

I nearly make it all the way to the marina before history repeats itself.

HAYDEN

Rhys takes command of the boat the second we hit the open water.

Parker looks at me with a rueful grin, but neither of us object as Rhys barks out orders. He knows *Frida* just as well as we do, and despite the years he's spent away, sailing is in his blood.

I understand the need to connect with it—to return to the sea. So Parker, a six-time state champion, doesn't object to his big brother's domineering. Neither do I, despite the fact that I've been a lieutenant in the Navy for years.

Parker grins at me, nodding to where Rhys is turning the winch to release the spinnaker. "He sure as hell wasted no time."

"He rarely does."

"He's also in one hell of a temper. Nearly bit my head off when I asked him if he'd arrived yesterday or this morning."

Damn. "Yeah, we had a bit of an argument earlier."

Parker nods, and there's sympathy in his eyes—sympathy I don't deserve. "About you pulling a disappearing act on us? Yeah. Rhys isn't quick to forgive, you know, but he'll come around."

"You weren't angry at me when I returned," I say, knowing I'm going to have to tell Parker about Lily. It's only a matter of time until Rhys says something, and judging by his clenched jaw, it's not going to be in complimentary terms.

Parker shrugs. "Look, man, I'm sure you had your reasons. Was I angry at you? Yeah. You didn't even say good-bye, Hay."

"I know."

"But look..." he says, and there's more depth than I'm used to seeing on his face. His eyes are dark with earnestness. "I get it. Your situation was different from ours. It fucking sucks, but it's the truth. I'm not going to blame you for that."

"Thanks."

"You could've called every now and then, though."

"I should've, man. I'm sorry."

"Apology accepted," he says, putting a hand on my shoulder. For a second, it feels like we're sixteen again, side by side at the back of *Frida*. It's easy to imagine Henry and his father at the front of the boat, Lily lounging on deck somewhere, Rhys reading a book next to her.

I take a deep breath. Getting this right might be the most important thing in my life. Michael Marchand's approval means absolutely nothing to me—but his sons' approval does. More than that, it means a lot to Lily, despite her insistence to the contrary.

Besides, I'm not overly keen on being tossed overboard.

"There's something else, though."

"Oh?" Parker leans against the railing and holds on to one of the beams.

"Yeah. Lily and I are dating. We never meant to keep it from you, but we wanted privacy." I meet his blue eyes, wide now in surprise. "I hope you can understand, man."

Parker blinks at me a few times. "Dating? Like, you're *together, together?*"

"Yes, we are."

"Wow." He shakes his head, and I let my hand drop from his shoulder. "I never knew."

"I didn't mean to go behind your back."

Parker shakes his head again. It's in disbelief, but so far, there's no anger on his face. "And I thought she didn't like you."

"She didn't, for a while," I say truthfully. "She was angry at me for leaving."

"I literally had no idea."

I nod, glancing to where Rhys is standing at the front of the boat. He has his back turned to us, but I can see the tension in his shoulders. It's clear his younger brother isn't having the same reaction.

Parker follows my gaze. "Rhys didn't take the news well."

"No."

"Well, he's always been thorny. Ignore him. He'll come around."

"You think?"

"Absolutely." A wide grin splits Parker's tanned face. "You're family in more ways than one now."

"You're okay with this?"

"Okay? Fuck, man, there's no one I'd rather see my baby sister with."

For a moment, all I can do is stare at him. It's the absolute last response I was expecting. Parker, despite his usual smiles and laughs, has always been protective of Lily. He'd nearly been as bad as Rhys, despite teasing her when they were children.

He sees my confusion and breaks into laughter.

"What, you think you were good enough to be one of my best friends, but not good enough to date my sister? Get your head out of your ass, Hay."

I can't help the surprised laugh that slips out of me. "Mind telling your brother that?"

"Rhys will come around," Parker says. "Damn. I'll have to tell Turner to stop mooning around after her."

My hand instinctively tightens around the railing. I know she doesn't have any interest in him, but the familiar feeling of envy at his name and status is hard to ignore.

"What about you?" I ask. "I haven't heard anything about women in your life lately, Parker. Your mom mentioned something about a girl…"

Parker's eyes narrow but he doesn't say anything. Instead, he looks over at Rhys, who's blatantly not paying us any attention. "I'll talk to him," he promises. "Text Lily and tell her to meet us at the marina when we get back. We'll get a beer at the Yacht Club, all of us."

I watch as he ducks under the beam and heads to the front of the boat to stand next to Rhys. They're polar opposites— one dark and one light—but next to each other it's clear that they're cut from the same cloth.

I shoot Lily a text with the invitation. Reception is dodgy at best out here, but I watch as the little tick appears. *Delivered.*

It's several hours later when we finally set course back to the marina. Rhys has, somewhat reluctantly, begun to talk to me again.

"I can't believe Parker let you off easy," he murmurs beside me, our hands moving fast over the rope, the knots as familiar to us as our own names.

"I guess he's the smarter brother."

Rhys sends me a sour look, but it's tinged with amusement. "We won't get rid of you this time around, will we?"

"No, you won't."

He nods, glancing out toward the glittering waves. "Good."

The sun is low in the sky when we finally spot the marina in the distance. It's been good, this, being out today. Reconnecting with her brothers. Gaining—somewhat surprisingly —Parker's unequivocal support.

I check my phone again. I haven't had service for hours, but the closer to shore, the higher the likelihood. I watch as my phone gets one... two bars of service. A text comes through from Lily, sent hours ago.

I'll be there when you get back! And please ignore my family. It's still just us, Hayden. You and me.

I smile at my screen at the same time as guilt rolls up inside me. She's still afraid I'll run or spook, like a skittish horse. I've given her reason to feel that way—my brave, proud girl, who was never afraid of charging headlong into new situations. Who climbed the tallest trees and woke up in the intensive care unit with a smile, who bought an art gallery on a whim.

Rhys, Parker and I barely need to communicate when we sail into Paradise Shores Marina. We know the boat and we know the docks here. It's automatic, the movements and the teamwork.

Parker jumps onto the dock first, and I throw him the rope, holding a hand up to signal to Rhys to cut the engine.

We cruise to a smooth halt alongside the dock. The place is nearly empty, most people already done for the day or at the Yacht Club. I can see the lit terrace from here. There's a faint sound of laughter and music.

I jump down from the boat, closely followed by Rhys.

Lily isn't waiting by the Marchands' dock.

"Didn't you say she'd be here?" Parker asks, and I nod, finding my phone in my pocket.

"She said she would. I'll call and see, maybe she went ahead."

"Is this what we have to get used to now?" Rhys murmurs to Parker. "Hayden handling communications with *our* sister?"

Parker just shakes his head. "Shut it, man."

"Whose side are you on?"

"*Lily's*. Just like you should be."

I shake my head at them and call her. Two dials go through before I'm clicked off the line. A chirpy, electronic voice tells me that the subscriber is unavailable.

"Her phone is off."

"Damn it," Parker says. "She always forgets to charge it."

She often does, but I still feel uneasy. Lily wouldn't say she'd be here and then not show up—or at least text one of us.

We head up to the Yacht Club. It takes me only a few seconds to scan the terrace. There's no auburn hair in sight.

"She's not here either."

Rhys shakes his head. "Damn it, Lily."

My mind runs through a list of things that might have happened, and for a second, I have to fight to keep the unease from turning into panic. We don't know. She's probably just late, even if it's not terribly in character.

One of the girls at the Yacht Club stops us on the way out and throws us a winning smile.

"Heading out so soon?"

"Yes. Thanks."

"No worries. Avoid Ocean Drive on the way back," she says cheerfully.

My heart goes cold in my chest. "Why?"

"Haven't you heard?" An uncertain note creeps into her voice as she looks at me. "There was an accident. The police have closed off the street entirely, no traffic in or out."

There's blood ringing in my ears.

If the waitress says anything else, I can't hear it. I'm already out the door.

My hands are clenched at my side as I break into a half-run, heading to the parking lot. I'm aware of Rhys and Parker by my side, but if they're speaking, I'm deaf to that too.

An accident.

Ocean Drive.

This can't be happening again.

We get into Rhys's car in silence. I want to strangle him for the extra few seconds it takes for him to turn the key in the ignition in his old Mustang. Fucking rich kids and fucking statement cars and goddamn fucking car accidents.

We're halfway out of the marina when Parker swears loudly in the backseat. He answers the phone a second later.

The world spins when I hear his response. "Yeah, we're already on our way there, Mom."

Rhys speeds up.

It feels like a bad dream when I see the blinking lights in the distance. A police car is parked sideways in the middle of the road. Rhys hasn't even pulled the car to a full stop before I'm out the door and running.

It's her car. It's her car, damn it, and it's totaled. Crashed into one of the iron-wrought lampposts that line Ocean Drive.

A policewoman is roping off the area. She looks grim, hair pulled back. "What happened here?"

"An accident," she says, clicking her tongue at my brusque tone. "A motorcyclist and a car."

"Was anyone hurt?"

"Yes." Her eyes are stern, but they soften slightly as she looks at me. I don't know what I must look like to be pitied, but I'm beyond caring. "One of the civilians involved had to be airlifted to the hospital."

The edges of my vision flicker.

"Who?"

She shakes her head. "I couldn't possibly—"

Rhys interrupts her. "Lily Marchand. What happened to her?"

"Over there," the policewoman says with a nod. An ambulance is parked nearby. A woman is sitting on the back, a blanket around her shoulders.

I would recognize that hair anywhere.

"This is the scene of an accident. You can't go inside —Hey!"

Nothing matters—not the angry shout from the police officer or the sound of her brothers behind me—as I run.

Images flash before my eyes of a different night, a different street. There had been so much blood then. We'd been alone, just her and me, my hands pulling her out of the wreckage. This is not that time. She's whole—she's safe.

Lily stands up to greet me, a faint wobble in her steps that sends my heart racing. I wrap my arms around her and pull her close. It's need, pure and simple, to know that she's safe.

Panic and adrenaline still pound through my body.

"Are you okay?"

Lily nods against my neck. Her hair smells like it always does, the same shampoo she's used for well over a decade. "It was so stupid," she whispers.

"And you're *sure* you're okay?" I loosen my grip, realizing I might be holding her too tight.

"Yes, yes. Just a few bruises."

"God, Lily…" I pull back and tip her head up. Her eyes are wide and green as they stare into mine, but there isn't a trace of pain or fear in them. I brush my thumb over her cheekbone, putting a hand on either side of her face. Her expression softens as she looks up at me.

"I'm okay," she murmurs again. "I'm okay, Hayden."

I lean my forehead against hers and close my eyes. My heart is beating fast, like I've run a marathon. "I thought…"

"I know. I know. But I'm okay."

The decision to kiss her isn't conscious. I need to know she's okay, I need to feel it, and she's just as eager as me. Our lips meet with soft, heated urgency, my hands pulling her closer against me. She's real and she's safe. I let my hands travel up her back to make sure, just in case.

Lily puts a hand on my neck and pulls me in closer, like she needs the reassurance just as much as I do. Her scent, her body, her taste is everything I feel—all of it telling me what I rationally know. *She's all right.*

But more than that, I'm reminded of just how much I love her. How my life would come to a grinding halt if something were to happen to her, if I failed to keep her safe again.

Lily's hands slide down my chest. I brush a final kiss to her lips, soft and sweet, my body aching for more of her. I'll never get enough of her closeness.

She blinks up at me with a dazed smile on her lips. "Hayden, I—"

"Lily!"

We both turn to see her parents. Her mother's eyes are frantic, sweeping over her daughter's form, assessing her just like I did. I can see Rhys and Parker standing next to them. Both of their eyes are wide.

Shit. Well, at least they all know now. Really, properly know.

"I'm okay," Lily says, loud enough for her entire family to overhear. "I'm completely okay."

"What happened?" Rhys comes closer, the family in tow. "Lils, your car looks…"

"A motorcyclist was going crazy on the road," she says. "Switching lanes, losing control of the motorcycle… I had to swerve, or I would have hit him." She puts her head in her hands. "He had to be airlifted. I don't know… it didn't look good."

I put my arm around her shoulders. I know I should let her parents get to her, her brothers—but I can't let go of her yet.

"We'll check on him, Lily," her father says. "Don't worry about that. God. You're never getting in a car for the rest of your life." He says it with as much sincerity as I feel. Twice is two times too many.

Rhys chuckles, but I can hear the strain in the sound. "Damn it, Lily. Why didn't you call us right away?"

"My phone broke in the crash."

Eloise Marchand sends me a curious look but says nothing as she leans in and hugs her daughter fiercely. "Let's get you out of here," she murmurs. "I've had enough of seeing my daughter in ambulances."

I couldn't agree more.

My car is towed—Parker and Rhys handle that, while my parents follow the ambulance to the hospital. Hayden rides with me. I feel fine, but the doctor takes a bunch of tests to make sure, X-rays and a CAT scan and a careful exam of my reflexes.

All the while, I see the same haunted, gaunt look on Hayden's face. He's a quiet shadow next to me, holding my hand. This is too much of a déjà vu. I can see it in all of their faces, bearing the same worried expressions I'd witnessed a decade earlier.

But it's not like before. I'm barely hurt, yet it doesn't matter how many times I say it, they don't truly believe it until Dr. Rashid confirms it.

"You're all clear," he tells me.

Hayden clears his throat. "Is there a risk of delayed onset whiplash?"

My dad shoots him a surprised look. He hasn't commented once on Hayden's steady presence beside me.

"Not likely, no," Dr. Rashid says. "But Lily, I want you to call me if you feel any pain in your neck in the coming days or even weeks. You can come in right away and we'll take a look."

"Okay. Thank you, I'll do that. Do you know what happened to the motorcyclist?"

Dr. Rashid's smile fades. "He's in surgery. I don't know more than that, Miss Marchand. But if it sets your mind at ease, I believe he had a history of epilepsy, which might unfortunately explain the erratic driving behavior."

"Oh." How terrible. "May I send him flowers somehow? Or is it all confidential?"

"I can ask his family for you, if you'd like."

"Please do."

It's very, very late at night when Hayden finally opens the passenger door to his car. He's still quiet—has been since we said goodbye to my parents.

He pulls out of the parking lot and onto the road back to Paradise Shores. His hands are clenched tight on the steering wheel.

"I'm taking you home," he says. "And I'm staying the night."

It had seemed like a foregone conclusion that he would. I try to smile at him, but his gaze is focused on the road ahead.

"That sounds great."

Hayden nods once, but his profile is stark against the passing streetlights. His jaw is clenched, and tension radiates from him.

Tonight… It was too close to what happened a decade ago. It was too close for the both of us, but I know that while I wear the physical scars from that accident, Hayden mostly bears the psychological ones. He had been the one to pull me out and call 911. I have very little recollection of that night at all.

"Hayden… Are you all right?"

There's faint surprise in his eyes, and then he reaches out and puts a large hand on my thigh. The connection between us is as it always has been—a safe anchor in a stormy sea. It calms me immediately, and I can see how his own tension lessens slightly.

"Don't, Lils. I'm not the one who was in a car crash."

I lean back against the seat. The adrenaline has left me, and together with the painkillers, all I feel is tired. I can't wait to have his arms around me and drift into sleep.

I put my hand on his. "I know. But I also know it was… It was similar," I whisper. "To what happened before."

The tension is back. I can see how he locks down and retreats into his shell. "Not until we're home," he says, and I understand. He can't break apart until we're out of the car.

But I can't help but notice that he called my place *home*, or the corresponding warmth that blooms in my chest.

We've always been home to each other.

He parks the car in silence and wraps an arm around my waist as we walk to my front door. I'm not hurt, and I don't need the assistance, but I need the connection as much as he does.

Hayden gently takes the key from me and unlocks my front door. I shoot him a tired smile. "I'm fine, Hay."

"I know," he murmurs. "I know."

He closes and locks the door behind us. I kick off my shoes and throw my bag to the side, and then we stand there, in my little hallway, just looking at each other.

Hayden's eyes are a storm. There's fear there, such furious fear that it nearly takes my breath away. I take a step toward him, and he toward me, and then I'm in his arms and he's carrying me toward the bedroom. His arms are wrapped around me tight, like he's afraid I might disappear. I'm holding him just as tightly.

"Christ. When I saw those flashing lights today…"

"I know. I know."

"I can't handle it, Lils. Not again."

"I know." I pull his face down to mine and press my lips

against his feverish ones. "Neither can I. But I'm okay. We're okay."

"Thank God for that." Hayden lays me down gently on the bed despite the urgency coursing through us both. He pulls me close, hugs me against his chest. I understand his need to touch me—to know I'm all right. I feel the same with him… touching him to know he's here.

"God," he murmurs again. "Lily, I love you so much." His eyes are dark with emotion and something else, something uncertain and vulnerable. I can't help the flutters in my stomach or the way my lips curve into a smile.

"I love you too. Always have."

"I never stopped," he says, voice low. "Not once, not ever, not since I first saw you."

"When we were kids?"

He nods. "I just didn't know it right away. All I saw was a girl with hair like fire and knobby knees, challenging me to rise to her level."

I put a hand on his chest. His heart beats fast and strong beneath my palm. "I loved you too, from the start. Even if you were terribly grumpy."

"Not with you."

"Especially with me," I say, smiling. "But I learned how to make you laugh eventually."

"You did. God, Lily, no more car accidents." He rests his forehead against mine. "My heart can't take it."

"No more," I agree. For a long time, all we do is breathe together, our bodies intertwined. His arm is strong beneath my head. My own fear and adrenaline subside, here in his arms, where nothing can harm me.

"How was sailing with my brothers?"

He shakes his head, but there's amusement in his voice. "You want to talk about *that*?"

"Yes." I slip my fingers inside the hem of his T-shirt and stroke the hot skin beneath. "They didn't scare you off?"

He brushes my hair back and leans in to kiss me. I respond in kind, both of us drawing reassurance from one another. "No. They never will. Lily, I'll never leave you again."

"I know," I murmur, warmth spreading through my chest. I finally believe him. "I spoke to my father today. About what he told you after our car crash, years ago."

"You did?"

"Yes."

"Lily, I never meant for that to drive a wedge between you two."

I shake my head and rise up on my elbow, fighting tiredness so heavy it makes me dizzy. This is important—and some of my old anger resurfaces.

"He had no right to," I say. "Absolutely no right. You had just been hurt yourself, and I..." I shake my head. There will be more time to talk about this. "I told him to butt out of our lives."

Hayden runs a callused thumb over my cheek, and the look in his eyes nearly tears me apart. God, I love him so much.

"My brave girl," he murmurs.

"And none of it matters, anyway. My family... Your family... we'll figure it out," I say fiercely.

"Of course it matters," he says. "It just doesn't *change* anything between us. And baby, your dad did talk to me, but it was no excuse for me leaving like that."

"You were a boy. And you were scared... it's perfectly understandable. I had forgiven you even before I found out about Dad's interference."

Hayden lies back on the bed, his hand playing thoughtfully in my hair. "I didn't think I was good enough," he says softly. "But it's no excuse for leaving."

"But you are! You always have been."

Hayden grins, and it's the first true smile I've seen from

him in what feels like forever. "I'm not, but it's okay. I've stopped trying to be noble. I'll be here, loving you, for as long as you let me."

I kiss him, and he groans into my mouth, tucking me into the curve of his body. His lips are soft and gentle against mine. I want to keep going, but he breaks it off, smiling against my ear.

"No more," he murmurs.

"No more what?"

"Excitement. There has been entirely too much of that these past few days."

I chuckle against his ear, so glad to have him here, to be close to him, to be able to run my hand through his thick hair. There's nothing like the warmth of his skin against mine and the faint scent of his soap.

"I agree." Tiredness threatens to undo me, pulling at my eyelids. I stifle a giant yawn. Hayden pulls me closer and I rest my head against the crook of his neck. His chest rises and falls strongly under my arm, an anchor in all the chaos.

"Tomorrow," I murmur, "we should talk to your uncle."

"About what?"

"Us. It's not fair that he's the only one who doesn't know."

Hayden's chuckle is a soft whisper against my hair. "Oh, he knows, baby. He's known forever."

HAYDEN

Ralph Cole is buried in August, under the hot midday sun, in a quiet service attended only by close friends and family.

I'd debated for a long time if I should go or not. It didn't feel right to attend an event to honor his life—not when I knew there'd been so little honor in it. There had been nothing but hatred in my heart for him for so long.

But as it turns out, going to his funeral didn't have to mean I forgave him. It was Lily who told me that.

"Just because you go doesn't mean you condone what he did," she'd said, her tone matter of fact, one day when we were painting her new gallery. "It can be for you to say good-bye. To close that chapter of your life. Maybe to ensure you have no regrets later on. It only means what you want it to mean, Hayden. He's gone. You do what you need to do—for you."

She was right.

And now I'm standing at the back of a small church, a tie chafing around my neck, with Lily next to me. Gary didn't want to come.

The framed picture on his coffin looks like a stranger. The image is nearly twenty years old, my father healthy and smiling with the wind in his ink-black hair. Lily had smiled immediately when she saw it, and I know why. I can see the resemblance myself.

But for the first time in many years, it doesn't scare me. I might be my father's son, but I'm also my mother's, and Gary's. My father doesn't define me—not entirely, at least.

There are only a few other people in the church, and none I recognize. It's not surprising. Dad's lifestyle wasn't exactly conducive to long-lasting friendships.

I feel hollow when the priest concludes the service. It was short and to the point, much like Dad had been. In part, I feel relief, like a vice has loosened around my heart. Like I've put down a burden I've been carrying for a very, very long time.

Lily slips her hand into mine. "Do you want to stay?" she murmurs. "For the reception?"

I look around at the handful of people in black gathering their things. "No. I don't want to make small talk about him."

"All right." There's no judgement in her gentle tone. "I think the people here know who you are, regardless."

"They do?"

She shoots me a soft smile. "I've seen a few of them glance at you, yes. Your hair, Hay… it's pretty clear who you are."

I reach up and run a hand through it self-consciously. I've let it grow. I guess I resemble the old man more than I thought.

"Well, they can guess all they want," I murmur.

We're out of the church and halfway to the parking lot when a voice stops us in our tracks.

"Wait!"

A girl runs toward us. Her dark hair goes down past her shoulders and unusual, wide eyes stare at us. She can't be more than eighteen.

She just looks at me.

"Hello," I say finally. "Can I help you?"

She nods once, a jerky movement, but when she opens her mouth to speak, no words come out.

Lily offers her a kind smile. "My name is Lily," she says. "This is Hayden. Were you also at the service for Ralph Cole?"

The girl nods again. "Yes. Yes, I was... You're Hayden Cole?"

"I am." An unspeakable emotion comes over me, looking at her. At the familiar set of her cheekbones and the faint curve of her mouth. It takes effort, but I manage to soften my face into an expression I hope looks welcoming. "And who are you?"

She swallows. "Stephanie Cole. You're my half-brother, I think?"

The ground goes a bit unsteady under my feet.

"Stephanie..." I repeat. I've never heard of her. Not once. Not through Gary, not through Dad's sporadic texts. "How old are you?"

"Sixteen."

"I've never heard of you."

She flinches, as if I've said something harsh. "Well, I mostly grew up with my mother. I didn't have much contact with... with our father."

"Good."

"He mentioned you," she says, and there's hope in her eyes. "He talked about you a lot."

"He did?"

"Yes, he was very proud. You're in the Navy?"

I give a slow nod. "I was."

"Yeah... well. Yes." She shrugs, and she's looking at me expectantly.

Damn. I'm fucking this up royally—I can feel it. This needs to be handled with more tact than I've ever used before. Lily's gaze feels heavy. *She believes in me.*

"Stephanie, is your mother here?"

"Yes. She's back at the church."

"Would you two like to come with us to dinner? We could talk."

The smile on Stephanie's face makes some distant, painful part of my heart ache. It's tentative, a bit shy, and filled with a lot of fragile hope.

A sister. *I have a sister.*

"Yes," she says. "I'd love that. Let me just go get her."

"We'll be here," I say.

Lily and I watch as Stephanie runs back to get her mom. Lily's hand tightens around mine, and I grip it back, grateful for the support.

"My father had other children," I say.

It's not a surprise, really, when I think about it. But it never struck me to look for them. I never even thought to ask.

Lily's eyes are wet. The incredulity in them mirrors my own exactly. "Hayden…"

"I know. This is…"

"A blessing," she finishes. "Family always is."

———

The weeks pass quickly after that.

Stephanie comes to Paradise Shores a few times, getting ice cream with Lily and me. She's shy, but I learn more about her history, and tentatively share some of my own. It's not going to be an easy process, but we're both willing to take it slow. Talking with her mother had been the hardest— someone who had seen the monster my dad could be and had escaped. Someone my mother should have been. But it's the good kind of difficult. The one that means wounds from the past are healing, that I'm getting stronger.

Lily decides to work part-time at Harris Properties and devotes a lot of time to her gallery. I'm there most evenings too, hammering and painting and distracting her.

It's great.

We spend the nights together. Either at her oceanside cottage or at my house on Elm Street, but so far, I haven't slept a night without her by my side in weeks. I hope I never have to again.

She tells me to come to the gallery one afternoon, after having barred me entry for days. *It's almost done,* she'd said —*and I want you to be surprised.*

I'm excited when I knock on the gallery door. It's freshly painted and put back on with new hinges. Gary helped me with that, sanding the old door down in the garage at my house.

Lily opens the door with a wide grin. It's the same smile I'm used to from childhood—the wide, beaming one, without restraints or pretension. Her auburn hair is up in a bun and she's wearing paint-stained overalls.

She's hung all the art. The walls are filled with photographs, with paintings—there are even a few sculptures. The sound of soft music wafts from the hidden surround system.

"Lily, this is gorgeous."

"You think?"

"Yes." I've seen the art she's been working on, the pieces she's sourced from others—but seeing it all come together? It's a love letter to both art and the ocean. Each piece is different, but the story they tell… it's beautiful.

"This one… I haven't seen this one before," I say, stopping in front of a painting of a beach. The sky is tumultuous, a mixture of reds and purples. Two children are walking along the shore.

"I just finished it," Lily says, coming to stand next to me. "What do you think?"

I lean in closer. There's something about the children… they're only silhouettes, but they're familiar. The girl is walking in front. Even though she's stuck in a painting, her body is portrayed with motion in mind, energy evident in her stride. She's reaching back, her hand clasped tightly around the boy's.

He has shaggy hair. His shoulders are slumped slightly, but he's turned toward her, letting her drag him across the beach.

"It's us."

"Yes. From ages ago."

The sky is darker on his side of the painting. She's pulling him toward the light, toward the sky with a gorgeous sunset.

With a start, I realize it's not actually a sunset. It's a sunrise.

"It's beautiful," I say, wrapping my arm around her. "You in the lead, and me following?"

"I couldn't take *too* much creative license," she says, and there's laughter in her voice.

"Mhm." I bend down and press a kiss to her lips. She's too much, this woman. "Well, it's true. My heart and my soul are yours. They were, even back then."

Lily gives a little moan and turns to me completely, wrapping her arms around my neck. She feels like an extension of me—the two of us one person. My strength and my courage, my conscience and my sanity. In the months since I returned, I've learned the true meaning of a relationship. Of being partners—lifting each other up. Of being good enough together.

"I love you."

"I love you too," I say. "And I love this painting. Is it for sale?"

Lily shakes her head. "I was planning on putting it up for sale, but now, I don't know. It doesn't feel right."

"You should sell it," I tell her. "Definitely."

Her eyes dim. "All right. If you think so, maybe I should."

"I do. I already know of a buyer, actually."

"You do?"

"Yes. He's a big fan of your work." I wrap my arms

around her waist, walking her backwards. It's no effort at all to press kisses against her cheek, her neck, her skin warm under my mouth. "He's very interested."

Her laughter rings out in my ear. "Is he?"

"Yes. Very, *very.*"

"Good, because as it happens, he might be my favorite fan."

"He'll be happy to hear that."

Lily kisses me, long and deep, before she breaks into laughter again. "If it makes you this happy, I'll paint you over and over again."

"You make me happy," I say. "Just you."

Her hand stills on my cheek. Her green eyes glitter with love and trust, and my chest feels so full of emotion that it might burst.

"My handsome rogue," she whispers.

"Very handsome," I agree, bending to whisper in her ear. "I'm still waiting for you to hire me as your nude model, you know."

Lily grins. "I'm not done with your gentleman portrait yet, the one with the hounds at your feet."

I chuckle at the mention of that old joke. "Something for my mantlepiece?"

"Yes, or you can hang it in your office."

"Mmm." I run my hands down her back, finding the soft curve of her spine. She feels amazing in my arms—always has—like she belongs here. It's still hard to believe we spent so many years apart, when I'm close to her like this. And I know I'll spend the rest of my life making sure we're apart as little as possible. "Move in with me."

"Really?"

"Yes. Into my house, or me into yours, or we sell it all and buy something else. I don't care, I just never want to say goodbye to you."

"I like the sound of that. A place just for us." She presses a soft kiss to my lips, the feeling like home. "People will say it's too fast."

"People?" I know exactly who she's talking about. But her parents haven't said a negative word about us, not since Lily told them. I think they know they risk losing their daughter forever if they do.

"Yes, people. But they'd be wrong. I've loved you since I was ten years old, Hayden Cole."

I bow my forehead to hers, closing my eyes. Her words never fail to stop me in my tracks completely. "There's something else I'm going to ask you one of these days," I say. "I'm trying not to move too fast in that regard, though."

Lily's breath catches in her throat, and I hear her swallow. "That's interesting."

"Yes."

"Hypothetically," she murmurs, "I think you'd get a positive response, if the question is what I'm thinking it might be."

"*That's interesting,*" I echo, smiling at her. "Expect it when you least expect it, that's all I'm saying, Lils."

"You're good at keeping me on the edge of my seat, aren't you?"

"Always," I say, kissing her softly, holding the first and last girl I've ever loved in my arms.

———

A few months later…

Michael Marchand is quiet next to me on the large porch. The ocean is calm in the distance, the sun beginning its slow descent. It's late fall, and the air is cold. We're heading for winter.

I asked him out here for a reason, and judging by his

silence, I wonder if he suspects. But he always was difficult to read.

"Well, Cole? What did you want to discuss?"

"I've been back for months now," I say. "Lily and I live together, and I'm going to ask her to marry me."

Michael looks at me. There's more gray in his hair, and I'm two inches taller, but he's still able to look down his nose at me. It used to bother me once—intimidate me at the same time as it raised my hackles.

It doesn't anymore.

"Are you asking for my permission?"

"No. I respect Lily and her opinion far too much for that. I don't need your permission." I face him fully. "I would, however, appreciate your blessing. We both know it would mean a lot to her."

"And to you?" His eyes are narrowed, but only slightly.

Ten years ago, his approval would have meant anything to me. The symbol of finally fitting into Paradise Shores—into the family—and proof that I was finally good enough.

Now, I know I am.

"It will make family get-togethers a hell of a lot easier," I say dryly.

To my surprise, Michael laughs. It's a dry, throaty sound. "Damn, Cole. You always did swim against the stream."

"You asked me to leave once," I say. "But I won't leave again. For as long as Lily wants me, I'll be here for her."

"I know that," he says calmly. "I saw that the second you returned. And that's good. My daughter deserves no less."

"She deserves everything."

"Spoken like a man truly in love." He puts a hand on my shoulder, and I try to hide my surprise. "I was wrong about you once, son. You've made something of yourself."

I meet his gaze head-on. "I have. But I'm not too proud to recognize I had help along the way. My uncle. Lily. You." I incline my head, struggling past my pride. "I've never properly thanked you for my tuition all those years."

Michael's eyes glitter, like he's seeing exactly how difficult this is for me. "You don't like being in someone's debt."

"No," I say, gritting my teeth.

"Neither do I." His gaze turns thoughtful. "A self-made man. Just like I was, once. That's something none of my sons can say."

I don't nod, but I don't contradict him, either.

"You're not in my debt. You make my daughter happy, and you're strong enough to keep her safe. That's more than repayment enough." He gives my shoulder a last pat before taking a step back. He opens the lid to the grill, inspecting the lobster tails lined up in a neat row. "I know I haven't been easy on you. Never tried to be."

I scoff and take a sip of my beer. "No, you definitely haven't."

"I'll give the boys hell, too, when they bring a woman home, don't you worry."

I think of Henry in his ivory tower in Manhattan, working so hard for this man's approval. Of Rhys's use of sarcasm as a shield and his nomadic existence. Of Parker's string of romantic attachments and cheap smiles.

"I can't wait," I say, knowing that this time, there'd be someone to have their backs against this man—me.

EPILOGUE

ONE YEAR LATER

Lily

Two ticks.

It's positive.

I sit down on the edge of the bathtub and put my head in my hands. I'm going to be a mother. *I'm going to be a mother.*

It's taking all my effort to stay calm and let my breathing slow. A child. We're going to have a child. A little mini-Hayden, with dark, shaggy hair and gray eyes. A big smile.

Happiness unfurls inside me. A child. *A child.*

It isn't planned, but isn't exactly a surprise, either. We'd discussed it briefly... and we hadn't been as careful as you're supposed to be. We'd slipped on the honeymoon, and not just once. Hayden had whispered to me that it would make him happy, and I'd reacted in kind. But that had been in passion—in moments of bliss.

Now it's real.

For two weeks, after the wedding, Hayden and I had been on a paradise island in the Caribbean. Just the two of us and crystal-clear water, white sand and a rented sailing boat. It had been like a dream.

His business is doing better than anyone had expected, including himself. The company now has a team of nearly ten consultants whom Hayden regularly receive reports from.

I look down at the engagement and wedding ring on my finger. It still feels odd to look at, even if they complement each other perfectly. I'd worn the engagement ring for almost a year, ever since he proposed last fall, and all through the planning and preparations for a summer wedding.

We moved into a house of our own, with all the planning that came with it. The house next to my cottage had unexpectedly come onto the market just a few months earlier. It had fantastic ocean views and a large backyard.

I'd stood outside it one night, looking at the shutters and imagining painting them dark blue, expanding the upstairs terrace, a children's playhouse in the garden, a spare bedroom for when Hayden's half-sister visited. He'd wrapped his arms around me, still warm after his evening run, and kissed my temple.

"Should we get it?" he'd asked, and there had been nothing to say but yes.

It still isn't fully renovated, but we live here now, together. Married. I stand on shaky legs and look into the mirror in the master bathroom. Carefully, I put the pregnancy test on the counter with trembling hands and look at myself.

I look flushed. Happy. A bit scared.

Hayden still struggles with feelings of inadequacy and dark thoughts. The memories of his childhood run deep, even if he's a master at hiding it—and pushing it away. And a child… it's hard to forget the doubts he's expressed occasionally about being a father himself.

I wash my hands and walk through our master bedroom, down the stairs to the living room. My laptop is open, the spreadsheet with the gallery's upcoming events still there. It's gone better than I could ever have expected—so good that I've even had to hire someone to help me run it.

The house is empty and quiet. Hayden is at the marina. Rhys and Parker had needed him for something, they'd said, and he's gone on the *Frida* for the day. I'd chosen to stay home, because I wanted to work on the gallery's schedule. *And* because I had been suspicious, my period over a week late.

I drum my fingers along the kitchen counter. I'd wanted to check it alone, but now I want Hayden here—right away. I don't want to be alone with this knowledge for a second longer.

So I grab a book and a sweater, and then I head down to the marina. They've already been out hours. Shouldn't be long, now.

The words on the page swim before my eyes as I try to read, sitting by the Marchand dock. I'd brought the book on our honeymoon, but Hayden had been very adept at distracting me from reading it. He'd roll over, slip a hand across my waist and whisper something amusing or loving in my ear, and I would put the book down without a second thought.

It's a calm day in late August, and the waves are soft against the dock. Our kid will grow up here, just like I did, and just like Hayden. Will she love sailing as much as her father? Or will he want to spend his days painting?

I put the book down and close my eyes. The possibilities are endless. And Hayden... I can see Hayden as a father, a child riding on his shoulders, small hands nestled deep in his thick hair. Always teasing and playing, but he would be the first to pick his son or daughter up if they fell, strong arms lifting up and brushing off.

The image makes me smile.

The *Frida* sails into the harbor just past five in the evening. They've rolled up the sails, and she's cruising on motor alone. I can see all of them—Henry at the steering wheel, tallest of the lot. Parker's head of blond hair as he sits at the front, preparing to jump onto the dock to tie the rope. Rhys is standing next to Hayden, the two of them shoulder to shoulder as they spot the distance and shout instructions to Henry.

My family. It's so rare that all my brothers are together in Paradise Shores at the same time, especially since they'd already been here in July for the wedding. I was the first who had moved back permanently, and if I had my way, I'd make sure they all did the same.

I help Parker tie the knots and anchor the boat along the dock. "Didn't know you'd be here, Lils," he calls. "Hayden said you had to work."

"Changed my mind," I say, using a half hitch knot. "Was it nice out there?"

He wraps an arm around my shoulder and gives me a half-hug, and we stand watching as the others get off the boat. "It was amazing."

Rhys's hair is wet, and when he gets closer, he shakes it like a dog. I laugh as the droplets fly. "You took a swim?"

"Of course I did. The others are cowards."

"It's called being *sensible*," Henry says, his voice low. "We can't all be rebels."

Rhys snorts. "Ignore him. He's been in a terrible mood all day."

Both Hayden and Parker laugh, but Henry just shoots them a dark look. I'm not surprised, though. My oldest brother has been acting oddly for weeks. It's not difficult to guess the reason.

"Is this because of the girl you brought as a date to my wedding?" I frown at Henry. "She was lovely."

"No, it's not because of her."

"Liar," Rhys says, voice teasing. "Faye unsettles you. Admit it."

"I am *not* going to talk about this." Henry stalks off down the dock, his wide shoulders looking tense. He's so regimented, so focused, that he sometimes forgets the important things in life.

Parker drops his arm from my shoulders and nods to Hayden. "You going back with Lils?"

"Yes," Hayden says smoothly, bending to pick up the book I'd dropped on the dock. "It's getting late."

"It is," I agree. "But would you guys want to come over tomorrow night? Board games and wine? We can dig out some of the old ones."

Rhys grins. "You want revenge?"

I smile back at him. "I think I'll be considerably better at Monopoly now, yes. You guys always had the advantage of age."

"We'll see about that."

We reach the parking lot and say our goodbyes, Hayden's hand on the small of my back.

"See you tomorrow!"

Hayden gets into the driver's seat and reaches over to put a hand on my knee. "Didn't know you were going to wait for us."

"I hadn't planned on it," I say, looking down at his broad, tan hand. "But I wanted to."

"I'm glad."

"Was it fun?"

He snorts, but his voice is warm when he answers. "Yes. It's been a long time since all of us were out on the boat together."

"It has." I put my hand on his and watch his quiet contentment with a smile. My brothers are Hayden's, too; they've accepted him as my husband as readily as they did when we were children, and Hayden was a new playmate. My family feels whole again.

He shoots me a smile. "Although I prefer just the two of us on a boat... I like your brothers, baby, but I like you better."

His eyes flash with heat and amusement, his hand tightening on my knee. I bite my lip at the memory—the boat rocking softly amongst the waves, his body on top of mine, warm lips against my neck and his deep, powerful rhythm.

"I prefer that too," I say.

Hayden's smile turns a little bit wild, and I can see in his eyes that he has plans for when we get home.

But so do I—and I don't feel like I can wait much longer. He parks the car and I grab his hand, pulling him inside the house.

"I'm sweaty," he says, running a hand over my back. "I should take a shower first. Join me."

"Gladly. But first… I need to show you something."

"Oh?"

"Yeah." Nervous butterflies flutter in my stomach, alive with excitement as we head up to the bedroom. I gesture for Hayden to have a seat on the bed, and he scoots back, running a hand through his hair. He would look relaxed if it wasn't for his amber eyes, fixated on me.

"Is something wrong, Lily?"

"No."

He frowns. "I can tell something is."

"Nothing's *wrong.*" I head into the bathroom and grab the pregnancy test, still by the sink. The two lines are still as clear as they'd been hours ago.

I walk back into the bedroom, my bare feet sinking deep into the carpet.

Hayden looks at me in silence. "Lily…"

"So, you know how we haven't been… very careful?"

He frowns, but then his gaze sharpens, alert like a predator. "Yes?"

"It's paid off, so to speak. I think I'm pregnant." I hold out the test to him, showing the sign. "I took it a few hours ago."

Hayden stares at it for a long, quiet moment. Then he leans back, arms braced against his legs, and says nothing at all. My heart is beating so fast in my chest that I fear it might leap out and tackle him to the ground. *Say something!*

"Well? What do you think?"

There's something warm and excited in his eyes, something that's growing by the second. "Come here," he says quietly, waving me closer. "Let me hold you."

He catches me around the waist, strong arms pulling me along his body, and buries his head against my shoulder. I hold on to his T-shirt and can't stop myself from tearing up.

"A baby," I murmur. "Can you believe it?"

Hayden pushes my hair back. Warm lips touch my forehead, my cheek, my nose, finding my lips. I kiss him back through my tears, feeling so happy I might burst.

"No."

"Are you happy, Hayden? Is this good news?"

A rough hand cups my cheek, his thumb smoothing away one of my tears. His face is so dear to me, the cheekbones, the thick hair over his forehead, the unusual eyes.

"Yes," he says. "It's amazing news."

"Really?"

"*Yes*." He closes his arms around my waist, lifting me up and spinning me around. I grip his shoulders and smile down at him, seeing my own joy reflected back at me.

He doesn't let go when we stop spinning, instead lifting me up and onto our bed. I pull him with me so that we're side by side.

"Were you afraid I wouldn't be happy?"

I run a finger along the sharp edge of his jaw. "A little bit. I was scared you'd… I don't know. That it would freak you out."

"How little faith you have in me," he murmurs.

I slide my hand into his thick hair, running my fingers against his scalp the way I know he enjoys. "I know. I'm sorry. It was only a small fear."

Hayden's smile fades, even if the happiness in his eyes doesn't. "But you're right. I might fuck up, Lily."

"You won't."

He sighs. "What if I do, though? There's a risk I could become—"

"No, there's no risk at all. Do you know why? Because I won't let you."

He closes his eyes, our foreheads touching. "I know."

"But more importantly, *you* won't let yourself fail. I know you, Hay. You're one of the most driven people I've ever met. I know you better than anyone, and I have complete faith in you."

"Thank you," he says dryly, a smile in his voice. "Besides, I know that if I screw up, I'll have to answer to not one, not two, not three, but *four* angry uncles, not just the kid's but my own as well."

I laugh. "Not scared at all, huh."

"No." He kisses me softly, his hand finding the curve of my waist and the still-flatness of my stomach. "With you as my wife? Never."

————

Do you want to find out why Henry Marchand, Lily's composed older brother, was so distraught?

Read his story in "Ice Cold Boss," an office romance between a billionaire boss and his fiery assistant. Turn the page for the first chapter!

THE STORY CONTINUES

Ice Cold Boss

He's ruthless. He's my new boss.
And he's used to getting what he wants.

I'm drunk when I send my job application to Henry Marchand. *"It's not like you're going to consider hiring me anyway, you elitist."* Yep—that's actually what I write. Excuse me while I start tunneling to China.

When he summons me for an interview, I'm floored. But I'm also unemployed, so I say yes. Yes, absolutely, *yes.* He offers me the position of his personal assistant.

Is it the job I want? No. But his firm is brilliant, and I'm determined to work my way to the top. Nothing will stand in my way, not even an inconvenient attraction to my new boss.

He's competitive, ambitious, harshly good-looking. His new favorite sport is challenging me—my limits, my wits. The chemistry between us soon sizzles and burns.

Lines get blurred. Boundaries are crossed.

He's not as cold as he seems.
And he wants me.

CHAPTER 1
FAYE

What do you do if you're a broke architect who's been wrongfully terminated from your job? Throw in a large amount of student debt for good measure, an even bigger dose of ambition, and the humiliation of being turned down by most of the major architect firms in New York.

The answer? You drown your sorrows in wine.

My best friend comes over and we open a bottle of white. Technically, we open two, but it's the light and bubbly kind of wine, so it only counts half as much.

"To my latest rejection letter," I say, and hold up my glass for a toast.

Jessie holds up her own. "At least you're out of Elliot Ferris's office. You could still have to work for that jackass, Faye."

"Yes, and I'd be getting paid," I say sadly. "But you're right. Here's to being broke—but at least there's no one ogling my ass!"

"To no ass ogling!"

We toast, and giggle, and descend into the kind of madness we've always gotten into. Silly and funny and entirely harmless.

Well.

At least it *starts* harmless.

But then Jessie leaves, and I open my laptop for a little bit of midnight fun. Maybe watch my favorite YouTuber break down yet another shopping haul, or a tutorial for braids so intricate I know I'd never manage to succeed on my own. Perhaps do a spot of drunk online shopping.

The job searching website pops up—I'd left it open. There's a new ad, posted in the day since I last checked.

Marchand & Rykers is the firm name. They're a small, boutique architect firm uptown, one I've only heard about but never encountered. It's not one of the big players, but they're well-known for taking on expensive, prestige projects. It's also a firm that hasn't rejected me yet.

My heart sinks as I read the job description. It's not even a position as an architect. Assistant. They're hiring an assistant to the executive partner.

It involves all the usual sort of stuff—event managing, calendar work, email and phone. Damn. This city is killing me, not to mention this profession. Five years I'd spent with Elliot Ferris, and in the end, what did I gain?

Nothing. No recommendation letter, no promotion—nada. Zilch.

Is assistant the best I can do now? Have I really sunk that low?

Drunk anger rises up in me as I press the giant blue button that says "apply." I have my CV ready, so it doesn't take long to attach it and finalize my application.

Please submit a cover letter. Hah. As if they'll hire me anyway!

An idea forms in my mind. It's so silly that for a moment all I can do is grin at the empty document on my screen. Yes. Why not give them a piece of my mind too? It's not like I'm realistically going to get this job. I have no background as an assistant and not a single recommendation to my name. I'm twenty-seven years old and live in a studio apartment in Brooklyn.

I start to write. *Dear...* Damn it. Who's the head of the firm? A quick internet search pulls up the name. Henry Marchand. Probably a mean old bastard, with a pudgy stomach and graying hair. Another Elliot Ferris, with his clawing hands and sickly-sweet smile. Ugh. They're the elitist dragons guarding the building industry in New York, making it impossible to gain a foothold as a young female architect. Assholes.

Dear Mr. Marchand (what kind of fancy-pants name is that?), I start typing.

You're not going to hire me, you old stooge, and let me list the reasons why. Intrigued? You should be. I'm about to tell you everything that's wrong with this industry. You're welcome.

———

I wake up with a pounding headache and a mouth as dry as the Sahara. My sheets are stuck to my cheek, and I can tell without touching it that my hair is a complete mess.

Sunlight streams in through my window. By the looks of it, it's late already.

"Damn," I murmur to no one and sit up, putting a hand to my forehead. I knew drinking with Jessie had been a bad idea, but then I'd received the letter of rejection from Ford & Sons...

God. That made it a total of six rejections. All major architect firms in New York had rejected me. Me. And I'd been valedictorian of my class at university. Sure, it wasn't Ivy League, but it had been the best I'd been able to afford on my scholarship and loans.

I stand on wobbly legs and make it out to the kitchen to grab a glass of cold water. I glance over at the potted palm tree in the corner. "Looks like we might have to go back to Ohio if this continues, buddy," I tell it.

The tree looks morosely back at me. The leaves are turning brown at the edges, despite my tender loving care. I've killed every plant I've ever bought, but I'm determined that this one won't suffer the same tragic fate.

"Hang in there," I tell him. "I'll find us something. I know you'll feel better when I have a job."

Not to mention, so will I.

I take a seat at my kitchen table and open my laptop. There's a new email in my inbox.

Automatic: Thank you for your application!

I frown and lean in closer. I didn't apply for anything.

Marchand & Rykers has received your application. We will be in touch as soon as possible regarding—

No. No, no, no, no, no. There was no way.

That was a joke. A drunken, stupid little joke, just to amuse myself.

I open the documents that I sent in, one by one.

My heart is pounding when I open the cover letter—the one I vaguely remember typing in drunken, self-righteous anger.

Dear God. I actually sent it.

OTHER BOOKS BY OLIVIA
LISTED IN READING ORDER

New York Billionaires Series

Think Outside the Boss
Tristan and Freddie

Saved by the Boss
Anthony and Summer

Say Yes to the Boss
Victor and Cecilia

A Ticking Time Boss
Carter and Audrey

Seattle Billionaires Series

Billion Dollar Enemy
Cole and Skye

Billion Dollar Beast
Nick and Blair

Billion Dollar Catch
Ethan and Bella

Billion Dollar Fiancé
Liam and Maddie

Brothers of Paradise Series

Rogue
Lily and Hayden

Ice Cold Boss
Faye and Henry

Red Hot Rebel
Ivy and Rhys

Small Town Hero
Jamie and Parker

Standalones

Arrogant Boss
Julian and Emily

Look But Don't Touch
Grant and Ada

The Billionaire Scrooge Next Door
Adam and Holly

ABOUT OLIVIA

Olivia loves billionaire heroes despite never having met one in person. Taking matters into her own hands, she creates them on the page instead. Stern, charming, cold or brooding, so far she's never met a (fictional) billionaire she didn't like.

Her favorite things include wide-shouldered heroes, late-night conversations, too-expensive wine and romances that lift you up.

Smart and sexy romance—those are her lead themes!

Join her newsletter for updates and bonus content.
www.oliviahayle.com.
Connect with Olivia

[f] facebook.com/authoroliviahayle

[o] instagram.com/oliviahayle

[g] goodreads.com/oliviahayle

[a] amazon.com/author/oliviahayle

[BB] bookbub.com/profile/olivia-hayle